THE

BUDDHA

BOOK

ALSO BY ABRAHAM RODRIGUEZ

Spidertown

The Boy Without a Flag

THE

Abraham

BUDDHA

Rodriguez

BOOK

A NOVEL

PICADOR USA
NEW YORK

Picador® is a U.S. registered trademark and is used by
St. Martin's Press under license from Pan Books Limited.

www.picadorusa.com

For information on Picador USA Reading Group Guides,
as well as ordering, please contact the Trade Marketing
department at St. Martin's Press.
Phone: 1-800-221-7945 extension 488
Fax: 212-677-7456
E-mail: trademarketing@stmartins.com

Library of Congress Cataloging-in-Publication Data

Rodriguez, Abraham.
    The Buddha book : a novel / Abraham Rodriguez.—1st ed.
        p. cm.
    ISBN 0-312-26299-X
    1. Comic books, strips, etc.—Authorship—Fiction.
2. Bronx (New York, N.Y.)—Fiction. 3. Children of prisoners—
Fiction. 4. Male friendship—Fiction. 5. Teenage boys—
Fiction. 6. Murder—Fiction. I. Title.

PS3568.O34876 B84 2001
813'.54—dc21
                                        2001021902

First Edition: August 2001

10 9 8 7 6 5 4 3 2 1

"To The Fifty"

The Great Escape is a classic American film about Allied prisoners of war who are confined to a high-security German POW camp. Escape artists all, they manage the largest escape in history— seventy-six prisoners. Most all are caught. The German SS execute fifty of them outright. The film, directed by John Sturges, is dedicated to their memory.

This book is dedicated to another group of prisoners of war.

1

TAG: Jewelry item, usually a diamond bracelet worn by street girls to show they enjoy the special benefits and protection of a posse moneyman.

The fight led them into the bathroom. The tub was full of water. She had just stepped out of the bath when he came.

She ended up under the water.

Jose couldn't say how it happened. All of a sudden Lucy was under the splash frantic rocking. He had been thinking about how it all had to end somewhere and here it was, no way out. Even mouthed the words as Lucy's moves went slow motion and bubbles streamed past her lips. Then, the sudden sinking down of everything. The eyes straight up, forever.

And then the quiet, dripping.

HE SAT ON the toilet. Droplets on his baggy pants. Arms weighing, so hard to lift them. Legs aching as if he had done laps at the gym.

Went into the kitchen. Two wine bottles on the counter. Bread. Cheese. Cold cuts. Crystal stuff. Like she had been expecting him. (Not him.)

Went to the window to look down on the street. A UPS truck squeezed past parked cars. No sound. Couldn't hear salsa music blaring from upstairs. A dog on the corner stomped with every bark, but it was still a silent movie.

Hands numb, not feeling right. Picked up the wine bottle. Walked it along the edge of the counter. It fell with a crash that he really didn't hear.

Pause.

Sound?

Stared at the red splatter on the floor. Nausea. Strolled the other bottle to the edge. (How it seemed to fight him.) Made sure to watch the twirling spiral real good this time so he could catch the crash. The red rose splash.

Jose tweaked an ear. Nada.

HE WANDERED THROUGH the apartment, expecting her to pop up from somewhere. Towel-drying her hair maybe, with those quick, irritated strokes.

She had been getting ready. Her clothes were laid out on the bed. Had smelled all soapy fresh her hair squiggly wet when she answered the door. Didn't even ask who. Like who else could it be? Her face all glowy like she couldn't wait

and then she saw that it was Jose. In a flash her face went cold, the eyes narrowed. That terry-cloth robe shut tighter.

"He's gonna kill you," she said.

Tried to close the door but he pushed his way in. Stood in the living room like he was searching for something. She stared back as if she had forgotten her lines.

"So you finally took a bath," he said.

She was tying that robe *absolutely* shut.

"You shun't be in here, man." She sounded tired of him. "He'll kill you."

A *chispa* of laugh from him.

"Maybe I'm the one gonna kill him."

She laughed in that way that she had that was like knives and daggers, the look of an adult smirking down on a little boy who messed himself.

The rest was blur.

They wrestled, they push shoved just like old times, the tag on her wrist flashing every time she blocked his fists. Enough diamonds on it to make you choke, she had bragged the week it premiered on her wrist. The official brand of Angel's ownership. Title deed. Sparkled every move, every mannerism. It even made a chiming sound.

He went into the bathroom, floor wet with slippery. Turned off the tap. Pulled her arm out from water and tugged at the diamond bracelet. Water splash. Her body seemed to buck. When he got the bracelet off, her arm fell and knocked against the tub like a stickball bat.

The tag was *his* now. Dried it off with a towel. ANGEL, it read. Gleaming blue so fire. Checked to see what Lucy thought of that, but there was no laugh, no sharp snappy comeback this time. Her terry-cloth robe tried to float free. Little bubbles clung to her underwater face. Like looking into a marble.

Jose was going to wait for him to come home.

Opened the knife Dinky gave him and put it on the coffee table. Dinky had tried to talk him out of all this but couldn't, so he dropped the knife on him almost like a last resort, a laugh, even. The knife was such a teeny toy thing. Sunk Jose just looking at it. He'd have to move pretty fast to use that. When the bastid comes in, lunge from cover. Slash throat cut across so swift and deep-thrusting that there will only be blur stab and sting.

(Lucy standing there. Her robe dripping soapy water.

"You'd better be swift," she said so smug.)

For a second, she was. Then not. The empty kitchen doorway. Made him go check that tub again to find her still under, her feet up against the tile. Those sloppy-painted toenails.

Was he really going to get a drop on Angel with that teeny pocket knife? Jose schoolboy sat back down on the couch with trembling hands.

A sound.

Turned. Lucy by the kitchen door again, robe streaming water.

"Wow. Big man makes his move. I gotta stick around to watch this."

Where were the laughing children, their thumps of play on stairwell steps? The dogs barking in the yard, the wild dueling saxes from the *merengue* in the alley? It was all gone. There was only Lucy, still laughing. Holding up that wineglass like she was toasting him. Hadn't he smashed all the wine bottles?

"There's another in the cabinet," she said.

He scooted past her laughter, into the kitchen to check. Sure enough, one more bottle, green and chubby. Flung against a wall with a flash of shard splatter. The sound jarred him. Noise rushed in whoosh. Felt a wave of nausea, but it was worth it. She was gone.

Back to the couch. To play with the remote, mute the images. Gloria Estefan unbearable even with the sound *down*. Stuffing handfuls of M&M's into his mouth from the bowl on the coffee table. Where he had left the little knife.

What he needed was a gun.

How was Angel, big-time drug-dealing mothafuck *not* going to have a gun somewhere in his crib? Jose got up and searched. In the bedroom, he checked drawers and closets and shoeboxes. No gun. He did find money, a bag of smoke, that monogrammed lighter, and this picture of Angel and Lucy which he did snatch snatch snatch. Good to have those big thigh pockets on those baggy pants. About to overturn a big black tote when he heard somebody tapping on the door.

Jose raced through the living room, creeping up the hallway with wooden squeaks. Was right behind the door before he realized he had left the knife on the coffee table! No way to go back for it. The tapping was more frantic now. Soon maybe the key would enter the lock. Soon the doorknob would twist. Jose peeped through the peekhole. Wasn't Angel. Was instead well-known female chatterbox named Diana, who stood on tippytoes to peer in as he peered out.

"Lucy. Come on, man! Open up! I know you there."

Jose exhaled, tension springing loose.

"Lucy!" Banged the door with a fist. "I need my workout clothes!"

Jose quietly left the door. On the couch again, he fumbled with the knife. Noticing how strange his hands looked, like they had swollen from the act.

"Lucy, gawdamn..." Could hear the whining from afar. "Just 'cause you in there fucken don't mean I gotta wait for my shit!"

Rattled the knob one more time before thumping away down the stairs. Jose choked on too many M&M's. Could hear everything now. There were pots and pans clinking in someone's sink. There was a *drip drip* like rhythmic baby congas. The screechy vestibule door opened and closed.

Jose held the tag up to the light. ANGEL. I belong to ANGEL. And after all the trouble she went through to get it! Now she don't belong to anybody.

Tears. Blind for a moment. Went to the bathroom again to check on her. Was it that he kept hoping she wouldn't be in there?

He ran into the bedroom. There had to be a gun, a gun, all those drawers he pulled open. His clothes, her clothes fluttering down. Pants, T's, blouses, socks. The balls of pantyhose were scented. He pulled down another drawer.

That sudden phone ring almost set off his sprinkler system. He froze. Three rings, and then the clicking of the answering machine kicking in.

"We're not home right now," Lucy's happy voice announced, "so leave a message. Maybe we'll get back."

"Lucy." Angel's voice. "Lucy, you there? Come on, pick up. I know you there, don't do this. Look, I won't be able to come. I got some shit comin up, a'ight? Where the fuck are you, anyway?"

Jose stood right by the phone, like he might pick it up. Just wanted to say, Nah, Lucy can't come to the phone, she's in the tub. Should I take a message?

"Lucy, man! Don't play me like that. Pick up."

Jose pressed the speakerphone button. The light came on. He pressed it again. The light went off. And there went Angel.

Now Jose paced like he needed the bathroom bad. Was Angel on the way? Everything was moving too fast, he couldn't breathe. He had come to teach Angel a lesson. Hadn't he done that by floating his prize guppy? A good opening scene, but with a knife like that he realized there was no reason to ruin such a good beginning with his own demise. So he scooped up Dinky's knife along with a few M&M's for the road.

Time to jet.

It wasn't until he got to the street that he noticed he had a ball of pantyhose in his pocket.

2

S treet.

The springy knees. Like something in him had emptied out. Remembered walking in the drizzle with Lucy, after fucking. Now the same feeling but. Something worse. Stunned slow, and even the hands didn't work right. Was it written on him? He checked himself in storefront glass, but nothing.

Everything muted and soft focus. Congas played a sensual strut from the shack on the empty lot. The rock dealers looked mellow, crackheads shrinking from sight the moment they scored. People seeming to whisper. A dog about to bark settled on a growl. Lucy laughing, or was that birds? Jose wandered like he was trying to put off the home scene. He took the long way, hoping to find Dinky, but he ran into Jeeps. Would've ducked him but he got spotted first. The frenetic crazy Jeeps and his crew love to spring out from cover. Jose jumped back, parried thrusts kicks elbows, dodged and spun back with dukes up like it was rumble time. Then Jeeps stepped out, wearing that gold tooth smile.

"Hey, bastid! It's just Jeeps. How come my man be so jumpy tonight?"

They slapped hands and finger-snapped. Jeeps gave Jose a long hard look.

"You look funny, slick. You sick?"

Jose nodded.

"Damn, lookit'chu! Look like you seen some ghost."

"Get off. I'm lookin for Dink. You seen him?"

"Nah, man." Jeeps snorted like he resented being asked for info. Checked up and down that street like a good cornerboy. "I think he's with his brother today."

"His big brother from the marines?"

"Yup. Johnny's his name, right? Guy used to run shit out here. Dinky always hangs with him when the bee hits town."

Damn it! Just when Jose needed Dink the most. His teeth started chattering.

"Damn! You sick. Hey, Measles! You got any cold stuff?"

A skinny freckle face kid came over. He searched in a pocket and took out two boxes of cough drops.

"You want lemon, or cherry?"

The kid's eyes, too close together. After every word, a sniffle. That hoppy urgent NOW about him. Jose grabbed the lemon flavor and popped a couple.

Jeeps studied Jose carefully while his crew jumped up and down stoops like kids on recess. He stood calm, rubbing his baby goatee like he was too adult for such romp.

"So tell me, Jose," he said. "Why'd'ju do it?"

Jose couldn't breathe. "Do what?"

Jeeps looked real serious. "Why'd'ju do it, bro?"

Jose reddened. Tried to brush it off.

"Maan, what the fuck are you talking about?"

"I'm sayin they just found another stiff. This afternoon. That makes three already."

"Ah Jesus." Jose exhaled with relief. "Gimme a break."

"It's that serial killer dude thass been runnin around," Measles put in, a little too loud, a little too close so there was lozenge stink. "He popped somebody else today."

"I was in school," Jose said.

Jeeps started to laugh, his hand on Jose's shoulder.

"I was only jokin about'chu bein a killer. We all know you such a good boy."

Jose felt something inside quiver. He fought the urge to say. There was Lucy in that tub. She was going to be in that tub forever. Maybe he would've said, if by that time Jeeps and crew hadn't skittered away laughing, and what a cackling bird sound that was, all up and down the street.

PHONE BOOTH.

The coin would not go in for the longest time. Were they making those slots smaller now? Too many rings before a voice.

"Is Dinky there?"

"Nah." A slightly sleepy tone. "He's out with his brother. This Jose?"

"Yeah."

Dinky's ma was good people. When her drug-dealing husband ran off with the four kids, she stayed alone in the house, vowing to fight. The two youngest shared their own place, and Dinky crashed with his brother Johnny. Once his big brother left to join the marines, Dinky started crashing with his mother. Started going to school, stopped doing street time. She was happy enough to have him living at home so she let him live as he pleased. The thing was that she was drinking too much. (War takes its toll.) Sometimes she had that medicinal smell on her. Always clutching that teeny dog with the permanent shakes.

"Yeah, he's with his brother. You know what the two of them are like when he comes around."

"Listen, can you have him call me the minute he comes in? It's kinda important."

"Okay, sure."

SIRENS. THE COPS could already be at his house, who knows? Made him want to put off the home scene just a little longer, taking that turn up Avenue St. John. There was a brick wall facing an empty lot that was shrouded by tree leaves and tall grass so it was safe to spray-paint dedications without being spotted so quick. Tags, crew insignia, broken hearts, posse scrawls. Vows of love and forever fealty. The intertwinings of hearts and scribbles like some kind of living narrative. There was always something new, some old life rubbed out crossed off blackened by some new promise. There was a come and go to the messages, layers on layers. Some lasted only a night. A few became fixtures, like that silver heart in the left-hand corner with the words across it like a forever vow:

ANGEL LOVES LUCY 4-EVER

How happy it had made Lucy to see it! How she bragged and pulled friends down to see it, even Jose, like she had to prove to him she was worthy of a fucking drug dealer. (Shit, the things that make Puerto Rican girls proud.) For close to seven months, that silver heart had been throbbing on the wall. In that time Lucy went from posse-girl hopeful to Angel's wife, complete with crib, tag, and beeper number. How many times had Jose stared at those words? Seven months those words had been burning holes into him. What was the point in coming over to that wall, hoping that someone might have written over it? But that never happened. No one would touch Angel's heart, a true sign of respect from taggers and street scribblers. Had he expected tonight to be any different?

Why hadn't he brought a can of spray paint so he could finish the deed off? He was still cursing himself out when he heard the clatter-rattle of one. Jose turned, thinking maybe there was a whole posse behind him, but there was only Anita, stepping out from the tall grass. The loose minidress she was wearing did not go with the empty lot decor, the busted rubble the shards and tins. This did not present a problem for her. Jose thought about the last time he had seen her, how she had seemed stumbly, cloudy-eyed. Now her face was free of crack bumpies, her eyes clear and bright even in this low lighting. The fine cotton and silk blends she wore hinted at a stable flow of cash from some meaningful employment.

"Well, little brother."

She always talked to him as if she had just seen him yesterday, but her appearances have always been cameos.

"What brings you to the wall, hmm?"

A year ago, Jose didn't even know he had a stepsister. He had just gotten a new stepdad when he started sighting her under a bodega awning or sitting on a stoop as he passed, her eyes glued to him. Saw Dinky talking to her once. Asked him about her, but he only shrugged. "Just some skeez I know." Then she started talking to him. You the boy in 3-C? Is that ya moms? That green-eyed dude is ya father, right? (*Not* mine, Jose pointed out fast, he was new and sure acting like a father, but Jose didn't call him that yet. His mother hadn't bothered to poll him on the issue or even ask for his vote. To Jose, the man was still just a Pedro Vega. And he was still a Jose Rodriguez.)

"This makes you my new little brother," she said. She had the same green eyes in her face. A long-lost daughter finding her real daddy? "Just tell him you saw Anita," she said. When Jose did that, the results were gratifying. Pedro blew his top, while Jose's mother kept asking, *Quien coño es Anita?* The two of them argued all night while Jose sat out on the fire escape, figuring the breakup would be imminent. Yet the rift was patched, the past married to present. Pedro made what looked like an obligatory statement in front of them, under his mom's watchful eyes.

"Anita was the result of a relationship I had with a woman who was already married to a bottle. I can't even really say I'm the father for sure. It was that kind of thing. You know"—fake laugh—"I used to run around a lot in those days. That whole Puerto Rican manhood thing."

Anita's appearances were not so regular. He hadn't seen her in months. Wasn't there something so secret agent about her, the way she slipped out from behind bushes tall grass and stoops? It never bothered him to see her, but tonight was different. His hands trembling like that, better stick them into pockets. Slink down a little into that windbreaker to maybe find some way to hide from probing eyes. Her fucking eyes. Seemed to suck meaning out of everything, pulling, pushing, knowing something. Again the fear: could people see what happened, what he did? There must be Lucy all over him.

Anita scanned him, head to toe, her eyes going from him to the tribute wall as if she was trying to add it all together.

"Maybe you come down here tonight to make your big splash, is that it?"

The tease in her voice did not disguise the something digging deep underneath. Better walk slow.

"I'm looking for Dink," he said, the only thing that would come out. Why did her face change like that? What was that shine in her eyes? Now she seemed grateful.

"Dinky." It was like she was weighing the name. "I remember now."

She laughed as if Jose had brought her a present. It calmed him.

"This such a small world, right? Dinky. Shit. Does he ever talk about me?"

"Nope."

"You don't have to answer right away. You can think about it first."

"It's still nope. He never talks about you."

The happy went out of her face. "He hasn't been around on the streets. You know, like sometimes I look for him."

"He goes to school now. With me." Jose was glad to talk about anything. Anything other than. The trembling would not stop.

"I'm sure thass why. He don't mention me, I mean. But I think thass gotta be fate that he turned his back on the street, you know? Just like me. I left that shit, little brother."

She was shaking that can like an afterthought, her eyes scanning the wall. Jose watched the filmy silk dress. How it moved with her shake. Jose was arrested by that certain female something that always hypnotizes boys. She noticed his stare, put a hand on hip like she was modeling.

"Do you like wha'chu see?" A little bit of primp. Coming closer. Putting the spray can away in her shoulder bag. Pulling out that pack of cigarettes. Two unlit cigarettes dangling from her lips. Eyes glued to his like she could feel his trembling.

"My brother," she whispered so close, "you look like you got somethin'na hide."

Jose shifted his weight, fighting the tremble in his legs. Trying not to look into her liquid brights.

"Was that Angel's crib I saw you coming from, or do you just know somebody in the building?"

She lit the two cigarettes in one swift motion. Jose took one even though he wasn't much of a smoker. Puffed because he knew smoke was a good shield and it kept shaky hands busy. Plus he knew Pedro would smell it on him and get mad.

"You cold, Jose?"

"Huh?"

"Your hands are trembling. An' you look awful pale."

"I have a cold," he said.

She moved away, as if liars sickened her. Walking right over to that silver heart of Angel's. She touched it, fingertips.

"Do you believe in happy endings?"

Jose's eyes felt full of wet. Maybe it was the cigarette smoke sting. The look of that ANGEL LOVES LUCY 4-EVER heart.

"No," he said.

"Me neither. I had such a thing for Angel, once. Until he got him-self hitched, I mean. So much for happy endings. I come here an' look at this heart an' I think, well, looks like he got a happy ending." She turned to look at him. Her eyes were wet. "You think he has a happy ending?"

"No," Jose said. The flashing image of Lucy in that tub set off new trembles.

"That fucken heart. I been wantin'na blot it out for a long time. You see I brought my canna paint, right? You think tonight should be the night?"

She pulled out that can.

The cigarette made him sick. He tossed it away and watched the lot undulate like a field of boiling lava.

"Yes," he said.

She was headlights. The headlights were coming up the hill. A cop car siren that made him start. The red and blue flashes sped over the bushes.

"What makes you so jumpy, little brother?"

The siren getting louder.

She shook the can frantic and then black, black came pouring from its thin teeny spout, black spatter over silver heart, black blot-ting out Angel-Lucy blotting out forever with a steam hiss. Left the wall dripping black. Jose suddenly began coughing. He had been holding his breath.

Her eyes were full of all those blinking car lights. Stage lighting for her big show.

"So Dinky," she said, recapping the can and tucking it into her bag. "Does he still hang out on Longwood?"

"Yeah," Jose said, hoping that was all that was required. She was leaving all right, but she turned to him one last time.

"Tell my father you saw me," she said, like always.

She headed for those blazing cop lights. As if they were Times Square.

3

H ome.

The *novela* started at eight. Every apartment in the building was tuned to it. Could hear it outside on the stoop, up and down the stairwell like ghost talk. Words, forming in his mind. Lucy was speaking them. Whispering like she used to in the dark. Muffled by blanket by pillow, by his kisses kissing back. What was she trying to say to him? He could not separate her from the soap opera blaring from every doorway every floor.

No, María Elena. El no te quiere como te quiero yo. Tratando de impresionarte con prendas y joyas. Pero el no te necesita como te necesito yo. Ríete ahora, que pronto vivirás la prueba...

The *novela* escorted him right to the door. Into the living room, where the words sprouted into stereo. His parents were snuggled on the couch super cozy. They didn't look at him until the commercials came on.

Jose stooped to kiss his mother's forehead. Pedro never gets a kiss. He only gets a look, a certain nod that comes from the back row of the theater.

Tu no le perteneces a el. Eso lo sabrás . . .

Pedro's eyes flick off him and back to the screen. Almost like dismissal. That suited Jose just fine. Had made it to his room when Pedro spoke up.

"Hey. I need to talk to you," he said.

"Okay. But I gotta use the head."

"Well. Be brief."

The tone. Commanding deep resonating stuff like he loved to use at school, walking the hallway as the principal's number one pigeon in waiting. It made something in Jose seethe. Like something from a picture book. The fat Spaniard *patron* on his hill, talking down to the dark-skinned *peon*. It made Jose turn to deliver a quick salvo.

"I ran into Anita tonight," he said.

Jose's mother unsnuggled herself, a certain hard to her face. (That battle wasn't over.) When her face got like that, Jose thought no wonder her name is Dolores. *Dolores* means "pains." She went into the kitchen with not a look back. Pedro glared at Jose.

"You should know better than to bring that up when she's around. Can't you be considerate about her feelings for a change?"

"What do you want me to do," Jose yelled, "pass you a note? The girl popped up. That ain't my fault."

"Can't you at least wait until we're alone so you can tell me? Doesn't the word 'teamwork' mean anything to you?"

Jose stared back blank. Better to shut up than have something slip out.

"But why don'chu just tell him?" Lucy asked.

"I gotta piss," Jose said.

Ducked into the bathroom. Ghost face in the mirror. It felt good to shut that door, to try and breathe. Rinsed his face but no color coming back. Watched water rush into the tub all torrent. Lucy, under the churning. No bubbles from her lips now, just air bursts from her open eyes. Teeny globules clinging to her face, her neck, her hair. She was holding her breath but when she saw him pissing, she laughed, sending up a jagged water burst. All of a sudden her head was above water, her laugh reverberating.

"Stop that," he said, but it made her laugh harder. He turned the taps on full blast to drown her out. She kicked out at him. Water splashed the wall.

"Say. Wha'cha parents do if they find me in here? Hmm?"

Watched the water rush over her. She obediently slid under but wouldn't take her eyes off him. Untying her robe so he could see the fields of bubbles camped out on her tummy her belly button tangled in her black muff.

(And how seeing him stare made her smile.)

He turned off the water. The calm *drip drip.*

"Lucy."

Yank. Tried to pull her up from under but she was like made of stone.

"I take it back."

Pressing his eyes shut like he was making a wish, squeezing

eyeballs deep trying to erase the picture. When he looked again there was nothing but drain, sucking down the last of the water.

Shakes, trembles. Like chills.

Jose stepped back into the living room. Pedro was alone on the couch. The credits rolled up on the screen.

"Well well." Pedro wouldn't take his eyes off the screen. "Another late night, ah?"

Clicked channels with the remote. Dolores in the kitchen. The sound of dishes in the sink.

"I didn't know you were working tonight."

Neither did Jose. Had he mentioned going to work tonight? It was Jose's night off. He had gone somewhere to murder someone, that was all. Would his "father" be able to tell somehow? He still hadn't given Jose a good hard look. If he did, maybe he would see how the color was gone from his face, how the flavor the spice the brown of Taíno was gone. How Jose was white white white as a sheet, a ghost, almost an UNspick. (But NOT nearly WHITE ENOUGH to anchor a show on Univision.)

"Sorry, pops. I was gonna call."

Something about the way Jose said "pops" that always sounded like a demotion. Even his mother hated to hear it.

"I thought if we treated you like an adult, you would act like an adult. Don't you think a little more responsibility on your part is called for?"

"Sorry, pops."

"You don't even remember to call me Pedro."

"I'm sorry, Pedro."

Silent fuming. Pedro kept flicking channels. Jose thought it was just like sitting in front of the principal. It wasn't even like dad talk. Pedro seemed to have learned how to talk to young people from a textbook.

"Don't you think of your mother? Why put her through it? You could at least call. Doesn't the place where you work have a phone?"

"I'm sorry. I just had a lot to do tonight. I cop the extra shifts at the pizzeria when I can. It don't pay enough just three days a week, pops."

"Pedro."

"Pedro. Thass why I crib all the extra time I can."

"Can you do me a favor and drop the ghetto speak? What's wrong with trying to express yourself like an articulate, well-educated Puerto Rican?"

"Okay."

"Very good. So next time if you're going to be late, you'll call so Dolores won't worry herself to death, right?"

Jose nodded slow. With Pedro, it was better not to say anything. Same with adults in general. They were just not getting it. Every year it got harder to talk. Jose couldn't care about what they had to offer, what they held up as an ideal. Being talked to this way constantly by adults made him think he was in training to be a sheep.

"There's something else."

A pause like something big was coming. Jose's stomach throbbed.

"This is the thing," Pedro said, like a bandit with a proposition. "I have my foot in the door. I'm not officially the assistant principal just yet, so they'll be watching my ass all the way to June. I don't know how they feel about me having a son at the same school so you just keep calling me Mr. Vega when you see me in the hall, none of that 'Hi pops!' stuff. Who knows? Maybe one little slipup and I'll be going down those stairs so fast my ass will have ridges. I won't talk about maybe transferring you to another school just yet. We'll see how it goes. But I'm sure you agree that the family should come first. Wouldn't you like us to get that house out on Long Island?"

Like the picture from the brochure. Three bedrooms and a deck. Dolores had pinned it to the fridge with grinning veggie magnets.

"Sure, pops. Mister Vega. Pedro."

"This is why I need your behavior to be exemplary during this period. With that in mind, can you explain that little fracas you got in last week?"

Jose leaned back into the *butaca.* Couldn't tell if he felt relief, or annoyance.

"What do you need to be getting into fights for, anyway? Don't we pay for you to go to the gym? That's all I need, for you to be standing in a corner of my office—my very own son!—during *my* probationary period!"

Jose cursed under breath. The silly-ass shit that is daily part of being teen. It hadn't even been a fight, just some punch and kick with that asshole, Shakes. Jumped Jose and Dink to show off some new moves. Then it turned into some big thing, and guess who got the note?

"Just don't let that happen again."

"Okay."

"Just keep out of trouble."

"All right!"

Dolores entered from the kitchen. Brought Pedro a cup of

coffee and that plate of soda crackers he loved to dunk. She also brought a can of soda for Jose. Patted him on the head like a good doggie.

"Thank you, Dolores." Jose mockingly. Dolores made a face.

"Tu te ves cansao." She passed a hand through his hair. "Oye, tu te ves mal. Tu tienes catarro?"

"Si."

Jose didn't want to look her in the eye too much. Mothers have weird discerning qualities. He popped open that soda can, but before he could drink, she swiped it right back.

"Si tienes catarro, pues no puedes beber soda. Te es lo que necesitas." And she headed back to the kitchen like a nurse tending patients.

Pedro dunked a soda cracker, eyes on the kitchen doorway like he resented the interruption.

"I don't understand this lack of community feeling with young people today. We're all in the same boat, aren't we? You know, I have a cousin who fought in the Korean War. The feeling of unity and brotherhood among soldiers. Maybe that's what this lazy MTV generation needs. A good, hard war to bring them together."

Jose stared. This was NOT a veteran of the Korean War talking. He was NOT in the fighting 65th Infantry, no spick soldier in olive drab. He cheered spick soldiers from the sidelines as they went off to war. He was NOT at bloody Inchon, where Puerto Ricans bravely proved themselves—all those young farm and backwoods boys from Montana Wisconsin Iowa The Peach State and now these NEW American boys from Caguas Santurce Bayamon Rio Piedras, all eager to make the grade. How did Pedro manage not to get called up? (This part was always sketchy.) Seemed Pedro came from the kind of family that could stay out of such things. Pampered and soft-bellied, Pedro makes speeches and does not fight. Just like his hero, Luis Muñoz Marín.

"Maybe there's nothing to be united about," Jose said.

"What does that mean? Aren't we all Puerto Ricans?"

"No."

"What are we, then?"

"Did you ever kill somebody?"

"What makes you ask a question like that?"

"I was just wondering."

"Well, you already know I wasn't in the war."

"Neither was I, but the question is did you ever kill anybody?"

Dolores came in. Put the mug of tea beside Jose on that little table by the lamp that said I LOVE CAGUAS on its bulby round tummy. She went right back to her kitchen sink without a word. It must have been the look that Pedro shot her.

"So look," he said to Jose, "this thing about Anita."

Jose sighed. One thing after another. The tea stink brought back the nausea. Pedro turned the TV up a little louder to be sure the wife didn't hear.

"How far from here was she?"

"What?"

"Was she nearby? Does she know where we live?"

Jose should've said yes. Instead, he only shrugged like it was beyond him.

"Well, I hope you listen to me good. Whatever you do, just don't lead her here, you understand? You have to take my word for it. That girl is dangerous."

"Dangerous how?"

"Can't you ever just take my word for it? She got in trouble with the law some years back. Trust me, it's a sick story. The court tried to involve me in that mess. Not me. No way." His hands brushed it off. "She's probably after money. She's cheap trash like her mother."

Dolores walked in as if she had timed it perfectly. She gave Jose another careful lookover. "Nene, te pasa algo? Tu te ves triste."

She wanted to make soup for him. Maybe he should stay home from school tomorrow? (Nah. Couldn't do that. Had to see Dinky.)

Jose drank as little of the tea as he could get away with. Dumped the rest, then headed to the bathroom. There, he turned the taps on full blast, and vomited into the toilet.

4

Astronomy. Jose's first class of the day.

Mr. Taylor had pulled down his map of the constellations and pointed out stars with his yardstick. The forty-nine kids crammed into that small classroom weren't listening. There was a constant murmur and buzz that caused Mr. Taylor to smack his desk with the yardstick from time to time.

"Ahh, chill, teacher man," Shakes said from his spot atop the cabinet in the back. He was one of the lucky few that got to stretch and lounge on ledges cabinets and even atop bookcases because of the lack of desks. "You make too much noise with that stick, man. You keep wakin me up."

"That's enough of that." Mr. Taylor's voice boomed over the laughter. "We have finals coming up, gentlemen in the back, and if you wish to fail then that's your privilege. I'm not reviewing this material for my benefit."

The girls started to protest as Mr. Taylor stood by the blackboard and did nada.

"You such an asshole, Shakes," Toothy Barbara said, hair wriggling as she spun to face him.

"Yeah," her friend Dezzie said. "Can'chu see we got a test?"

"Go ahead, Mr. Taylor." Toothy Barbara shushed the class and motioned to him like she was the film director. "The scene opens with the teacher in front of his class, waiting for them to shush. Suddenly, shots splash the windows—"

"I'm waiting," Mr. Taylor said as a dozen voices cut in spoke up yelling frantic before everybody was shushing everybody.

Jose put his head down on his desk. Couldn't deal with being a teenager today. The day felt unreal. That morning, Jose had checked in the mirror. Pale. Eyes crusted with UNsleep. Dolores felt his forehead again and asked how his cold was. The scrambled eggs made him nauseous. The few bites of toast left a flat, burned taste.

Pedro's new morning style. The well-suited crispness of him, the cleanshaven respectable look. Didn't used to care much about being late but now that he was up for assistant principal, he was always forty minutes early. Memorized every memo, spoke often of the grand job the principal was doing, didn't mind subbing for some sick teacher. (Was the union hearing about this? Saved the school some money.) Had never been the type to wear suits, maybe shirt and tie at best for those auditorium moments. Now he was suiting up sharp, with goop in his hair shiny. Clinking spoon against coffee mug which has a map of Puerto Rico looking like a strip of torn newsprint. Dolores could not stop kissing him.

Jose felt like he would burst.

"Look. I'm in trouble. I murdered a girl last night."

Said it. But it was only a whisper, drowned out by Pedro's last slurp of coffee.

"The Earth moves around the Sun at a distance of about ninety-three million miles. It is about eight hundred miles in diameter and is a member of what we call the solar system. It is not the only planet. Mercury and Venus are closer to the Sun while Jupiter, Saturn, and Mars are farther."

The uptight was still in Jose's stomach as if he had taken some of that speedy acid Dink sometimes got ahold of. Where was he? Jose worried, thinking about nights they would run around smashing phones with crowbars. (Not just any phones, but the ones used exclusively by drug dealers for business.) Dinky knew which posses used which phones. Would usually wait until the boys ran off camera. Then they would rush in like commandoes, and do the deed, sometimes chased by bad guys. Shit, who knows if Dinky didn't go on some joy ride last night and got his head blasted open? And right now that Jose really needed to talk to him.

Because last night, no sleep. The hot angry toss and turn. The instant replay. The way her words still burned. He kept taking it back. Chanting into the wet pillow. Falling in and out of vivid Lucy dreams until he woke for good.

He started to draw. Jose was good at hiding in the lines and swirls, all the inner mechanics of his strict comic-book-style panels. He could be completely lost for hours.

Jose had twelve pages of panels. Couldn't stop the story. Perfected those panels all the way to sunlight, then brought them to school, where he sat drumming his fingers and staring at Dinky's empty seat.

THE PRINCIPAL'S OFFICE. The one room in the whole building with the most feel of strangle, of air being stolen. There were those humming banks of fluorescents above. The neat piles of piles, the stink of people who shit bricks every time the boss man walks in.

The principal was a big man named Rolando Reyes. *Reyes* means "kings." He was the kind of man that gave everything a grave look, even when saying thanks. When he walked in, *he* was where all the eyes went. He sucked attention from a room, and ran a tight ship with that tight asshole.

Dinky was sleepy. He tried to keep his eyes open and focused as he stood before the principal's desk. The man was blowing into his coffee as if he hadn't yet decided to acknowledge another presence in the room.

There were two copies of *BUDDHA BOOK #3* sitting on the desk, each one wrapped in its protective Mylar. The splash of color blasted through plastic with a vibrancy that made Reyes squint.

"Well, Mr. Robles. What have you got to say for yourself?"

There wasn't much interest on Dinky's face.

Reyes leaned back in his chair. It was made of leather and had seventeen settings.

"Fine, don't talk. It doesn't matter. Mendoza is going through your bag with a fine tooth comb."

"Yo. Wha'chu gotta go through my shit for, man?"

"You don't use that tone of voice in this office. Or words like that."

"Why'd you confiscate my stuff?"

Reyes laughed. Pointed, as if Dinky had just scored one.

"That's rich. 'Confiscate.'" The humor escaped his face like it was made of vapor. "Did you learn that kind of convict talk from your father?"

Dinky exhaled. (So it would be the usual act.) The infinite patience on his face infuriated Reyes. Whenever it was apparent he wasn't feared or respected, he took it like a cold slap. And Dinky could read that on his face.

Reyes slid the comic book from its plastic sheath. Flipped through it like he knew exactly where to go.

"No. Maybe you got the word from here, page twelve, where the young teacher, distraught over her affair with a seventeen-year-old student, is forced to face the 'big, burly' principal of the school? 'When she saw his face at the door, she felt like he had arrived to confiscate her whole life.' Does that sound familiar?"

Dinky did not react. Infuriating, to a man who grew up on *Perry Mason* and was always looking for that revealing reaction shot. It was not good news for a principal, the head of state as it were, to find himself in a student comic book. (And naked, fucking Andrea Colon in a broom closet, as depicted in *BUDDHA BOOK #1, THE BONAFIDE RUMORS ISSUE*.) That first one had upset him, but it had been a little black-and-white thing that made the rounds from hand to hand and then vanished. The rumors in there were filthy. Hardly a teacher escaped unscathed. Reyes tried to forget about it, but when the second issue came out a month later, he realized this would be a regular thing. Bigger format, more pages, and a centerfold! Copies were seized, students grabbed, and there were a few general assemblies that led one teacher to comment on Reyes and his "Mussolini style." Could hear a pin drop after his impassioned oratory, but no cheering followed, no cries of *DUCE,*

DUCE! Only the staff and faculty applauded, their desperate applause sounding like spit on a griddle. There were no arrests. The students were not talking.

"So come on," he pressed Dinky. "What have you got to say about it?" Slapped down the comic. "Why don't you come clean and save us both a lot of trouble?"

It was already a lot of trouble. Reyes was determined to find the culprits. The third issue was no fantasy, no rumors. This was the true story of Carmen Arroyo and her love affair with seventeen-year-old Boots. Real story, real names, real scenes. The new issue arrived with a splash, spilling from teachers' mailboxes and lockers and desks. And this issue was in color!

Dinky shrugged. "I told you already. I didn't have nothin'na do with this shit."

"I told you about using that kind of language in here!"

Dinky scowl. "This ain't a church."

"What would you know about a church? Why don't you explain to me how somebody who has nothing to do with it is found in a bathroom with fifty-eight copies?"

"I told the gorilla that grabbed me. I went in there for a leak. The comics were in there. I din't go in there withum."

"You was framed, is that right?"

Dinky waited a moment to let the sarcasm pass unnoticed.

"I'm sayin I don't know anything about it."

"Oh yeah? Tell me then, what does the masthead say, there, on the first page, ah? Can you read it?"

Reyes shoved the comic in Dinky's face. Dinky grinned like he was proud.

" 'Produced by the students of Luis Muñoz Marín High School!' "

"Not *that* part!"

Reyes snatched back the book. "Look what it says there, there! 'Art and story by SPIK-EE BOY and SLINK-EE.'" He tossed the book down, like the prosecution rests, your honor.

"So?"

"So, Slinky! Isn't that what they call you, ah?"

"It's Dinky." He did not mask the contempt. "Dinky. Not Slinky."

"I think that's close enough for my books."

"You'll never prove it. Thass circumstantial."

Reyes opened his eyes with mock amusement. "Wow. Another ten-dollar word! Yet somehow it doesn't surprise me you know that one. Tell me, is that what you think they nabbed your father with? Circumstantial evidence? Is that why he's in jail now?"

"He'll be back," Dinky said unhappily.

"I believe in three to five, isn't that right? Don't talk to me about needing proof. A principal is one of the world's last uncrowned monarchs. You think I need proof? You forget yourself. Maybe there was a time when you thought you were hot shit because of your daddy the drug dealer. And how the streets all bow down to you when you pass like you're gutter royalty. But you know what? Those days are over. Nobody needs to romanticize your shit anymore, making you look like some urban heroes. You're just little hoods. And when you walk into this school, you're on *my* turf. You cease to exist when you come in through those doors. Can't fly with your props in here. You are just a student here. You have no rights."

"You had no right to confiscate my stuff."

"A student on probation can be searched at all times. Students suspected of engaging in illegal activity can be searched—at all times. So you're saying I *don't* have a right to search the son of a convicted drug dealer on school property? What judge do you plan to dope with that story?"

"I just want my shit back."

Because the last time he was searched, they kept a few of his sketches. Could be the proof they needed if the bastids got wise—good thing they were rough and unfinished. (Jose and Dinky managed to swipe them back before they could be studied.) Now Dinky didn't take chances. Carried no art, no doodles. He had to warn Jose, who had the bad habit of carrying completed panels around with him. Fuck, who knows what he might have on him right now! Jose's stuff was always comic-book ready. If they came across those pages, it would be curtains for SPIK-EE BOY.

Dinky knew that if he was going to be searched regularly from now on, then anybody with him would be open game. (After all, how do they know the son of a drug dealer hadn't just made a sale?) They wouldn't find pages on him, or drugs either for that matter, but the thought of that flat-face fuck Mendoza going through his stuff infuriated him. His notebook, his DJ tapes, and what about that new Dinky Toy that his brother brought all the way from some shop in London? (When you become a marine, you see the world.) Dinky was always happy to see his big bro, but when he stuck that hard-to-find Dinky Toys all-metal Sd.Kfz.251/10 armored personnel carrier in his face, Dinky almost bawled. Didn't he just see that shit listed in some hobby magazine for two hundred bucks? The treads work, the layered bogies turn, the mounted 37mm traverses. Dinky had hoped to show it off to Jose. Now it was probably in Sweaty Mendoza's hands, a sniveling froggy type whose style includes swiping stuff from student bookbags whenever he led a search. The worry brought a frown, the first sign Reyes could see that he was having an effect.

"Not only am I going to keep my finger on you," he said, flipping open his cigar box to pull out a choice Macanudo, "I'm going to find your friend, this SPIK-EE BOY."

His fingers, fat stubby removing the wrap on that thick cigar brown. His special cigar cutter ivory and pearl, that made a *snap* sound. The shiny chrome lighter clicked flame. The ventilator system that he installed in his office so he could smoke there cost the school $3,588.

"Ahora se acabo el relajo," he said, blowing out that first cloud of smoke while flicking on the ventilator with that special button on his desk. "You've gone too far. I'm not going to have the reputation of this school tarnished by a pair of thugs."

Dinky showed no emotion, but when Reyes smiled, he felt his stomach twitch.

"THE STARS ARE not genuinely fixed and have extremely high velocities relative to Earth . . ."

Suddenly, he had grown.

He didn't know if for better or worse, he had just changed sizes. Jose looked around him at all his classmates and felt they were kids. Their kid fingers fumbling with pens, with notebook paper. Jose was beyond them. He had just done something that set him apart, that put him in a different league. Nobody knew. They would look at him and not know. He didn't know if he liked that. Maybe he wanted people to know, to see the shock on their faces, to enjoy their confusion. The feeling of being above everybody lasted a little while, but when his eyes fell on Dinky's empty seat, he felt alone. He felt the bigness of what he had done, big because he couldn't ever take it back. He fought the trembles.

The back door squawked open. It was Dinky, droop-eyed and sluggish. Mr. Taylor made a mark on his attendance sheet without breaking his rap on the stars.

"So, Mr. Robles. Can you tell me the distance between Earth and its natural satellite?"

Dinky squinted. "What?"

The class erupted. Like sea against a rock.

"I said can you tell me how far away the Moon is?"

"When?"

Mr. Taylor whacked the desk with yardstick for quiet. "That's it, laugh. You can all laugh hearty when you can't answer that question on tomorrow's quiz."

The class groaned. Sneakers tamped hands banged tables.

"That's right. Surprise quiz. So you can all see how badly you're doing. Maybe Brainiac over there can help you get a lower grade."

He motioned at Dinky with his chin, a throw-off gesture like he was set to just pack his shit and jet.

"Hey, that ain't cool," Shakes said amidst the disgust. "The guy can't help it if he's a Ricky Retardo, man."

Mr. Taylor waited again for the laughter and claps to die down.

"Well"—his smile bitter—"if that ain't the pot calling the kettle black."

"Thass old an' cold, man." Shakes put an unlit cigarette to his lips. "You make a dude not wanna stick around, bro."

"I know the feeling," Mr. Taylor muttered, going back to his stellar map. More details about gasses and swirls and high temperatures.

Jose couldn't focus. He tried to lock eyes with Dink, but he just put his head down on his desk like Jose didn't even exist. Whassup with that? Jose tore a page and scribbled. Folded it small, waiting for Mr. Taylor to turn his back before nudging Toothy Barbara. She grinned and read it first before passing it on to Dinky.

Hey. WAKE UP!
I need to talk to you, bastid.

Dinky didn't look at him. He scribbled and passed it back to Toothy Barbara, who again inspected the contents before delivery.

SO WHAT'S UP?

"The Moon is only 239,000 miles away. Ten times the distance around the Earth's equator. Its distance shifts constantly because the Moon has an elliptical orbit. By the way, Mr. Robles, it's an oversimplification to say the Moon revolves around the Earth. The Earth and Moon revolve together around the barycenter, or center of the system."

So WHAT'S UP? Is that the best that Dinky could do? Did the bastid get so wrapped up with his brother that he forgot all about his going to see Lucy "to finish it"? He scribbled frantic, the letters almost pressing through. Toothy Barbara gave him a questioning look when she read that one. He motioned for her to get on with it. She nudged Dinky without taking her eyes off Jose.

I killed Lucy last night.

"Damn."

Dinky turned to give Jose a look, to see what kind of joke this was. Toothy Barbara hadn't taken her eyes off him. Jose was about to write another note telling them to stop staring at him when Mr. Taylor stepped over, yanking the note out of Dinky's hand. Nailed the three with a dirty look before checking out the note.

"Hey, wake up, I need to talk to you bastID? So what's up, I killed Lucy last night."

The laughter hit like a wave splash. (Dinky ducked.) Loudest of all was Shakes, going, *Yeah Right you wish.* Dinky hid his face but peeked at Jose, who looked stunned and blank-eyed. The rifle shot sound of yardstick striking desk made him start.

The laughter trickled down to titters. Mr. Taylor looked out at all the faces, then went over to his little book to start handing out little red zeros.

"It wasn't *me!*" Toothy Barbara screeched. "Why should I get a zero?"

Mr. Taylor didn't even look up as he scribbled. "Come come. Don't you know the messenger always pays for the message?"

"Hey, Teach," Shakes said, "is the faggit's love letter gonna be on the quiz?"

The class laughed the bell rang the chairs scraped. Mr. Taylor scrunched up the note and tossed it into the basket, scurrying to the board to list chapters for the quiz. Dinky stared at Jose like he didn't get it. There was a joke, wasn't there a joke? Jose was on his way to him amidst the general scurry when Toothy Barbara stepped right in front of him.

"Hey you with the notes. Whass this about bein a ladykiller, hmm?"

"Yeah, whad is that?" Dezzie put in, over her shoulder.

"Don'chu wish you knew, Tooth head."

Toothy Barbara grinned, her magic eye turning from hazel to green. Nothing she loved better than a challenge. "You know I'm gonna find out the story anyway, so why not save yourself some trouble an' just tell me whassup now?"

"Get the fuck."

"Jose," Dinky said, hoping to calm him.

Toothy Barbara grinned.

"You know the case I'm working on now, don'chu?"

There was flux all around them, students rushing out every place, but Dink and Jose stood riveted. Toothy knew how to get attention. She planted that look on them, like she was on to something.

"I'm hot on the trail of the comic-book bandits. You know, *THE BUDDHA BOOK*?"

"Yeah well." Dinky pulled on Jose. "We got places to go."

"I just have to find this SPIK-EE BOY. 'Cause you know, I already got this SLINK-EE dude figured out."

Dinky glared. "Oh yeah?"

She only had eyes for Jose.

"How come you look so fucken *jincho,* baby? You been listenin to that white music again?"

"I have a cold."

She checked his forehead. "You feel too cold to have a cold."

She didn't like the way he pulled her hand off. She never liked that.

"The school newspaper is sure the culprits will soon be caught," she said, like she had written the lines herself. (She had, actually.) "Their identities will be discovered, and their deeds punished."

"And the entire story will be broken by *The Sentinel*'s two star reporters," Dezzie said with great flourish. She had that weird quality—people only noticed her when she spoke up.

"You mean star finks," Dinky said.

"That sad Ms. Arroyo. She was nice. I liked her. Did she help you put the story together?"

"Fuck off," Jose said, as he and Dink walked away from her. She and Dezzie followed behind as they hit the crowded hallway.

"I'll find out, Jose. You know that. An' this thing about bein a ladykiller? Evidently some type of fantasy deal, right? Like maybe you imagine yourself in some low-budget porno thriller?" She adjusted her pointy glasses. Imitation ivory frames with teeny rhinestones. "Jose Shlong? Long-dong Vega?"

Dezzie laughed out loud. Jose and Dinky turned around just long enough to trade looks with them as they made the left turn to math class. Barbara gave Jose that deep, probing stare. He and Dinky watched the flutter of her pleated skirt, and stayed pensive.

"That girl got it in for you," Dinky said.

"How much you think she knows?"

"I don't know. But if she's on it, they won't need a torture device to get her to talk. The bitch'll spill everything."

Dinky pulled Jose along the crowded hall. His eyes were on the lookout for hall monitors that knew him on sight, that were apt to stop him. He wanted to avoid getting Jose searched. He was thinking about that just as Jose nudged him.

"I got new panels to show you, bro."

"Ah Jesus," Dinky said, pulling him down the stairwell fast.

5

Luis Muñoz Marín High School stood on a lonely stretch of Southern Boulevard. It was a big brown bunker of a building just off the Bruckner Expressway. It had stood empty for years until some school board member started to agitate for a new "target" school. It opened two years ago as a school for "troubled teens" that eventually became just another overcrowded, understaffed, underfunded South Bronx high school. Luis Muñoz Marín made all the papers, but it wasn't because of great achievements. A flurry of unfair practices suits from unions. Four city council members forced to resign after it was discovered they sold interest in the school to private companies. Two assistant principals ousted after they used school money to see the world, and the school's first principal was fired. He had talked a lot about the grand new computer room the students were going to have, thanks to the generous support of several corporations. A year later and still no computer room, though the office staff did receive equipment upgrades and an entire new bank of MAC COMPUTERS SWIPED FROM STUDENTS, the paper screamed. More indictments.

Rolando Reyes stepped in with a flourish. A member of the local school board and three-time candidate for a city council seat, he talked about creating a new kind of school, to imbue youngsters with a sense of culture and heritage. He led a march, burned a drug dealer in effigy, and threw a school "night rally." "This is what's waiting for these drug dealers," he cried, brandishing a baseball bat.

The bat did not stop the shootings. Six students hit in or around the school so far this year. Two deaths. There was a boy who evidently "jumped" from a school window. Every week they took at least three guns off students. Reyes refused to install metal detectors. He would've had to move that huge bust of Luis Muñoz Marín, his personal hero—and he wouldn't hear of it. "The image of that man should be the first thing they see when they come in. This is a school, not a prison," he said at the city council hearing. There would be no more scandals at his school. He would stake his reputation on that. At his school there would only be an unswerving loyalty to the younger generation of Puerto Ricans. Taíno specific. RicanCENTRIC. The bust of *El Gran Hombre* in the entrance hall the definitive symbol of Puerto Rican ascension.

"We have arrived, as Puerto Ricans," he told the students on his opening day in the packed auditorium, which was draped in bright red Coca-Cola flags. "Every time you pass the bust of this great man of democracy, you should think of where he has brought us." Reyes gestured grandly under the big red banner proclaiming "THE CHOICE OF A NEW GENERATION." "Of how you wouldn't be here if it hadn't been for his heroic effort to bring Puerto Rico together with the United States as a strong, vibrant partner in this grand, democratic experiment."

The students, who studied history from books published in

1979, did not seem so honored. They wrote on walls, spray-painted the bust three times, shot out the ground-floor windows. The bathrooms got vandalized so many times that Reyes refused to fix them. The school was overcrowded. Students sat on window ledges, countertops, on tables, and even outside classrooms in the hallways. Each year more and more students got sent there, including those tons of black kids that Reyes didn't know what to do with. "This is a Puerto Rican school," he told the city council at an appeal hearing he called to complain about the overcrowding. "I'm sure the black students will get a good education, but I'm wondering if this system wouldn't be better served by sending us those students who need a Puerto RicanCENTRIC school the most— Puerto Ricans." The council warned Reyes that he could go complain to city hall if he wanted, but if they slapped him with charges of racism the council would dump him. (Reyes stopped protesting.)

Teachers came and went so fast that Reyes interviewed young teacher hopefuls daily. Especially now, for Carmen Arroyo's position had not yet been filled.

Carmen was a youngish twenty-six. She taught English and lived in the "hood," on Kelly Street. The students liked her. Not only did the boys appreciate her showing off her fine legs in those short skirts, but the girls liked the way she could sit with them for hours to gab about boys. Cute boys. (She had her favorites too.) Could sometimes spot her after school, sitting in a booth at the Cuban sandwich shop. Girls clustered around her, all gabby about the dilemma of boys. There was a true girlfriend chumminess to the way they shared lovelife talk. (Carmen spared no details. A good source for condoms, sex advice, and makeup tips.) Was that her at the big roller rink on Bruckner? That's where she first got her ass spotted with Boots, the cutest boy in school. He was no Ricky Martin, just a scruffy-haired reckless type no doubt headed for jail "unless he could be saved," and some girls can't resist a challenge. Evidently this was a *big* challenge for Carmen, judging from the after-school rap sessions in her car and all that counseling. The night those posse boys said they would kill him, he slept over at her house. That was the morning Toothy Barbara happened by, working on a tip. To find Boots there, quietly sipping his coffee.

"No doubt about it," Toothy Barbara announced grimly to the concerned cluster of girls. "The poor woman is in love." They drafted a resolution to pull their teacher aside and warn her to cut that shit out because talk could get around and it could be big trouble. Before they could get to her, a jealous girl went right to the principal's office and ratted on Boots. Soon he had been pulled from class and was animatedly bragging. That led to Carmen Arroyo standing before Reyes.

Carmen arroyo left quietly.

The closing panel of *BUDDHA BOOK #3* showed a beaten, tear-streaked Carmen Arroyo sitting by her window overlooking the old Prospect Hospital. It was this last page that incensed Reyes the most. That whole office scene, exactly where did they get that dialogue, which seemed authentic? It was *this* issue that he passed around the conference table to the six teachers he pulled from classes the five hall monitors the two supervisors and his security chief, who sat beside him. (The students called him "Sweaty" Mendoza because his face got slick any time there was action.) And now, while students poured out of classes in loud scurry, Reyes prepped his people.

"I need all of you to think like intelligence experts. Do you know students who draw? That doodle aimlessly across notebooks, workbooks, scrappaper? Collect all scraps. Check wastebaskets. Search for similarities in style. Remember that every artist has a distinctive touch. That is where we have them."

Mr. Peterson, the art teacher, flipped through *BUDDHA BOOK*. Smirked. "My students sure don't draw like this." There was a dry unbelief in everything he said. "It's as if now everybody wants to show they *can't* draw."

"Well. Keep looking. You hall monitors and security personnel have all been briefed on our little friend, Alonzo Robles. Refer to the police photos. Remember he's the son of a convicted drug dealer. He is suspect at all times of being engaged in illegal activity. So search him, and anyone he is seen with."

There was a deep quiet. The student bustle in the halls outside. The teachers seemed almost like kids who were praying for the bell.

Pedro Vega raised his hand. He had been in the room all along although no one noticed, a problem that seemed to dog him. He was the only staff member not to appear in the comic so far.

"Yes. *Pedro*."

(Liked the way Reyes said "Pedro." In Spanish. Like a *compai*.)

"I just wanted to mention that not all students of this fine school are involved in this. My son is working with me, to find the culprits."

"Oh yes." Reyes brightened. "Very good. I recall that you have a son here with us."

"That's right. I've spoken to him about this, and he has pledged himself to our cause."

Reyes smiled at Pedro's choice of words.

"The key here," Reyes said, "is to confiscate every copy of this thing that you see, anywhere. Reiterate to the student population that these people are criminals that need to be handed over for the good of the community. That their actions reflect on all of us, and that they make us look bad."

"How do they ever," Sweaty Mendoza said with wonder, turning his copy sideways to check out that Carmen Arroyo centerfold. Lingering there.

"Color copier," Miss Perez, Puerto Rican Studies, said.

"You mean like *our* color copier?" Mr. Peterson got screechy. "We just got some new ones in the office!"

Reyes shut his eyes for a moment.

"*Calma*," he said.

The student scamper. Like mice in the wall. The lights buzzing. The feel of waiting.

"There must not be another issue."

Reyes gave each person in the room that look of determination that was supposed to inspire them to action.

The late bell rang.

Reyes did not move.

No one moved.

6

"Where the fuck were you? Dinchu get my message?"

They were in a second-floor bathroom. The late bell had just rung, and classroom doors slammed all up and down the halls.

The bathroom was empty. A large puddle shimmered like a brook, over by the urinals. Flies buzzed in and out through the open windows. The sink lay on the floor, surrounded by plaster and bricks.

Dinky checked all the stalls, just to be sure. He seemed more uptight than Jose, which should have been impossible.

"I was in King Rat's office. Thass why I was late. I got searched again. I thought it was about drugs, but it's not, bro. King Rat is all up about *THE BUDDHA BOOK.* The jerk thinks I'm SLINK-EE. An' now he's thinkin he gonna find SPIK-EE BOY by searchin me an' everybody with me. Do you read that?"

Jose was up on the windowsill, fighting the little trembles. Like all the words had flown past.

"Dink. Something happened last night."

Dinky was pacing. Tore off a bite of licorice twirl.

"Students don't have rights, he said. I'm on probation so he can fuck me all he wants! You hear what I'm sayin? I'm like some forever suspect. It ain't never gonna wash off! Did I ask for my pops to be a drug dealer? Huh? Why is that *my* fault?"

"It's not, bro."

"They took my armored personnel carrier, man! My brother just gave it to me. A rare Dinky Toy. I was gonna show you! That Sweaty Mendoza swiped it."

"So we can swipe it back." Jose hadn't ever seen Dinky so worked up. Jose had to grab him by the shoulders just to slow him down. "Dinky. Hello? We'll just swipe it back. We gotta make more copies, don't we?"

Dinky stopped shaking his head. Stared.

"Lemme check out'cha bag. Quick."

They both slid down to the floor, Dinky pulling out all Jose's stuff. The workbook was covered with doodles and art. There was a sketchbook full of Jose's unique cartoons. And there were twelve pages of panels Dinky hadn't seen before, completely laid out with captions, word balloons, and almost everything you would need to print it up. A girl held underwater. The streams of bubbles. The deep, charcoal black.

"Ah Jesus," Dinky said. "Panels. Ah shit."

"It's the next issue. I started work on it."

Dinky studied the pages. The face of that girl, underwater.

"Jose," he whispered.

They had already made that pact, that from now on everything in the comic would be real. No fake names, no rumors or fantasies. Dinky hadn't yet come up with anything. (He had at least ten or twelve pages an issue to fill.) And here was Jose dropping these ready-made pages of Lucy on him. A drowned Lucy.

"It had to end somewhere," the pages said. "Here it was, ending."

"What did'ju do?" Dinky whispered.

"It just happened," Jose said, feeling nauseous.

Dinky snapped out of the daze, picked up the sketchbook. Stuck the panels inside, then took the stuff over to that hole in the wall behind the shattered sink. Moved some bricks around in there, then tucked the evidence in snuggly neat before replacing the bricks. Jose crammed the rest of his stuff back into the bag. Dinky came back to squat near him, putting a fresh licorice twirl in his mouth. Passing one to Jose.

"You know, for a moment there, you really had me goin."

"Whachu mean?"

"I just mean," forced Dinky laugh, "you had me thinkin just now tha'chu actually popped that sorry-ass bitch."

Something in Jose was burning. He gripped Dinky, looking him in the eye. Dinky didn't want to look in there all of a sudden. His licorice stick drooped.

"Ah, nah. No way, man."

"Dink." Jose squeezed his arm. Not able to say it.

"Nah, man." Like he wouldn't even consider it. "You know we could only print that if it actually happened. Too bad, but we can't use it. No fantasy stuff. Thass the rule."

Jose pulled it out of his thigh pocket. Landed in Dinky's hand with a gentle chiming. Dinky shivered as if the ten diamond stones six carats each had given him a chill.

"Ah shit," he muttered, his eyes glassy as he fingered the tag.

Jose found his reaction hard to swallow. What he had expected from Dinky was hard to say. There was just disappointment everywhere.

"Did'ju need a story that bad?"

Jose didn't answer. He went into one of the stalls and shut the door slam. Pressed his burning face against cool metal. And that's when the bathroom door swung open. The walkie-talkie chatter. The tall white guy in the sweatshirt.

"Okay," he said. "You wanna get to class, or do I write'chu up?"

Jose flushed the toilet. Opened the stall door.

"Nah, man, we goin." Dinky handed Jose his bookbag.

"I have diarrhea," Jose said to the guy. Deadpan.

"You think I care?" The guy flipped open his pad as that walkie-talkie crackled. "You're that Robles kid," he said to Dinky. "Alonzo Robles, right?"

(Dinky flinched every time he heard "Alonzo.")

The monitor showed Dinky the photo in his pad, the mug shot the cops took of him when they busted him with his pops. Three poses for a buck.

Jose was impressed with how Dinky held out that bookbag, wearing that poker face, like he was used to the system dogging him, expected no less. Took the indignities in stride. Just another day on the job. Name, rank, and serial number. The guard threw Jose a look.

"Donchu move," he said, while giving Dink a cursory frisk.

"What." Jose said it with attitude. "You ain't gonna tell me *I'm* on your list, are you?"

The monitor snatched Jose's bag, peering in but not being too picky.

"Kiddo, anybody he's with is on my list."

"Can we get to class now?" Dinky was getting huffy. "Or are you plannin'na write a note for us?"

The monitor followed them all the way to Mr. Martinez's class. Watched them from the door to make sure they went in. At that moment, Mr. Martinez was standing against the blackboard with his hands clasped behind like he always did when he was annoyed with the class.

"Vamos a recordar que nuestro idioma es como piedra preciosa. Hay que tratarlo con respeto y cariño. Si no, lo perdemos."

The noise was everywhere, the class still restless. Mr. Martinez had the look of a neutered dog, bald and squinty. He was from Spain and talked with that accent that had something to do with castles and arrogance and fucking people of color up the ass. Everybody hated him. He never understood why the class cheered when he told the tale of the Spanish Armada getting sunk.

"Oye, vamos a ver si nos callamos, eh?" His words always sounding like imperious commands of white Spaniard taskmaster. Row faster, Taíno.

Jose wasn't looking at Dinky. Something tense there. Who was let down by who? He opened his workbook, and started to doodle real small. Dinky stopped him.

"Man. Din'chu hear anything I said?"

He snatched the pen. Jose exhaled, staring at Mr. Martinez, who still waited.

"Look, I won't make it look like the style in the comic book, okay?" Taking the pen back. Starting a sketch of two girls down by the beach. Dotted bikinis. Big round eyes watery sparkle like on those Japanese cartoons.

Mr. Martinez was going *shhhhhhhh*. They hated when he did that. It only made everybody go *shhhhhhh* right back. Then the laughter would start again.

"Did'ju use my knife?"

Jose didn't look up from his craft. "No."

"How did it happen?"

"One moment we were talkin. The next . . . she ended up in the tub. In the water." Jose stopped sketching. A wave splash hit him. The forever tense trembling in his stomach. "An' I held her down. Just like that."

Dinky's face was blank. "Just like that."

They weren't looking at each other.

"So instant, I didn't believe it even while it was happening."

What were they talking about? Sports? A video game? A girl they both knew. Unreal. Lying in a tub of water.

"I cun'ta made it happen if I tried. If I had gone there plannin'na kill . . . plannin'na do that, it would never happen. It was always like that with me an' her. Things would just . . . take off."

Dinky's eyes looked watery as he stared at the blackboard.

"You mean like that time on Coney Island?"

Jose nodded. "Yeah. She . . ."

"Bueno." Mr. Martinez walked to the back of the classroom where the projector was set up. "Pasen la tarea al frente. Luis? Amontonamelos ahi encima de mi escritorio."

It had been a humid summer day. Jose and Lucy had double-dated with Dinky and that black girl named Candy who had blue nails three inches long. Couldn't stop talking about all those event-ful trips to the salon. Jose and Lucy were dressed alike, in brown baggies and big loose shirts. Fighting and necking and then fighting and necking. Jose especially remembered the street smell of her, the way her hair was squiggly wet from the pool.

They kept setting each other off all day, but when Jose refused to get on the Cyclone, she freaked. That was it, the last straw. She was getting on that shit no matter what. What kinda man was he, not willing to get on the roller coaster with his woman?

They had it out right by the concession stand. She splashed him with soft drink. He squiggled mustard in her face. While he stood fuming, she found herself a young guy to sit with her on the Cyclone. Side by side they went, up and down and over. Twice. Three times. When she finally came over, she had the guy's phone number on a slip of paper.

"His name is Derrick," she said in hello. "He's from Kingsbridge!"

Jose was quiet on the long train ride back. Like that was it, the end, no more. He rode between cars looking down on blurry dashing streets. Thought of how it would be to throw her off the train. It was the scene he drew when he got home. A whole strip. Threw her right off, train wheels screeching on a slow curve. She landed like glass. Shards of Lucy scattered everywhere. The thing was, it hadn't happened. He drew the panels just to get it out of his system. It was fake, imagination, release. These latest LUCY panels were the real thing. The thought gave him chills.

"It's all in the panels," he said to Dinky.

THE MOVIE WAS called *EL HOMBRE SIN PATRIA*. It was about this guy who said, *"MALDITO SEAN LOS ESTADOS UNIDOS!"* and everybody went apeshit. They put the asshole on a boat and shoved him on an island and everybody there that knew him was forbidden to have congress with him or even senate. No one could say a word about like how the Mets were doing, or whether Oprah was fat again—and absolutely *no* references to Michael Jackson whatsoever. The guy spent a lot of time going from shore to shore on this boat, but the more he traveled the more he realized how much everybody on the planet hated him for renouncing his own country. Without a good press secretary or even James Carville to help, he was sunk. Felt like shit and mumbled to himself a lot. In Spanish, which they made sure to translate. Big yellow captions for all the Puerto Ricans.

Jose started another sketch. A wide-eyed Asian girl. Underwater. The flickering film light and half-dark was perfect for talking, even though Mr. Martinez kept shushing the class to point out interesting scenes.

"Did anybody see you?"

Dinky's question hung in the hazy flicker. Jose immediately thought of Anita, of what she had said about seeing him. The thought of anyone knowing or even suspecting gave him some burn, but he decided Anita was no threat. She was a bit player, not even a daily occurrence.

"Nah. Nobody."

"What about the body?"

Dinky sounded like a cop. Real professional. Had he accepted it already? Was he that hard? Jose found it difficult to swallow that lump.

"Did'ju just leave it there?"

"Nah. I dressed it up an' took it with me. I mean what the fuck was I supposed to do?"

Dinky exhaled. The man without a country was dancing with a woman in an elegant ruffled dress. She spurned him. The guy couldn't even get a blow job.

"So you're tellin me that Angel's gonna come home, expectin'na find his little honey all wet for him. An' what he's gonna find is Lucy in the tub instead?"

Jose had been trying not to think that far. There is always a strange math to everything. Many times Jose just didn't want to find *x*.

"You know whachu did? If this really happened like you say—"

"What do you mean 'if'—?"

"—you just walked into the crib of a big-time drug dealer. An' you popped his wife."

There was a matter-of-fact about his voice, a sheen to the stare, that made Jose feel more and more queasy.

"You know how many posses would love to slap that bastid's face like that?"

Dinky was getting sparkle-eyed, as if Jose's act set off dreams. Dink, after all, was a guy who busted drug dealers' phones. Who spray-painted their dream mobiles and swiped their hubcaps.

"There are people who would throw you a party for this. Posse boys would hail you like a slick eraser. Dealers and squad leaders would offer you candy, pussy, car rides an' limos. They might even wanna hire you if you make a career out of it. You'd be cruisin in your own Jag in no time."

Jose felt a chill crawl up his back.

"I din't think you'd take it like this."

The man without a country was on his deathbed. Boy, was he

ever sorry now! Praying for the president of the United States. In Spanish.

"I'm just sayin, you know, it beats smashin phones, bro. My own pop would wanna shake your hand."

Dinky's eyes jumped around the half-dark, like he had gotten a good burst of energy from somewhere.

" 'Cause look. Just whachu think Angel's gonna do about this? I mean, when he comes across that body—whachu think he's gonna do?"

They exchanged looks. It was like the thought hit them at the same time. (Or maybe it was Dinky that put it there.)

"Nothing," Jose said. "He ain't gonna do jack."

"Right." Dinky whispering urgent under corny sound track as the credits rolled over the man without a country's lonely, untended grave. "He'd be a chump to invite the 5–0 to come sniff up his crib. No matter how tight he may be with Mr. Pig. He'd be openin himself up, makin himself look messy. The 5–0 could even squeeze him for more green."

"Or maybe they just sicka him." Jose's mind filled with story possibilities. "Why shun't they think *he* did it? She's lyin in his tub! They'll just pin it on his ass, take the credit for bringin in a big dealer!"

"He'll say he didn't do it. You think they gonna believe him? Alotta these guys just disappear their wives when they get sick of them."

Jose felt the anger swell up. The point of his pen pressing through paper.

"He never gave a fuck about her. I told her all along but she wun't listen. I was the only one that gave a fuck about her."

The film got tangled. Screeched caught in the projector. Mr.

Martinez started to panic, talking rapid Spanish. The film hopped back into place.

"You probably right about him. Maybe he'll do like I heard he did to that guy Renaldo."

Jose's eyes flickered with gangster footage. "Yeah. Renaldo."

"Used to be Angel's donkey. One day he did the hundred-meter dash with the week's take. I heard Angel pumped in the six bullets himself. Then he an' his boys dumped the body off the Triborough Bridge."

Jose nodded as if watching the footage. "Maybe thass what he'll do to me."

Chaos. The film crunched and mangled. Mr. Martinez appealed for help from one of the boys, who shrugged. Wasn't the film over anyway? The lights came on. A couple of boys pulled at the ripped film strip. Mr. Martinez groaned.

"How's he supposed to know it was you? Didju leave a note?"

"Nope."

"Some kinda callin card?"

"Nah, nah."

"He'll think it was some other posse. He sure ain't gonna think it was some skinny faggit schoolkid like you."

"Excuse me?"

"I mean how is he ever gonna know?"

Dinky's wonder increased with every word. It was making Jose feel stranger still. The tingling in his stomach got worse. The way Dink was looking at him didn't help, either.

"What? Why you lookin at me like that?"

"Bro." Dinky had on a fuzzy smile. "You just mighta committed the perfect crime."

The chill was painful passing through. Jose clenched jaws tight.

Mr. Martinez was at the front of the class. Shades on windows flew up with hysterical squeals.

"Ahora. Vamos." Trying to calm the restless sea. Chairs scraping. The bell would ring soon and the class was fidgety. "Bueno. Quiero que me escriban un ensayo sobre *EL HOMBRE SIN PATRIA*. Oye, como me van a oir si no se callan? Yo, por ejemplo, puedo decir que soy de España. Que dicen ustedes, los que son Puertorriqueños? Espero ver los resultados mañana. Dos paginas!"

Dinky shut his eyes. Like he was flowing into sweet dream.

"It's like the perfect crime."

And then his eyes snapped open.

"I just thoughta something," he said.

"Whass that?"

"The fucken note. The note you wrote in class, man."

"Pssh. Fuck it."

"Fuck it? Shit, man, just when I thought this was the perfect crime! The whole class heard that shit aloud. Shakes heard it. He runs for Angel, don't he? All he gotta do is give the guy the note, an' you'll be doin the jump scene off the Triborough without a bungee cord."

"So what? So maybe I want Angel to know it was me."

"You want the 5–0 to know too?"

The bell went off like a fire alarm.

The Haunt was a gift from his father, Cesar. Payback for years of loyal service. The gift that kept on giving even though Dinky wasn't working for pops no more. The old man wasn't happy with Dinky's decision to live "at home" with his mother.

"Traitor," he said, "all I give birth to is traitors. I should kill all my sons now."

"That ain't it," Dinky replied. "I just gotta connect with school an' all that real-world stuff, pops."

"This is your real world right here. Your future's here. What the fuck have I been killing myself for, anyway?"

At times like those, his father looked more like one of Dinky's teenage friends, manic, pacing and swinging his arms like he was bugging on bad speed. Cesar was all natural, though. No drugs to break his concentration or steer him away from objectives. He was committed to selling them, not getting trapped by them. He had four kids, and that made him a dad. He was no Mike Brady. Not even once. No trips to Yankee Stadium or afternoons in the park. He was a brooding presence.

Dinky and his little brothers might never have learned how to laugh if it hadn't been for Johnny, the oldest. Cesar had set him up as the next in line, the one to inherit the shop. Worked for his pop right from the start, followed orders, failed. He might act up from time to time, like the day he abandoned his runs to swipe a van and take his brothers to Great Adventure. His eyes were all daredevil, his habit to find a way around every rule. He was the one who tickled the boys at midnight after a beating, who brought ice pops and bawdy jokes when Dinky had a fat lip from a daddy punch. His leaving to go join the marines was the sonic boom that scattered everybody.

The mom didn't rock with the firm. She worked at the Department of Motor Vehicles while her husband worked street scams, fenced goods, stole cars. She was another young, vibrant Puerto Rican woman that slept with trash and developed a loyalty to it. The street deals led him to crack dealing, and Ignacio Arturo Robles became "Big" Cesar.

The man found he was good at organizing, that he could build a team and make it work. Pretty soon, every weekend was Super Bowl Sunday. As he expanded, he began to "bite" the competition. They started calling him "Terror," "Push," "Wack Mack." On Fox Street the dealers he allowed to thrive bowed and payed tribute, but when he'd come home, his very wife would diss him. She would remind him that he was nothing, a thug with four kids. She never saw him at his best, dealing with crack-hoppy kids on corners, winning electoral votes with suppliers, devising new methods of moving product. He was a real business manager, but his wife didn't see it that way. All she did was bitch about how this was no life for a family and what kinda example was he to the kids and okay so he would let her blow all her steam out, maybe grinning a little or calmly smoking. When her energy seemed spent, he would beat her. The sobbing was no problem. "Women just cry," he would explain to the wide-eyed boys. "It's a device. They all use it. It's a trick. They pull a switch."

The rockum-sockum was a regular thing, until Johnny turned nineteen. One night Cesar was making his slap-happy response to her loud *quejas* when Johnny stepped in and just stopped it. He just got between them with his balled-up fists. It became a regular thing so that time and time again, Cesar had to postpone the match. He learned that although Johnny was willing to work, he was not going to put up with that beating-on-Mom routine.

It was becoming clear to Cesar that the woman was affecting the combat effectiveness of his men, so he gathered them together one spring day. A stoop meeting like any dealer might have with his troops. Johnny (nineteen) was the one chain-smoking. Alonzo (Dinky) at fifteen looked sleepy, stoned and uninterested. Luis (twelve) and Junior (ten) were the antsy ones, climbing up and down the steps. They liked making their own money. Nobody wanted to be a mama's boy, which was probably why they all accepted "leaving" home, though Johnny made it a habit to visit Mom. He always brought Dinky along, as if to train him.

"She's your ma, and don't forget it," he would tell Dinky in the car almost every time they went. "She's not like pops. She'll always be there, whether you work for it or not."

Cesar had a building on Southern Boulevard and another big one on Longwood. A couple of crackhouses and choice corners, and this trio of private houses overlooking the Bruckner Expressway.

He gave Luis and Junior their own crib, and set Johnny and Dinky up in The Haunt.

Living with Johnny was a blast. It was the only time that Dinky dug drug dealing. It wasn't about being kings or killers or the baddest on the block. It was the way summer scented those South Bronx nights. When every girl grinned (and when a Puerto Rican girl grins, the every inside of him blossoms), and music blared from *vayoneras,* whether hip-hop whether bachata whether that commercial Miami salsa shit, it was all movement. The greasy fried stink of those *pernil* sandwiches from that new Dominican place flavored the whole street. And it wasn't about being drug-dealing thug motherfuckers who never think before they slay. It was about brothers and smiles and shoulders that will always give you *espalda.* Will buck up your strength, will be *hasta la muerte* and, if you get popped, will wreak in your name—

"Business is business," Johnny would say, just like Cesar said it, only Johnny's face looked disgusted. Ducking bullets in Trans-Am screech, sucking vanilla shakes and speed-freaking down Longwood Avenue while the civilians tried to sleep. There were those times when they said FUCK IT I'm not gonna ask him for SHIT I don't need him I'm gonna do it MY WAY I'm gonna let him see just who the fuck I am, and soon that became every day. Soon it looked like Johnny was his own man, cutting his own deals, running the boys *his* way, building his own turf right under Daddy's nose.

Did Cesar pick up on that? Were they more Johnny's boys than his? One night, after a big scream-out with Cesar, Johnny's car got chopped by rapid fire. Lucky thing Johnny only got chipped off the old block, but his pal Hamper tomato-sauced the windshield with lettuce cheese pickles onions. Johnny even had some on his jacket when he showed up at The Haunt. Dinky had to roll three joints just to calm him.

"He tried to kill me; he tried to kill me." Like a mantra. The trembling hands, the jittery eyes. Dinky had never seen Johnny like that.

"I'm gonna kill him," Johnny said, and then he covered his head with his trembling hands for a long time. He sank out of sight, not working for a few days, until that scene on the roof. Cesar and Johnny face off by the parapet. Who would throw who? Dinky had watched, shivering under a stairwell by the roof door. Johnny left Cesar standing by the edge. Stormed past Dinky like he didn't even know him. Dissolved right into the U.S. Marines. One day he was there, the next he was gone, finding other digs to crash at with some friend from New Jersey until he had to report for training. One last visit to the moms in the story, a few quick handclasps and hugs for the troops. Not many words, not much to say. Luis, Junior, and Dinky all watching him get into a car for the long ride away.

"You shun't work for him," he said. "He doesn't deserve it."

The very last panel of the story showed Dinky yelling, "What are we supposed to do?" Because, who's got a choice? Cesar's glaring eyes followed them around like one of those cat clocks from the seventies. It wasn't love that bound them to him.

Now there was no more Johnny and Dinky in The Haunt. It was Jose and Dinky. The two of them up on that fire escape. Jose looking over those six pages of Dinky story and nodding, going yeah, and the sound of traffic mellow, another slow joint to make his eyes chinky. But his face looked strange and there was no getting around it. Something had happened to that boy. Dinky was noticing the new lines and craters.

"It's good," Jose said, "though the panels need work. But we should put it together with mine, bro."

"No way," Dinky said. "No way we gonna publish that Lucy shit."

"But we have to." There was a sound. A sob, a cough, something that came from Jose. It stopped the words for a while. Gave Dinky the time to relight the joint.

The Haunt was thus: Sandwiched between rumbly-tumblies. Boarded-up stoop so entryway only through the house next door. From all appearances, just another empty boarded-up, but first floor was an active crack hole where you had to be on the guest list. There was a posse haunt in the basement where Dinky used to DJ parties to keep the local action squads happy. The second floor was all warehouse, piled high with all those items that need piling when running a healthy drug op.

The third floor was all Dinky's. Separate entrance along the third-floor apartment from the house next door. The stairwell was sealed, no trespass without key. ALONZO'S WORLD (wooden sign painted by Johnny). Dinky's Haunt. Three big apartments plus access to the roof. From there he could hop from building to building, or run out through one of the many escape hatches in case of. This gift from Cesar was an open door for the boy to remember that the torch had been passed to a new generation that shouldn't ask what your country can do for you, ask what you can do to make the country—

How could Dinky *not* jump back into the biz now that his father was in the joint? Wasn't it his duty, now that Cesar was sitting all glassed in, bug in a jar, staring through that plastic barrier like he was still home? His eyes still had the authority, his voice that bite and sting. Jail was no shame. It was stripes, rank, honor. It was where officers got promoted. Cesar always got cockier in jail, like he enjoyed the chance to earn more stripes. He always said the joint was a good place to make new connections, spread the faith, get new tats. (Last time, managed to get that serpent that goes from knuckle to knuckle to knuckle to.) "Maybe time for a new tat," he told Dinky the night he was booked, his nonchalance supposed to teach Dinky about how to act in front of cops. Dinky made him proud, wearing that stone face all through booking—after all, he was now the next in line.

Cops frown on family business, but they had nothing on him, so they took some snaps and let him go. Now father and son were on opposite sides of the glass. Cesar, like a good dad, tried to instil that sense of spine into his kid, and yet here was the kid doing that soft shoe. Trying to get away with that "Slick Willie" Clinton thing, to draw deep and *not* inhale.

"It's because of your brother. Ain't it?"

Dinky shook his head listless. "Nah, man."

"Oh yeah?" When Cesar wore that face, it was impossible to fob. The man wouldn't touch a book but he could read a face in a snap. Had that serpent on his knuckles and that snake just loved contact sports. Good thing the glass between them was so thick.

"He don't come to see me. He goes to see her, but not me. I wun'ta even known he was in town if you hadn't told me. You think thass right, that a son should treat his father like that?"

Dinky swallowed hard. Like he couldn't get that apricot pit down.

"He thinks you tried to kill him."

Cesar just stared back, forcing Dinky to have to rephrase the question. Another apricot pit going down slow.

"Did you?"

"Tell me something, little Alonzo. If Johnny jumps off a cliff, would'ju jump off after him?"

"Why don'chu just answer the question, man."

Cesar looked like he would spit through the glass.

"I know why you come here. I don't got time for people who think they slick. You gonna have to come down on one side or the other. The next time you come, you tell me which one."

And he motioned to the guard like he had his own private butler to open and close his door and shoo away the unwanted guest.

DINKY WANTED TO keep The Haunt. It meant freedom and space and no one to tell him when to go to bed. He could split his time between his mom's and there, and she respected his need for space. She trusted him. "You can stay there as long as you're not working for him," she would say, nailing him with a keen look. "You're not, right?"

"Nah, man."

"I mean, not even a little bit for chump change, right?"

"I don't work. I only crash there."

"It's not the safest place . . ."

"Ma, please . . ."

"I just mean it's good for you to be there. You can keep track of your brothers—" Her eyes all misty would suddenly turn hard, determined. "Do you see them at all?"

Luis and Junior never visited her. Dinky could only smile sadly when she brought them up. Her face would crumble if he took too long to answer, and then she would be reloading that glass, adding more scotch, less water. Dinky's old game of moving the glass around the table like a chesspiece, away from her, by degrees.

"I don't see them so much," he would say. Didn't want to tell her Cesar was making a point of keeping them well hid from him because he saw Dinky as just another Johnny, another traitor that might lure the boys away. "You know I'm not runnin with that. But they are. So I don't see them."

"But'chu should see them," she insisted this time. "You're brothers. Brothers take care of each other. Doesn't Johnny come to see you?"

That these talks always ended with Johnny made Dinky's head throb. Some nights at The Haunt, he couldn't sleep, sitting folded small on the fire escape. Watching posse boy cars trail sparks up the street. Wheels screeching engines roar. (The winner of the drag race gets the girl. He and his entire posse. Those boys do everything together.) Alone up there looking down, Dinky could feel angry about his big war-hero brother. The one who got out. The one who left him behind.

Lighter flick.

Dinky had the note. Opened it crisp, flattened wrinkles with his hand as if he needed to check it one last time. Thought Jose was watching him, but his eyes were scanning the horizon.

Hey. WAKE UP!
I need to talk to you, bastid.

SO WHAT'S UP?

I killed Lucy last night.

"You should watch this," he told Jose, whose eyes returned from the distance. Dinky felt it would be brief, so he put lighter flame to paper fast. The light breeze picked up on that shit and made that paper flash into ash like a magic trick.

Jose didn't say anything.

"Now nobody knows," Dinky said.

There were three apartments on Dinky's floor. One that he and Jose went into all the time. Two others that, for one reason or another, they stopped visiting.

Fourteen was the main Haunt. Mattresses, stereo, posters. The big table where they laid out the first three issues of *BUDDHA BOOK*. Comics, magazines, video games scattered everywhere. A twenty-seven-inch TV they used for the Sega. Dinky covered a couple of walls with his spray-paint work. There was a Mickey Mouse that looked more like Mickey Rat, creeping over terrified tenements and derailed subway cars. There was a huge maze, now spreading to its second wall. YOU ARE HERE, stranded on a large South Bronx floating turd. Arrows point the way to get out but there are eight paths to choose from. All seem to lead to Nirvana, where that sad blond kid screams A DENIAL! Dinky was always spraying over the maze to keep Jose from figuring it out.

There was the Hubcap Room, walls lined with the results of their nighttime raids on posse cars. Dinky had so many of them he was starting to tack them to the ceiling. With the room painted black and that strobe going, it was almost like outer space, each hubcap a planet, a star. It was there that he kept fourteen of his prized die-cast metal cars and military vehicles, on display in that $800 antique bookcase with the glass doors. (Reminded him always of Johnny. How he drove Dinky to Gramercy Park in the Bronco to pick it up.) The treasured six-wheeled Panzerspah-wagen ($300) and that blessed Citroën ($450) among the others. That was where so much of his work money had gone. That, and DJ gear.

Stored that in Sixteen. Sound system mixers turntables crates of records CDs. Lights strobes digital effects, that dual CD player. Those posse parties in the basement are pretty tough turf to learn, but if you can make it there, you can make it all the way to white people buying you studio time so some rich client singer can tribe her honky-ass career further with your jungle mixes. Dinky became a master. Could pump the masses, then swing them low and crawly for some bumps and hinds. Could mold the mood. His fame spread from posse to posse, from block party to posse dive. The roller disco on Bruckner even offered him a go, but Dinky had been too full of posse life back then to even think of going legit. (Besides, Johnny had been like his agent, booking him with posses far and wee. And they always paid better.)

When Johnny left, Dinky lost the feel. Took his gear out of the basement and stored it in Sixteen. Could still mix tapes and sell them for six dollars. The perfect place to bring girls and get them horizontal. (Jose and Dinky would blindfold them like they were bringing them to the Batcave.) But the private parties had been over for a long time, and Dinky wasn't making tapes. These days he did not go in there.

Fifteen was Lucy's room.

Jose had brought her to The Haunt with a real need to impress. She had been buddy and pal for so long, until one night they started to do smoochies. He decided to introduce her to "his" world. (The blindfold routine was not enough for her.) He wanted to win her, and win her so bad that Dinky suggested he "give" her Fifteen. Why not? She was talking a lot of shit about posse boys having their own spreads and making all that money which they spent on their ladies. Diamond bracelets they called "tags" and gold belt buckles. A posse wife gets her own crib. Jose had to do something about that, so he and Dinky scrubbed those walls, tidied up like they were expecting royalty. Jose even repainted the living room. He hadn't thought about that for a long time. Why now? Was it Lucy, down by the chain link, reminding him? As Dinky burned that note all crisp, Jose watched the girl down on the street. *Crunch crunch* as she moved through the weeds. At least, he thought he could hear it the same way he knew it was Lucy. Lucy staring up at him enough to make him want to nudge Dinky, but he was busy talking.

"You shun't be makin mistakes like that," he was saying. "Writin it down on a piece of paper an' passin it to Toothy Barbara is out. You gotta get smarter. You can't be tellin people this shit. The cops ain't the problem. It's Angel. You lucky Shakes is stupid. Lucky that note was still in the can."

Jose squinted. The chain link quivered as if someone had just kicked it. There was no girl.

"Angel has to know," he said.

She had demanded a bed and sofa, like a posse wife trying to make the place more livable. Brought flowers, curtains, kitchen stuff. In Fifteen, they could pretend they lived together. A place to hang, a place to fuck, but she was always saying it was fake. Jose wasn't a posse boy, a drug dealer, wasn't even living on his own. Everything was "borrowed"—The Haunt belonged to Dinky.

Lucy filled Fifteen with enough of herself to make him miss her when she left. Didn't even empty out her little bureau. Left that portable stereo and those stuffed animals. The makeup stuff waited patiently by the mirror. When she left, she didn't bother to return for anything. Lingering last scenes were not her bag. (Capricorns let the dead bury their dead.) She had lit on Angel and now that she had moved on to the next level she had no more use for that childhood place. She had left Jose behind.

Dinky examined those LUCY panels with glassy eyes. Holding that tinkling ANGEL tag.

"What else?" he said.

There was the monogrammed gold lighter. There was that fat bag of smoke that Dinky unrolled to sniff the bouquet. There was the money—fifteen hundred dollars. And that goofy snapshot.

Dinky kept turning the panels like he was looking for some kind of confirmation.

"We can't print this," he said.

"Why not?"

"You know why already, man."

"But how else is he gonna know I did it?"

"Whass he need to know so bad for?"

Dinky's hard stone face. Weathered like a boxcar. Hard to read. Jose's face different. The jumpy eyes of a newfangled street kid who doesn't want to miss a thing. Who's just learning the rope.

"So you wanna hit him with this?" Dinky seemed mad. "You wanna cold slap the guy?"

"Thass right. Besides, it's my best work. Ever."

They were up on the fire escape overlooking the Bruckner Expressway. Cars sped by below. The words had stopped coming, and the rain breeze gave them shivers.

Jose couldn't tell if it was contempt or admiration in Dinky's voice. He felt awful alone up there on that fire escape. Jose hadn't talked about this to anyone, and now he couldn't say. He wiped at his face, pressed those burning eyes.

Swallow.

Dinky with those faraway eyes. Too lazy to go get paper so he used the bottom of a paper bag to roll a thick fat one that was surprisingly tasty. The smoke turned everything grainy like an old film. The rain fell. They went inside, Lauryn Hill spilling from speakers. Drumming their face with her fingers.

Side by side at the big table, like it was time to get to work. This time, a wordless slow dream. Dinky pulled out his paints, his markers. He had become an amazing colorist/inker. In the beginning, it was Jose who put it all together. Dinky couldn't do panels or word balloons. All his pieces were disjointed and scattered. Jose taught him how to word less and picture more. Dragged him to the comic shops in the East Village. Introduced him to artists like Tim Vigil Dave Gibbons Donald Simpson, that older stuff by Russ Heath Sam Glanzman Joe Kubert. Dinky's style woodblocky—used thick lines to create depth. Real good at drawing tenements bridges cars, anything with detail. His streets were very R. Crumb, his subway cars incredible.

The thing was that they drew well together. It was like the addition of each other made it perfect. Jose could Lennon and Dinky would McCartney right back. Jose drew the infamous centerfold of Carmen Arroyo, but it was Dinky who added the lines and background swirls that made her curvy form pop from paper like some 3-D hologram. It was a psychic link, a Gemini fuse. Two parts of the same nation.

The first and second issues had been put together that way, hand over hand, thoughtless instinct and wordless flow, but this third issue was a new rhythm. Jose drew the panels, Dinky colored them. Now he watched Dinky color the churning underwater of Lucy. The calm smooth was gone. The rain started to pour, the curtains snapping nervous.

"Jose. You okay?"

"I don't know," Jose said, pulling his eyes away from the panels. He couldn't watch. He grabbed a paper and began to sketch. It killed the tremble in his hands.

When the last page was finished, they all lay flat, covering the table. Dinky stood back to take them all in, his eyes checking details like he was an engineer. His eyes were buzzed, but not from smoke.

"You were right," he said. "This is our best work."

Jose didn't like the way Dinky was looking at him. There was a pressure from his eyes. For answers for truth for the reasons why. It was someplace Jose didn't want to go.

But he looked. He stood there beside Dinky and he looked at

his best pages. And he looked at drowning Lucy. And it was all together and that made it worse.

When the rain let up, they hit the street. They would meet again after Jose's shift at the pizzeria, but right now they slow-walked up Southern Boulevard. Dinky was chomping licorice and talking like maybe he was getting an idea for his story because if Jose had already done twelve pages, then they needed another twelve or so to finish the new issue and Jose had talked about how this time, it would be Dinky doing a *whole* story by himself, whether panels whether not it would have to be total Dinky, and so Jose should have been listening but he wasn't, or maybe it was that sound trick again where everything just got muted. There was a Lucy whisper on the street. The shake of shoulder-length hair, the *clip-clop* of her clogs on the sidewalk. Lucy hanging by the door to Ednita's Videos on Prospect Avenue. Jose nudged Dinky, hoping he would see, but Dinky didn't catch the manic energy in those legs, the swing of dark hair again. The girl turned and gave Jose that coy wave. A Lucy trademark.

"Whassup, Jose?"

But Dinky's voice was like so much background car horns and air brakes. Jose crossed the street fast. Dinky tried to keep up but there was this bus and that car and then a truck. By the time Dinky got across, Jose had gone into the video store. Dinky found him scanning the shelves with a blank look on his face.

"Jose, man. What the fuck?"

Jose walked past him, stopping by the open door to stare out at the street.

"Just missed her," he said.

"Missed who?"

The churning was on Jose. The nausea from the waves of crashing ocean. Dinky held him while he threw up that slice of pizza he had gulped down for lunch.

"I have to go back there," Jose said.

"Over where?"

"To the scene of the crime."

"Are you wack? Did you forget something? What makes you wanna go back there, man?"

Jose pulled away, broke free. Stared across traffic but didn't make a move.

"I shun'ta left her in that tub," he said.

Dinky turned him toward Prospect Avenue.

"Look. Go to work. You're late now anyway, right? I'll go cop a peek. See whassup."

The hug caught Jose by surprise. Triggered something. They were still on Southern Boulevard when the bus pulled to a stop across the street.

"I'll call you, man!"

Dinky hopped the back of the bus, clinging to large vents. His sneaks fought for grip on that wet, flat bumper. Jose waved as the bus got smaller. Glad the hug didn't last longer.

8

He just wanted to coast, to keep things simple. Why was everybody complicating his life?

Hadn't planned on another war, another campaign. Just wanted to keep The Haunt, collect those Dinky Toys, walk that fine line between street and not street. Wanting to grab from this shelf and that, to get better at the balancing act. The glass with the drink and how he had played chess with it.

"I resent you," his mother said.

"Why's that?" Dinky twirled the tumbler.

"Because all this time you *act* like you're trying to keep me from drinking. But you haven't noticed I've stopped." Her smile still a little unsure. "Nothing but soda in that glass. It's been that way for two months now."

Dinky sniffed at the tumbler. It made him laugh.

"I resent that. Like you're here and not here. Like you working both sides of the street."

"You sound like Cesar."

"Don't insult me. I wear new dresses, I wipe circles from my eyes. I even got the dog fixed so it doesn't tremble so much."

"Oh yeah?"

"That's right. I have the only toy poodle in the South Bronx that's on Darvon."

Dinky didn't like the intense look in her eyes, the way it all seemed aimed at him. She was reminding him a lot of Cesar.

She brought her hands up in an unconscious gesture of supplication.

"I want my family back, Dinky."

(Hoh boy.)

Dinky got up from the table like somebody spilled the lava. The living room bigger, maybe more sun. But she was right behind him.

"Now that he's in jail. Wouldn't this be the best time to make a move?"

"I don't know if I can do that," Dinky said, like he had said before.

"I understand completely," she said back like she didn't want to hear it. "Wouldn't want to give up that nice life, all those perks."

"For Chrissake. Why don'chu get Johnny an' his fucken marines to do it?"

Because seeing Johnny was nice this time too, always appreciate a visit. But something was changing. He made a lot of speeches about Dinky pulling himself up by his bootstraps—sure nice of him to drop by and bring presents. But maybe Cesar was right about the bastid deserting the family. Maybe Dinky expected the guy to want to do something to help. (Say it. Tell her.) Wasn't Johnny the oldest? Why wasn't it *his* mission, then?

"I'm not going to argue with you. You either care about your brothers, or you don't. That's up to you."

The sinking feel. The sense of loss every time she walked out of the room like that. The obligation of duty. It was the same trip Cesar was on. All Dinky knew was that he hated being in the spot of having to prove something to someone. Had to work for the love, earn that wage. Cesar said it was time to decide. Dinky just shut his eyes tight to keep the rain out as the bus shuddered dipped from curves from potholes.

And there was Lucy, underwater.

What made him feel guilt about what happened? Two issues ago, Jose did that strip where he throws Lucy off the train. Real vivid shit all right, but Dinky refused to have it in the comic book. He didn't want any Lucy-Angel-Jose thing. It might get them fingered. Lucy would definitely tattle and come after them. It would be too obvious.

"Besides," Dinky added, hoping to end it, "it didn't fucken happen!"

Jose's face went hard. Dinky stared, not knowing Jose could do that with his features.

"So you're sayin I should've thrown her off the train for real."

Dinky's face strained with disbelief.

"If I had really killed her an' given you the panels, then we could've printed them. Right?"

"Let's drop this." Dinky passed the joint like a peace pipe. "It's just that this thing between you an' her just gotta end, bro."

"Trust me," Jose said. "I'll end it."

That was the last time they argued about Lucy. Dinky had laughed, thinking it would never end with them. That was why he offered him the knife that night. Jose the most UNposse. Looked like a kid smelled like a kid. There was young and fresh all over him. Not the type you'd expect to hold a girl under until. The panels Dinky colored walked him patiently through the entire murder. Like he was there, adding the final touch. Brotherhood does strange things to a guy.

Dinky gripped the bus vent with rain-cold fingers. Hopped off on Longwood, crossing the slick street. This was old turf that he didn't visit very much these days. A few of the same olds gave him the look like they were surprised to see him walking that beat. Dinky only slow-nodded. Fox Street was quiet and wet like a post-card from some black-and-white time. On to Beck Street, where Angel's crib was. The same stoops and doorways that had pro-vided *esquina* when he needed shelter during those long days of work. Walking along slow, he noticed a small crowd near one of the stoops. There was a police car with dim pulsing lights. The way the scene appeared out of the drizzle made Dinky stop in midstep. There would be Lucy. Wet hair unblinking stare and that breathless open to her mouth. Was that Angel by the two cops, angry glaring as he explained, argued, raged?

Dinky blinked away film sequences. Approached the cluster of people, scanning faces. Kids standing with bubblegum stares. A cop muttered into talkie and eyed apartment windows.

It was a body they were looking at.

Dinky could tell by the faces. Humans get a certain way when they're looking at a body. It's the same with porno.

Couldn't make the stiff out yet but he knew it wasn't Lucy. It was a guy, sprawled across stoop steps. Three neat holes in his chest, punched through the blue *guayavera*. A cop appeared right then and dropped some waterproof tarp over the body. Threw it down without too much care so the stiff's face remained in view for all the gawkers.

She appeared out of the drizzle beside Dinky as if she had been there all along.

"It's no fun now," she said. Cigarette puff. "The bastids covered him."

Dinky stared.

Anita. Angel groupie. Hot pants stripper baby. Pouts so spoiled. Shot a guy with her midget .22 once. Walk on eggs with her. Wounds easy, never forgets. Eyes large and deep, don't fall in. She used to trail Angel—knew his ways, his days numbered on her clock. Maybe this was a break—wouldn't she know if something went down last night? For there was a tenth of Dinky, maybe a twentieth, that was hoping this business of a dead Lucy was just Jose writing a story.

She looked ten times better than memory. Those tanned legs, the clacky sandals. That minidress billowing out, silky pleats. There was a bow in the back, and lace on her shoulders. Back then she was just another street face, someone to kill time with. Shared moments, talk, a jay. This vestibule, that. The one thing he learned about her was that her appearances were never *una casualidad*.

"You shoulda been here when he was still with us." Blew a swirling circle of smoke at a cop. "Ahh, he twitched so pretty."

"What happened?"

She huffed. "He shoulda been mindin his own beeswax insteada playin at Inspector Clouseau. Stuck his nose in the wrong hive. So he got stung, right?"

She laughed at her own joke. For some reason while looking at her, Dinky recalled he hadn't been laid in over four months.

"He was pretty to watch." Came closer to whisper. "Just like in that *Phases of Death* video. You ever seen that?"

Dinky shook his head, scoping faces on the street again. Wanting to be sure he spotted them before they spotted him.

"I think watchin a man die is erotic," she said. Laughed at the way Dinky grimaced.

"I'm serious, Slinky."

He laughed. Words like that coming out of such a feminine pretty made him think how strange, how cool. Something sweet, something sick.

"Yuh fucken me," he said.

"Nah, I'm not. That *Phases of Death* video? Shows people actually dyin, actually gettin killed? Actually," she paused for effect, "I jerk off to it."

"Get outta here."

"I'm serious. Watchin a guy twitch like that. It makes me wet."

Rubbed one leg with the other. The clack of sandals.

"You should shut up with shit like that. Cop's lookin right at'chu."

She blew another perfect smoke ring. Dinky felt the warm smoke splash tender on his cheek. Almost a tickle. He coughed, she laughed, then gave the cop a come-hither stare.

"He knows tight pussy when he sees it," she said.

The cop looked away.

"Wha'cha doin, lookin for a date?"

"I told you, I get horny. Sometimes I ain't too particular."

"Tsk tsk. Whass Angel gonna thinka that?"

She seemed touched that he remembered something about her. Another smoke ring tickled his cheek. She sent them like kisses. Dinky rubbed the smoke feel off.

The detective. Bleary-eyed restless, he shuffled over to the stiff. Eyes not taking in the faces around him. He nodded to some other suit, then headed back to the car where the air conditioner was.

"Angel don't own me yet," she said.

"He better get smart."

Her eyes studied him. She touched his cheek.

"Damn, Slinky." (She used to call him that. Just like old times.) "Your skin's all cleared up."

Back then, he was a moonface. The acne cleared up when he started getting laid. Inés was first. After her, Bianca, Dina, Jenny. It was like he was in season. (Maybe it was a word-of-mouth thing.) The best acne cure ever.

Her leg brushed against his. He pictured himself fucking her. Made her smile, almost like she caught him at it. Got closer. Made him ask, "Whassup with you?" (She was so close.)

"I told you. Dead boys go right to my head."

"But I ain't dead."

"Ahh, Slinky. You kinda shy."

"My name ain't no Slinky."

"Slinky, 'cause you tall an' thin."

"It's Dinky, man. Dinky."

She stopped tugging on him.

"Dinky 'cause you got a tiny dick?"

"Dinky 'cause I collect Dinky Toys. The baddest die-cast metal replicas. An' I got the best collection in the whole fuckin South Bronx."

"Well." A huffy exhale. "Sweet, I imagine. But actually that don't do much for you, Slinky. A tag like that could give a girl the wrong idea."

A wall stopped Dinky's retreat. Only lovers stand that close.

"Look, Slink. I been starin at this stiff long enough. I got a freeze an' a half in my pocket. You wanna maybe have a blow with me? I promise you a nice surprise."

The tone of a hooker. Feels delicious, feels dangerous. He let her pull him away from the scene the stiff the 5-0 like mannequins they stood all cardboard cut-outs. Down the block she took him, into an alley. Pinned him against a wall between two Dumpsters. Almost wrenched his head off with that first kiss, such a press squeeze. Dinky wondered what the fuck made *this* possible. Sure, he knew her and that went back for some time, but it had never been lips and thighs and this hand pressing into his stiff.

"Whassup?" he said, swirling from peppermint lips.

"It's so perfect running into you. The way the pieces fall into place in my life. I couldn't ask for better plot development."

He was going with it. He wasn't sure why or for what purpose. Vaguely, something to do with Jose. Where did she pull the gun from? Couldn't have been concealed in that tiny purse, and no bumps no hiding places on her curvy surfaces. Like Bugs Bunny pulling out a hatchet. Dinky would've laughed, if only that midget .22 wasn't pointed at him with so much gleam.

"Ah man, whassup!"

"Shh. Don't move, Slinky."

"What the fuck is up with you pullin a piece, man!"

Her trembling grin. No smiling eyes.

"I just wanna know wha'chu doin on Beck Street today, Slinky."

"Wha'chu mean, man? I just been walkin—"

"Comin'na visit Lucy?"

Hearing that name come at him like that was a real shake. She was too sharp not to have noticed.

"I'm not here 'cause of Lucy," he said, watching that gun face.

"You're lying."

"I'm not. I'm here 'cause of Jose."

"Jose?" He couldn't read the grin. Looked bitter. "Is that why he came to see her last night?"

Oh boy. Dinky thought briefly about cornered mice. Cat's paws.

"Ah man, Anita. Put the piece away."

Against the wall between two Dumpsters, Dinky wasn't going far. He thought about all those times that Snoops used to pull a .45 on him, just for laughs. How Dinky learned to talk to a gun. Made him think he could talk his way out of anything. Not too sure about that now, watching Anita's eyes go angry.

"It just makes me sad, Dinky. That I've trusted you over the years. That I thought maybe I could look you up again."

"What the fuck you talkin about?"

"That we could be friends."

"We *are* friends," Dinky said, trying to calm the exasperation. Guns can go off under such circumstances. "Who's the one holdin the piece, anyway?"

"I talked to somebody about you yesterday. They told me you were in with Lucy. Do you know how much that shit burned, to find out that you were chummy with that bitch?"

"But I ain't chummy with that bitch. Whoever told you that is fulla shit. I don't hang with Lucy. I hang with her ex-boyfriend. Thass Jose. I chum with Jose."

"Jose?"

"Yeah, Jose. I think you know him."

"I know him sure, you tryin'na be funny? You tellin me he's Lucy's ex?"

"Yeah I'm tellin you. Him, not me."

"So he been sweet with Lucy?"

"She dumped him for Angel. How could he be sweet with her? Now you gonna shoot me, or what?"

Anita stood, processing. Could see those gears turning.

"Why was he over there last night then?"

Dinky felt a shiver. Too much coming at him. She had the gun but he had the information, so how could she shoot him now?

"Just shoot me already. I known plenny'a people pop their friends. It's why I got off the streets, man."

He watched the changes on her face. Carefulcarefulcareful. Tried to stop thinking she shot a guy she shot a guy. Put a gun against his head and squeezed for one big splash. She told Ronson she waited until the guy was asleep. Her body woke him with one long caress. (wake, baby. wake

> whass her name, baby. she better than me?
> I know her name. I know all about her.
> she ain't better.)

How long, Dinky wondered, did kitty cat play with her mousey before she did it?

"Small world, isn't it?" She seemed to be dreaming. "Angel. Lucy. Jose. Dinky." Her eyes sharpened on him. "Like we all been thrown together."

"Together," Dinky said. "Only you're holdin that gun on me."

"Thass right." Her grin trembled. "I'm a solo act. I already know that nobody takes me seriously. Like last week, when I saw Angel. He was lookin at me all pop-eyed, like he ain't never seen me lookin so good. An' I said, Hey, so now you got yourself a little posse wife, ah? Que bueno esta eso! Didn't my love mean anything to you after all that time? So how about if I go over to your crib an' just pop the bitch?"

The deep glow in her eyes gave Dinky the shudders, even though her gun hand was relaxed and she was leaning against one of the Dumpsters.

"You know what he said? He laughed, an' said he'd get her a bulletproof vest."

She was coming closer, gun hand behind her. A slow gradual approach that made Dinky feel a pulsing sex vibe.

"I don't think he was taking me too serious, you know wham sayin?"

"Yeah. I do."

There was a mellow something. A vague trembling to her. He would've guessed that she needed to be held. How fast the seasons change with her, how sunshine turns to rain.

"Like I would go an' shoot Lucy. Like I would do a thing like that."

Her hand was on his chest. Taking his pulse? He thought back now, to those old street days of his when they would sit in a vestibule to duck the rain, smoking a jay and talking like they were best friends. Only to soon be separated by duties. To find each other again maybe a week or two later, trading grins, sneaking some words in passing. He felt like it was like that again.

"He must think all women are alike. He must think he so important that some poor woman gonna throw her life away by murderin his wife. I mean that shit just don't work for ladies. I did the research. Carolyn Warmus, Bambi Bambenek, Amy Fisher . . . whass that, the look of success? Give me a break. The only one who wins is the guy. Why should I make him feel good? I end up in jail an' he can go pick up another chick."

The curl of her lip had the opposite effect, made him grin. Was like kiddy kontempt, an owl scowl. A kid who tries to look older. Dinky was completely disarmed. Forgot the sometime charm of street mates who come and go, the sudden birth and death of connections. That was the only thing worth living about the streets. Maybe Anita reminded him.

"What?" she asked, noticing his grin.

"Nothing," he said. "You were saying about Amy Fisher."

"Yeah." A pause just to look at him. "I just mean that I have a real career now. It's such a blast. I been dyin to tell somebody. The last thing I want is for people to think I been doin all this to impress some guy, to win some man. No way."

"No sir," Dinky said, getting into the spirit.

"Not me. I would rather shoot him."

"Shoot him?"

The calm that was Dinky sharpened into alert status. Faded newspaper clippings. Her hair was longer back then, her face more wounded. How surprised he had been to see the trouble she had gotten into. The defense played up her victim status. Dinky thought now about how he should've been harder on Ronson for daring to ever sell this woman a piece.

"Thass right. For havin made the wrong choice. I would shoot him the same way I would shoot a man who played me."

The gun was back. It was not smiling.

"Ah c'mon, Anita. With the gun, man."

"Whass your hand doing in your pocket?"

"What?"

"Your hand!"

"What, this?"

He pulled his hand out of his pocket, both palms up.

"I was just reachin for my last piece of licorice twirl, man! The doctor said if I don't down some sugar every twenty minutes, I'll pass out."

She closed the distance. The gun under his chin. A little too much muzzle.

"Easy, boy. If you gonna get anything outta your pocket, it's gonna be me that takes it out. Okay?"

She put a hand on his crotch.

"It's not that pocket," he said.

"But'chu got something in there."

"—"

"Hmm?"

"Right pocket."

"What?"

"The pocket on the right the pocket on the right."

"Whassup, Slinky? You don't like when I touch you like this?"

"I'd like it better if you take the piece outta my face."

She shifted, her whole weight on him. This was smart because if he made a sudden move, she could feel it and drill him. The gun was in his crotch while she searched, face to face. Breathing in short, hot tremors.

"Well. What do you know? The Slink don't lie."

Held the licorice stick up like a prize. Took a nibble of. So close he could taste her lips tasting. What was that baby powder smell? Gently she put that licorice stick into his mouth. Bit down on the other end, munching face to face. Until they were lips to lips. Hers, slick pink against latte skin.

Her quick candy breath gun pressed against his dick that black space in her eyes unreadable electric. Stood, standing still stopped dead in his tracks. Her fingers roving through his pockets. Too late he remembered. There was the sad clink and jingle of her find.

Color fled her face. She pulled back. Kill range, her eyes doing quick jumps. From the bracelet in her hand to Dinky's face. Reading what the ten diamond stones six carats each spelled out all sparkle.

"Angel," she said. Breathless flashing angry.

Dinky gauged the changes on her face. The change in fortune. How power slips from one hand to the other.

"Where'd you get this?" A whisper. It calmed Dinky, made him think she wouldn't shoot him. She needed his answers.

"Isn't that what you always wanted," he asked, "to have his name on your wrist?"

Now Dinky could even ask questions. But the biggest question of all was *why* hadn't Dinky given Jose that shit back? Jose couldn't possibly have offed that girl for a tag. Otherwise how could he dump it on Dinky and forget about it?

"What does this mean!"

The gun was trembling too much, quivery eyes. Eyes always wince before they shoot. "So you say you ain't tight with Lucy. An' now you show up with her tag?"

"Chill, Anita. It's not what you think."

"How'd you get this?"

The sparkle fire from the bracelet made him think of flames, flames in every window of The Haunt, flames blackening the edges on that underwater girl.

"Lucy's dead," he said.

An electric charge passed through them both. Having said it. Having heard. Unreal. She moved closer, checking his eyes for traces.

"Say that again."

Held that gun higher primed, like it would stop him from lying.

Swallow. The taste of her peppermint lips licorice taste baby powder scented cuddly sick.

"Lucy's dead."

"You think you can lie to a gun?"

Dinky slumped tired, sick of having a gun pointed at him. This meant he was getting pissed off and might soon do something stupid.

"You should learn to trust people, Anita. You might be closer to getting Angel all to yourself."

"Ohhh, don't fuck with me, Slinky."

"I'm not." (How she was coming closer.)

"You don't know wha'chu messin with, bro." (And closer.)

"I'm not playin. I know you. I cun't ever mind-fuck you."

"Thass right. You gonna have to do better than just a mind-fuck." (And closer still.)

The gun came up to his face. She clicked that pin back.

"You gonna shoot me now?"

She was breathing fast. "I don't know yet."

"Can't you hurry up an' make up your mind?"

"I'm tryin. Don't rush me. I just made a stiff."

"You what?"

Her licorice breath so cocky like she was dying to show off.

"Who you think blasted that guy on the stoop? Hmm?"

"Get the fuck."

"I'm serious." Drawing herself up a little taller. "That was me."

Dinky's face burned. A new step to the dance he hadn't expected.

"But you were standin right in fronta the 5–O!"

"Yeah. Ain't that a kick?"

She laughed like she had just shared a dirty joke (and was hoping for his buddy laughter too).

"I told you. I like to watch men die. I popped that bastid in the hallway, an' came round the back. The guy made it all the way out to the stoop!" She smiled proud. "I made like some witness."

He couldn't tell if she was lying or not. That was the scary part. Scary too the way she was close again. Scarier *still*, the way she pressed the gun to his neck.

"You ever do something to see if you get caught?"

Dinky closed his eyes for a second. Pictures of phone bashing, hubcap swiping. Spray-paint raids on the Dedication Wall where known tags would be obliterated. He and Jose blasting posse insignias into black limbo. Resistance fighters ducking sentries, spraying those walls ORANGE V FOR VICTORY—but no matter what, Jose wouldn't let Dinky spray over that silver ANGEL heart. No matter what he would not spray over that pumping LUCY name so happily entwined with Angel's. As if blotting her name out was some sort of sacrilege. What had Dinky done to lose Anita like this? Her eyes dim swimmy like she could no longer see him.

"Anita. If you shoot me now, the cops'll come in here."

"The fact is, I din't have to off Freddie, you know? The stiff on the stairs? But something inside me said, Why not, why not settle that too? I mean that the guy just gets handed to me. Yesterday you got put in my mind, an' here you are today, handed to me. Am I supposed to ignore the signs? I can't fight the urge. I've popped two people today, Dinky. I been settlin scores. Can I do three in a row, on the same day? Would that be a record for a woman? I just don't get these urges I have. It's like when a guy gets a bone. An' you're in that backseat goin nah daddy nah daddy but it's like the guy don't hear you an' then it's inside you an' it hurts. An' then after, he says, I cun't help it."

She grinned. Gun right up against his pulse.

"The cops are just up the street, Anita."

She motioned behind her.

"See that door? I could give you a bite an' then fly up those steps. These buildings here are all connected, did you know that? I know them all. I could disappear when I want. These buildings are my friends. They'll hide me. They covered for me lots of times, like real friends. Friends never betray one another. They don't hurt each other's feelings. Are you my friend, Dinky?"

"I've always been your friend, Anita."

Her eyes seemed to open up, like portals.

"Yeah. I always felt that. So why you wanna lie to me about Lucy?"

"I din't lie."

"Then tell me a story, Dink. A story about how two people find each other again, and what he does to make her trust him. One that lets her into how he got this."

Jiggled that ANGEL tag slow and musical. Dinky's thoughts choked up. Was he about to tell her what Jose did? Was it time to be spreading that around? Then all Anita would have to do is tell Angel. Then Jose wouldn't have to worry about putting out the story in the comic book.

The gun slid down to her favorite place again. Seeking out his dick amidst the gushiness of balls.

"Can you read that, Dinky? I killed two people today. One, two, Buckle my shoe. Three, Dinky? Don't good things always come in threes?"

His stomach tightened. The way she had him pressed there was no way he could make a move without her pumping a shot into his boyhood.

"I came to check." His voice sounded underwater.

"To check what?"

"I told you. Lucy is dead. I came to check see if there was anything going on."

Anita's eyes vague. Adding numbers, finding *x*.

"There was something going on last night. Late last night." It was like she was talking to herself. "People comin an' goin. Serious faces. An' Angel got outta sight right away."

She stepped back like she didn't see him. Turned around completely. Giving Dinky her back as she studied the tangle of coal black fire escapes above. Gun dangling from her hand as if forgotten. Dinky remembered her affection for Angel full blast and thought the worst thing that could happen now was for her to get protective about him, to take what happened as a move on Angel. It just might trigger her finger.

"It wasn't a hit on Angel," he said soft. "It was a move on Lucy."

She turned. Gun in one hand, tag in the other. Like she was weighing. All of a sudden the gun was pointed at him again, and her eyes weren't looking so good.

"Tell me how you know. How you know she's dead. Tell me who told you. Tell me how you got this."

"I'm sorry but I can't tell you yet." There was a sad surrender in Dinky's voice.

"You'd rather I shoot you?"

"I'm not a fink," he said.

The rainy smell to the wind burst. Sweeping garbage clatter in circular gusts. Her eyes glassy, not seeing him.

"Jose," she said. "Jose was there last night."

"I'm sorry but I can't tell you yet," Dinky repeated as if he had memorized the phrase.

She seemed to grin from afar. Some distance she had traveled.

"I just have to decide," she said. "Do you mean more to me alive, or dead?"

"I work better alive. Dead I'm not too good."

She grinned. Came close. Pressed the gun against his neck.

"She'll tell me what to do."

"She who?"

"Carlotta, Dinky. My gun is named Carlotta. She bites liars."

"Sorry. Carlotta. Whass Carlotta sayin then?"

"Carlotta says knees, Dinky. On your knees."

She pushed him down. Gun to temple. Kicked away a two-by-four with a brush of her sandal.

"I like how you look. All pretty and scared."

"I ain't scared."

"You ain't hard no more, either."

"This don't bone me much."

"Who cares if you get sprung? You gotta get *me* off. Thass what I would worry about if I were you. Okay, Slinky?"

"Okay."

"Thass what I like. A real responsive lover."

She pulled down her panties. Black lace.

"Munch," she said. Pressing him deeper. "I'll let you know if you pass."

Down the street, the cops bagged the stiff.

9

Hustle hustle turn around count the change careful dude you messed up last time hey yo better get over to the ices, man, there's a customer. I don't wanna see another one walk off 'cause you din't get over there on time HEY who was it had the extra cheese? SNAP that bag open with an arm twitch to shove in the steaming hot. YO JOSE MAN, you don't hear me callin you? YEAH I know it's your break but now is the WRONG TIME for a break. You gotta come help me. *Avansaa!* Put in another pie, that one there. His total is three sixty-five. Nah nah do that later get the phone *the phone*

(another order)

Jose reached for pad and started scribbling. Words passed through him. He had gone from worrying about what Dinky would find on Beck Street to just worrying about the guy, so any time the phone rang he hoped it would be Dinky. There were some pretty bad scenes in his head.

"Nah, we don't deliver anymore. The guy quit." Jose sketched on the pad as he talked. "I can take an order for pickup."

The voice an insect in his ear. Details pass through him straight to pen. Thoughts about permeable membranes. Mr. Brahma the biology teacher with his horrifying tests and surprise quizzes.

"About twenty minutes."

Jose hung up. Turned to a fresh pie on the counter when Anthony blocked his way.

"Whass this?"

Jose leaned against the counter to await the coming storm. There was always storm, no matter how smooth Jose ran things. It was just the way with some people. Anthony's face never looked untense, even when he laughed.

"Can I get a Coke?" a customer asked while cramming the last chunk of crust into his mouth. Jose picked up cup scooped some ice and shoved it under tap.

"I said, whass this?"

Anthony held up Jose's pad.

"It's an order."

Jose placed the soda on counter just as customer said, *I wanted a Large, man.* Jose without a word tossed the soda down the sink and grabbed a large cup.

"Jose. Look at me. Look at me right now."

Anthony was over by the cash register. Throwing nervous glances at the customers. A shave might do that man some good. The stubble seemed to always be the same shade.

"You listen. Is that what you do all the time? Pour my money down the drain?"

"The guy din't want it, Anthony."

"So what? Can't you use a little common sense? You could've poured the soda into the *bigger* cup an' then (big secret part) fill the rest with ice. But no, you'd rather throw my money away."

"Yo. Can I get my fucken soda please?"

"No," Anthony yelled at a clip, "you cannot get'cha fucken soda please. You can go learn how to ask for a fucken soda please! What the fuck shit is that?" He turned to Jose. "What is it with this place? Where do people learn to be like that?"

The customer walked out with a blast of napkins.

"You owe me a dollar," Anthony said.

"Nah-uh. That wasn't my fault."

There were two other customers waiting for slices, and a third who hadn't spoken up yet. There was half a pie in the oven and a customer on the way for a pie Jose hadn't prepped yet, so he flattened that dough. He smoothed out that sauce. Sprinkled cheese, onions, pepperoni. Found Anthony holding that pad again.

"So what is this? You haven't told me."

"I told you what it is. It's an order. The one I'm doing now."

"I don't mean that, I mean what is this artwork right here?"

Slapped down pad. Jose had doodled a pretty good rendition of Colt .45 pistol. Even got the metallic gleam.

"It's a piece, man. The piece I'm gonna get."

"Oh yeah? An' how you gonna afford it after I fire your ass? Ahh?"

"I don't think you're gonna fire me." Jose opened the oven door to pull out that half-pie.

"Que no? Yo sí te voy a botar!"

"Two slices to go?"

The money was already on the counter. Jose smooth with the pizza cutter. Had that way of gathering up the cheese along the edges that all the customers appreciated. A fold a snap a tuck and the man was out the door with his meal.

"You better get your act together," Anthony said, watching Jose do his thing, the swift professional to his every move. "Or I'm gonna fire your ass." The bluster was gone from his attack.

"You can fire me," Jose said. Snapping the register drawer shut. "I'll just take care of these last customers for you, okay?"

Dispatched the tall kid with the two slices. The quiet guy in the back finally spoke up. Jose split open a calzone and shoved it in the oven.

"You better nah get so cocky. You got that?"

"Yeah. Okay."

"You understand me now?"

"Yeah. I'm sorry, man."

"Sorry don't suck titties. *Majadero.* You keep busy out here." And with that last command, Anthony disappeared into the back.

Jose bit his lip. Almost six. Soon Monica would come. Then she and Anthony would lock themselves in that little room back there. Monica would come out at the end of Jose's shift, scented all whiskey sours and cherry-flavored condoms. It was a regular thing.

"For three hours I want it like I don't even exist. I don't want you should bother me for anything. You got that? You gotta learn to run the place like you own it."

Jose did that. He did that so well that Anthony could disappear into his nook with Monica, have a few *palitos,* crank that Daniel Santos and rock on that funky old love seat (which opened into a sofa bed). Jose liked having the place to himself. It was freedom, self-rule, and the girls sure liked to see him pounding that dough. But the world doesn't open up so fast when you're making four dollars an hour. Lucy was never impressed with his pizza-boy status. That was why Jose sold buddha.

She was always complaining about him being broke all the time. Why didn't he have wheels? How come he never took her anywhere? Should a girl be taking the subway all the time? How cool is that? "Show some initiative," she snapped. "There are guys out there makin three grand a week." And those boys have cars. Late night rides in dark backseats (the top down). The coal black bridges, the purple moon skies. Some gold sparkle for your wrist. Her pal Diana had introduced her to the world of posse boys. Now suddenly those trips to the Bronx Zoo on FREE ADMISSION WEDNESDAYS were no longer enough.

"You just like some boy. You gotta get outta that schoolboy shit an' get some props. In this town, you gotta get paid to get laid!"

Lucy could be pretty huffy when she got her mind set on something. He was going to have to shape up or ship the fuck. She even introduced him to a guy she knew named Michael, who could supply him with good cheap weed. Dinky had not been impressed.

"So what, now you wanna be a drug dealer?"

Jose tried to laugh it off, but Dinky stayed serious.

"It's not like that, Dink. I just wanna show Lucy up. I wanna see what excuse she gonna have when I got some green."

Dinky was unmoved.

"But, bro. What if what she wants is a posse boy?"

(the phone!)

Jose plucked that receiver up fast, but no Dinky. Another pickup order. Jose scribbled. The place was empty. Jose went into the back to check on Anthony. The candles were getting lit in the backroom, the sofa bed open. Flowered pillows, and that Claudio Ferrer bolero from the tape player. An old fogey voice, the sound of his liquored Spanish turning into English thanks to that American chip in Jose's head. He heard Spanish, but the words came out English: *I Too am Boricua. I too am a patriot.* Benign old-man guitars, their smell of beer and cigars and pure mountain sweat. *But if it means spilling the blood of a brother . . . then I don't want liberty.*

"What you want?" Anthony glared at the intruder.

"I came to get some dough."

Jose busied himself at the cooler across from the room, where he picked out three metal bowls of prepped dough.

"So how is it outside?" Anthony wore the hopeful look of a conspirator.

Jose grinned. "It's all clear, boss."

Anthony exhaled with a sense of mission. "Well. You send her in the minute she walks in."

(The thing is, the bitch married, Anthony explained during a lull, imparting some of that older generation Latino knowledge like *un tornillo saca a un tornillo* or when you got an itch, you gotta, etc. A man just isn't the same after a brutal divorce. Lots to prove lots to show. Jose always nodded patiently during these locker-room segments, the tales of old fart prowess. He kept that picture of Monica's husband in the cigar box by the register. Just in case, Chief. You can count on me just in case.)

Where was she? Things were running late. Anthony was already locked in his room, waiting. There was Danny outside, by the newsstand, waiting for the all-clear before coming in for his product. Jose never let his customers trickle in until after Monica arrived and he was sure Anthony wouldn't be coming outside. He reached behind the register and put the sign in the window: WE HAVE ICES. It meant, "Wait for the all-clear."

Jose could make between three and four hundred dollars a week, depending on how hard he wanted to work (and whether he and Dinky smoked up most of the product). Dinky was *not* into drug dealing but he did allow Jose to use The Haunt as a "safe house" to prep product so his mommy and daddy wouldn't walk in on him. (This was a big joke with Dink.) The fire escape the perfect place to clean and bag while expressway traffic flowed below. They prepped, toked, grooved to whatever tape Dinky chose to roll so it became more like private time than business.

Jose set up a system at school. Subtle. (He was the one into underground movements.) He could be passing Elmo that issue of *Tank Girl* in gym class, and right there—twenty dollars. Invited his regulars to come down to the pizzeria to get their fix, in hand-shakes while making change stuffed into pizza bag or floating in a cup of ice during those sudden hustle-bustle moments. He had specific sale days and scheduled his stops perfectly. No two days the same. He wasn't greedy. He connected carefully and steadily, counting the green rolling in. Up on the fire escape, laughing.

"This is better than selling *Grit*," he cracked, but Dinky only smirked tiredly.

"Thass how it starts," he said. "First you like the green. Lucy gonna like it too, but soon it won't be enough. She gonna say you could make more an' get more props if you'd only move up into the business world an' get yourself some *real* money action."

"It ain't like that, man."

"Yeah, sure." Dinky stared at the traffic below. "Just know the day you become a posse boy, thass the day we stop bein friends."

"Okay," Jose said in the heavy silence. "Bet."

They slow-mo slapped hands and snapped in the sullen evening dark.

(pang.)

He never should've let Dinky go to Beck Street. Hard not to worry. The guilt brought nausea. Claudio Ferrer's rum-hoarse vocal floating on those chattering guitars. Jose could not stand and do nothing. He had all those images that pricked like bug bites. He went to the window and removed the sign. Danny, waiting outside, flicked away cigarette and came in. Jose took a fresh glob of dough and started to stamp. Mold. Knead. Some small talk about Shruggie getting busted fencing stolen shit. There was Dinky, running down Beck Street. Dinky spitting up licorice as stab wounds made him go splatter. Little bursts of spit flying from Danny's lips.

"So what can I get you, bro?" Jose interrupted his flood of words. Danny made a peace sign.

"I thinka Coke, right? Make it small."

Jose drew two dimes from the thin leather jogging purse clipped to his pants. Small cup. Capping the jiggling ice rattle with plastic top. Young woman trooped in with little kid. Hair crunchy face freckled. Both of them.

"Yo. Lemme getta slice an' medium orange slush."

Danny took his change, waved bye to Jose as he stepped. Where the fuck was Dink? At least a call by now, something. Have to ask him about that tag. What if Jose lost it somewhere along the street? What if someone who knew Angel picked it up? The lady's slice was ready. Two more customers troop in to keep him busy, another quarter pie. Jose, standing by the oven door, hand on handle as he waited for the slices, waited for Monica waited for Dink waiting for word. A hope, a fear, a sense of having gone too far. Soon the ref would step in and call the penalty.

"Excuse me hello? Two slices to go."

Jose on automatic again. Carved out scooped poured inserted and shut that cash register drawer. There was Anthony, peeking out from the room. Jose shrugged—no Monica, no idea. If Anthony came around to hang outside with him, Jose would have to put that PLEASE COME AGAIN sign in the window to ward off his customers. Vague feelings of being forgotten by Dinky again, when suddenly there was Quique. Walked like slow motion, dreamy glazed eyes from too much smoke. He was trouble on a stick, bumble and fumble and trip. Should have ARREST ME stamped on his back. Leaning close to the window. Stamping with those bony fingers.

"Yo! Lemme get some icey!"

His thin digits struggled to loosen funds from pocket, everything in wads. Hardly a time he dug into pocket that some controlled substance did not tumble out. Jose quickly scooped up the yellow snow. The dime was in his hand when he gave the chump his change. Would you believe the fucker dropped it? Quique all grin, looking around like it's Allen Funt time. Pick it up pick it up, fucka, you wanna be some cop's collar? Jose sweating until the guy was out of sight.

(Dude. Phone order. Still not prepped.)

Jose pulled it from the oven. Formed it a nice box, cut into bubbling hot slices. The cheese dripping off the shiny cutter blade. Into the box, ready. Then, starting another pie. Spreading tomato sauce with ladle. Round and round bull's-eye. Blood red everywhere as Angel lets loose with long bursts right through the window. Twenty slugs as long as fingers.

(How's Angel ever gonna know? he could hear Dinky saying. And Jose would be saying back:

1. He could've found the tag again in some way that linked Jose to it
2. Shakes, who works for him, could've told him about the note in class
3. Somebody spotted him by the Dedication Wall just before Angel's heart was sprayed over!

"And after all that," Dinky says, "you still wanna publish this Lucy shit? I mean, are you fucken wack?")

Was good to always have a pie in reserve. To bake it up and then leave it out. Warm slices as you go and still have one in the tray. Jose always made one extra. (The homeless guy always gets what's left over.) And he worked on another pie and sold a few more dimes. The LUCY pages had to be printed up. He thought once Lucy's body was found, the comic book should appear on every desk. Then Jose would be walking down the hall with every student stunned and staring in silence—not a sound but his breathing. As he walks into his father's office and plants the comic book right down in front of him.

"It was me," he says, as the credits start to roll silently up.

And Angel is furious but can't do shit because the police whizz Jose away. And it makes the papers, his LUCY pages in *Time,*

Newsweek. The defense lawyer tries to make this big case about how Jose is this Puerto Rican geek kid driven mad by a high-performance school life and the pressures of society spoon-feeding him violence on TV until he just had to go out and prove it by killing a girl who only enters the story parenthetically. The judge found Jose's being Puerto Rican incriminating enough, and that's how he ends up in a jail cell at Riker's.

"That's a bad ending."

Toothy Barbara stared at him through her pointy glasses like she had him where she wanted him. The naughty pursed lips, like she caught him masturbating. Did she dress up for him? The leotard could not have been made to hold in so much top, the swishy skirt of her. Dezzie hid behind shades and that checkerboard dress. A matching blocky purse wide enough to play checkers on.

"I was just tellin Dezzie here what a bad ending you put on that short story you passed me today in class."

Jose gave her a look that definitely asked what the fuck she was doing here.

"I'm the pickup order," she said. "I may run Dezzie ragged, but she can't say I don't spring for dinner."

"Yeah," Dezzie said, opening the pizza box to sprinkle stuff on the pie.

"Besides, I'm worried about you."

"About me?"

She dropped a ten spot on the counter. Jose did change.

"Dez." Toothy Barbara didn't take her eyes off Jose. "Why don't you take the pizza for a walk? I'll catch up. I need to talk some business with Mister Stud."

"Okeydoke." Dezzie grabbed the pie, lowering her shades to give Jose a parting wink.

"What I mean is that it's an old story. That Lucy-Jose-Angel thing. It's old. You think people still talk about it? Not the way they talk about Andy Ramirez getting Yolanda Suarez pregnant, and that after a meagre fuck behind the gym bleachers. Are you listenin to me? This stuff about killin Lucy? Why don't you just let that shit go?"

Jose stared at her like he was looking at a ghost.

"What if I did kill her?" he whispered.

Monica stormed in breathless, laughing. Too much lipstick this time, bigger hair more eyeshadow. What makes a *trigueña* go blond? Hola amor, como estas? Polka dots everywhere, swimming on skirt on tank top on earrings.

"He's waiting for you," Jose said.

She leaned close, gave him an air kiss. Breathless thanks as she went into the back. Heavy scent of bath splash in her wake. The "patriot" Claudio Ferrer was replaced by a pussy-happy Daniel Santos, who, judging by the hyperactive woodwinds, was getting laid fine. The sounds boomed when the backroom door opened, then muffled when it slammed shut.

Jose started oiling a pizza pan, not wanting to look at Toothy Barbara anymore.

"So was that all you came to tell me?"

Toothy Barbara looked like she was going to say something. She exhaled with exasperation.

"Why did you do it?"

Jose stopped oiling the pizza pan. There was buzzing in his ears, sound coming and going. For a moment, he wanted to tell her everything. But she spoke first.

"Just don't get your ass slumped, okay?"

"What does that mean?"

"It means some little dick was stupid enough to paint over that ANGEL heart tag. And some people might think the stupid little dick was you."

A sense of relief flooded him so fast it burst out in a laugh. And he put the pizza pan down hard, laughing. And he stood there wiping his hands with a rag, relief almost making him cry.

"No way, Tooth. Nobody would think that."

"You just keep laughing," she said. "Stop lookin so nervous. I give Shakes at least two days to figure it out."

"Shakes would need a week to think it was me," Jose said, caught up in his own laughter. Then he saw how strange Toothy Barbara's face looked as she stood at the door. It was right at the moment when her one magic eye turned from hazel to green that he heard her say it. One moment, she was there.

"I don't care if you killed her," she said.

One moment, she was gone.

10

S he was behind him. Legs around his torso. The room faded to black and then filled with bright. Her breath in his ear.

She had asked him, black seams or fishnets? He thought she was going to slip them on. Instead, she used one to tie his hands behind his back. Made him toke on that fat white cigarette, whatever it was. "Truth serum," she called it. She was all arms and legs. Just her voice alone. Made him stiff.

"I like you, Dinky. So much."

The mix of arousal and fear made his body pulse like a lighthouse.

"Thass real good, Dinky." Nails raking the stiff. "But I know how to make it harder."

The other stocking went around his neck.

She strangled him at first in quick twitching pulses, then slow writhing times. Could feel her excitement rise with his every croak.

A lull.

Her happy laughing in slow waves.

"Stop," he said.

"Ahh, Slinky Dink. We just gettin started." Squeezed him pulsing like that. "Besides, you like it. Look how hard you are."

Her blow jobs accentuated by sudden bites and scratches. His trembling. From drugs from hyperventilating from heart attack from the way she squeezed choked gnawed. The room blackened. Like he was dreaming her so curvy bronze. Lighting candles, drawing shades.

"My arms," he said.

"*My* arms," she corrected him. A soft slap.

She put him inside, writhing him deep. The candle would blow dark. The candle would squiggle back to life. The candle would blow dark. Falling through rooms in black dream where all he could see were outlines in gray chalk

Dinky couldn't tell how long she was on top of him. Could feel his stiff somewhere long deep even through the choking pulls. How she adored the waves his body pulsed through her. Her pussy rocked with his spasms. When he started to panic, she came. (An endless falling.) Her cries. Seagulls swooping over foamy tips. Wave. Once it started, she made him. She made him so strong he passed out.

He was above water only for a second. A brief intake of air before he was shoved under. There were hands around his neck, pushing him down. The foamy green water like it was ocean. Dinky thrashed, lungs bursting. Came up briefly before he went under the gurgle of rushing green. Her face through the liquid shimmer. He was in the tub, and it was Lucy holding him down. Why did she let go? He sat up coughing, eyes stinging blind. The broken throat feel of all that swallowed her.

The bathroom was small. Looked exactly like the one Jose drew in his LUCY panels. It was even in black and white.

Lucy looked terrible. She was wet, her bathrobe soaked, her hair a mass of squiggle. Her eyes burned, the lips twitched resentful.

"Do you like it? Do you like the way that feels?"

All at once water whoosh as she pushed him under again, his hands slipping off the sides. The water poured in on top of him.

DINKY TWITCHED HIMSELF awake.

She was behind him, sleeping. Arms and legs locked around him. (He wasn't going far.) His arms were gummy numb with a shooting sting. The moment she felt him move she locked around him tight.

"Where you goin."

Her gravel whisper inside his head.

"My arms, man. They're sore. You gotta untie them."

He struggled because it was pissing him off. She choked him so hard, he saw colors. Red white blue blustering stars. Saw brother Johnny storming the beach with fellow marines and landing craft. Running fleeing arabs injuns gooks niggers spicks. Dinky felt the swelling numb, the panic like something was about to snap.

"You gotta say please first," she said.

The sound of her breathing.

"Please."

"Say it like you mean it, Dinky."

"—"

Loosened the stocking like she was annoyed, just tired of him. He wasn't playing along right. Watched him, chin in palm, while he tried to massage feeling back into his arms.

"I just don't know what to do about you," she said. Her fingers touched his lips. She seemed genuinely mystified. Dinky watched the ceiling vibrate. Tried to blink himself sensible. Where the fuck was he? A private house on Wales Avenue. Apartment Three. The creaky wooden stairs. She was lighting another one of those puffy white cigarettes. Dinky could tell she was only drawing flame and not really smoking. When she put it to his lips, he jerked away. It made her smile.

"Don't fight me, Slinky. Please do what I say."

(Where was Carlotta?)

Her eyes so dreamy dead blank. Dinky toked. Made him shiver from cold blowing into him.

"Good baby."

The shakes he was getting made her laugh and kiss him like she was so thrilled to come to his death throes. It was death, it was almost over the ridge. Dinky couldn't stop the goddamn shakes. He couldn't believe where she was taking him, each squeeze pull squeeze.

"I can't decide," she whispered. "Do you mean more to me alive, or dead? Dead. Dead."

Didn't like the way she squeezed when she said "dead." Had to keep her from saying that so much.

"Alive," he said. "You want me alive."

"Now how can you be so sure of that?"

The blank face. She got up off the bed like she needed to pace that energy out. At least the stocking wasn't around his neck, but in her hands. Still pulling and twisting. Dinky's body still bucking. He couldn't stop it.

"You guys are all the same," she muttered. Still pulling and twisting. "It don't seem like any of you are worth the time."

Dinky didn't like the sound of that, but when he tried to get up, he found his body only wanted to lie there and twitch.

"No," he said. Coughing. A feather stuck in his throat that wouldn't budge.

"I'm just too sentimental. Guys aren't. They pretend. They just wanna get fucked to death. They're dogs. Ice-T was right about that shit. A dog don't know enough to stop eating when it's full, do you know that? They'll eat 'til they burst! An' burst is just what men want, isn't it?"

Dinky felt like his throat was full of shards.

"Yeah," he said.

"I don't think it's sad to fuck a man to death. I think it's beautiful for a man to give himself up to please the woman he loves. Don't you?"

Those black orb eyes. Like Katherine Ross after they "fix" her in *The Stepford Wives.* Too much white. Was turning into dream. Her naked body and how it drew him. She was a spell. His body didn't need anymore. Didn't need didn't care what. His stiff clamored for her. She smiled at the twitches.

"Yeah," Dinky said, not knowing what. A sound. Caves. Rushing water. Angry Lucy eyes. "Not my fault," he was trying to say.

"That one big splash. Feel him emptying out. Into me."

She crawled over him, the feel of her a soft like never. She called, and his body followed. It was almost happening without him. No conscious thought, no mind. Dinky let himself be carried by waves. Maybe it was the kind of lust that could get him killed, but she was the most woman he had ever, ever. And he had managed to somehow keep Carlotta off the bed!

Dinky kissed her. He could feel the hardness leaving her body, the way she sank into him, opening up.

"Can we quit with the death talk?" He was whispering. "Don't you see? If you kill me, we can only do this once."

Her laugh a relief. She kissed his face, his neck, tenderly. Her eyes were wet. Dinky watched her kissing his hands. He was *in* something, deep. A little scared of her form of crazy, the way it swallowed everything and kept him on guard. And yet, he was letting go, released. Hadn't he always trucked with the mad? All those crazy kill boys he knew. And wasn't his father a killer? So Dinky turns his back on it, goes to school, meets his Gemini twin. A cool straight kid he can have adventures with. Only now Jose was a killer. Why did Dinky feel guilty, as if he had caused it, maybe carrying some sort of contagious gene? The sparkling tag on Anita's wrist was a constant reminder.

She slid out of bed and went to the bathroom. The sound of the shower, soft rain. What was she humming? Dinky felt soft-buzzed, his limbs slipping into a restful throb. The time was close to eleven. By this time, Jose would be cleaning up in the pizzeria, maybe putting out that leftover pie for some homeless guy. Dinky reached for the phone.

"Anthony's Pizza." Jose on barely the first ring, fast and frantic.

"A quick call," Dinky said.

"You fuck. Where have you been? I been thinkin bad thoughts, bro."

"I'm okay. Listen, everything's cool. But I think Angel found the body last night. I'm workin on that info right now. Anita saw Angel creepin outta sight last night."

"Anita?" Jose sounded bugged. "What's she got to do with this?"

Dinky was listening to the sound of the shower in one ear and Jose in the other.

"I ran into her on Beck. Don't you know she's got an Angel tit? She been stalkin that dude a long time. Why din'chu tell me she saw you comin from Angel's last night?"

"Well, where the fuck were you? I was lookin for you when I ran into her. She spray-painted over Angel's tag. An' I'm thinkin, shit man. I killed Lucy. You hear that? It's just startin'na hit me. I really offed somebody last night."

The song Anita was singing. Mouthing the words under running water. Love, love will keep us together. The sound of Jose's voice. No excitement no wonder no fear. It was almost trance talk. There were moments on his way to Beck when Dinky felt sure this was another fake Jose-kills-Lucy story, that Jose was only trying hard to make it sound real. But the sound of him now on the phone convinced him.

"An' where the fuck are you now? We were supposed to do *Hogan's Heroes* tonight. An' just where the fuck are you?"

"I can't talk now. I'm with Anita. She has the tag."

"What?"

The sound of the shower stopped. It was just the echoey squeak of faucets.

"Don't worry. I'll get it back."

Dinky hung up the phone fast but quiet. Her eyes were all snake charmer when she returned. A *Mona Lisa* grin that told him nothing. The soft jingle clink of those ANGEL stones as she slipped back into bed.

"Dinky." She rubbed him soft, her fingers kneading life back into his arms. "Is she really dead?"

He stared up at the ceiling.

"Were you thinkin'na Angel while you lyin with me?"

Her face tilted delicately.

"You sound jealous, Dinky."

Dinky kissed her. She let him. She closed her eyes. A long slow breath. Her lips open for him. Smile. She laughed. Silly girl. Silly girl to believe in such shit. He held her face still. He said the words slowly as if he were talking to a child.

"You must not go over to Angel." Softly. "You could be in great danger."

Dinky watched her eyes slowly go liquid.

"Danger how?" she whispered.

"You told him once you would like to go over there an' plug Lucy, remember? He might think this was you."

Anita was lost in thought. He knew enough to dread her sudden mood dips. Instead of an eruption, she seemed to sink into him. Not really what he had expected.

"Did anybody see you last night?"

She was nestling into him, gripping him arms legs fingers. Her lips pressing. Her wet face. Every breath was words.

"No. No one saw me."

"An' what did you see?"

She was kissing him. Every kiss was words.

"I saw him get there. It was two in the morning. He wasn't even there ten minutes before all these cars come. Nine of his heavy boys showed up like there was a bad smell. Then two by three come his general staff boys. Wearin those grim faces. They started stationing dudes up and down the street. I happened to find a good perch on this fire escape and I ate a bag of oranges."

This last kiss was big, a deep roaming.

"They snuck him out, Dinky. He went underground."

"You think?"

"I'm sure he won't be visible for a while."

What was she looking for in that drawer, her body laying across him? Something in her hand. Couldn't see.

"You came at the wrong time," she said.

"Shh." He held her restless form close. "We're in this together."

"An' what if I hand you over to Angel? Will we still be in this together?"

Her voice chilled him, but her eyes were not cold.

"I mean what if they're lookin for me right now?"

The way she held him. The way her body pressed.

"Just kill me now," he said.

The way her lips wrapped around him. He pulsed with gratitude. The sting of nails, the hundreds of electric currents. Slid over his face. The curve of her ass. The press into him deep. Lips on lips. His little bursts of breathing.

And the night got blacker still. The caress of arms and thighs. How does the moon do that? Float down from sky to hover behind blinds, a wide pale face. The streets whisper. Even trucks kept their voices low as they trundled past with a rattle of chain or crash of cargo. The passing fire truck flashes the room with red.

Deep strangle. Black pouring. The change in her eyes. She was not there with him. She was someplace else.

"Anita. Stop."

"I can't."

"But'chu gonna kill me."

"You're so sweet."

The faster he moved the tighter she squeezed. She wanted him slow. To feel it leaving him in waves.

A tremor spasm. Shook her happy. Her vague, throaty laugh.

Words croaked. But she heard. She heard even over the rocky rough sea of him. She stopped strangling him.

She was kissing him. Pulling the stocking off. Touching and kissing him frantic. Coaching him, coaxing his return back into body. "Breathe, baby. Breathe." What was it he said? Dinky didn't know. Must have been his body talking. The things she could force out of him.

"I love you too," she said. The desperate kisses, the grateful relief. Both of them.

The sleep rolled over their slick warm snuggle. Gripping as close as possible. Rolling back into their bodies.

The jingle of that tag. And how she made it dance in moonlight.

"Dinky," she whispered. Sleepy time little girl. "Tell me a story."

Dinky watched those diamonds flash ANGEL at him. He clasped her fingers, brought them down and under pillow, to keep that tag quiet.

"The fight led them into the bedroom," he said.

11

TAG: A symbol, name, or slogan spray-painted on a wall or sidewalk. Posses use tags to declare that they exist, that they own this land and should be feared. Anyone known to violate a posse tag could face death.

Gunfire. Hot prickly stings. The rush of an infantry assault right up Southern Boulevard, dark gray uniforms in a mad rush. Armored personnel carriers covered them with mounted MG-42s making that distinctive ripping sound.

The sidewalk exploded upwards in chalky bursts. The pharmacy on the corner gutted by point-blank tank fire, the pizzeria shattered to kindling. Troops firing into buildings, working slow and steady. A total cleanup operation. Bodies piled up near the subway entrances. (The army was down there, peppering one peppering all whether they had MetroCards or not.)

Jose started running. The supermarket exploded all glass and bodies. A splash of something gooey all over him. He turned to run back. Ran right into the armored personnel carriers. Jose hit the sidewalk, slithering over other twitching scrambling bodies. There, sitting in a command car not ten feet away, was Ralph Fiennes as Amon Goeth, removing his gloves and taking in the holocaust around him with quick bird blinks.

"I can't wait for this fucking night to be over," he said, as his car moved away toward Avenue St. John.

A smoky lull, with flames crackling everyplace. Jose got up to run again, but froze. There was a line of gray uniforms coming down the boulevard, and they weren't taking prisoners. Three beat boys that dared to show were stitched twirled splattered by gunfire. Bullets came his way—Jose ducked behind a line of cars. The Puerto Ricans all around him were running nowhere, heading down side streets only to find them blocked by tanks, by machine guns that spattered sidewalks, spun bodies apart. Run this way, run that way—cut to pieces either way, so Jose clung to wreckage. He would rather get run over by that oncoming APC than dance with bullets out in the open.

He was looking right at that advancing line of soldiers, flanking the APC slowly moving. They were field gray soldiers, firing their guns at everything that moved, their absolutely white faces turned grimy by sweat by dirt by blood by the dirty business of extermination. They looked hardened and experienced, almost unbeatable with their joyless eyes seeking out kills. Jose looked around him and realized there was not much he could do, nowhere to run. Out in the open they would stitch him. Hidden behind this wreckage they would find him in a matter of moments, the small turret on that APC turning this way and that like an animal snout seeking the scent of prey. Jose was thinking about what bullets would feel like cutting through him when suddenly he saw the line of soldiers buckling spinning falling. Bullets stitched through ranks. A series of loud bursts and the APC erupted in white flame.

More loud bursts. Two more APCs flamed crash, while a third

struggled to free itself from behind a burning Mr. Softee truck. Elation swept through Jose as he sighted a group of black men, firing
AK-47s from the hip. Now they poured from the rubble in their
khaki jungle gear, carrying grenades rocket launchers short-range
bazookas. They were loosing fire everywhere on the panicked
grays. Jose noticed them motioning to the Puerto Ricans to take
cover as they worked their way up the street. They clambered onto
tanks, pried open hatches, and tossed in grenades. One, two, three
tanks brewed up belching black smoke. The soldiers in gray were
now running for cover, dodging shells, jumping over walls of rubble.
They were running to catch APCs that were backing up along the
narrow side streets with grinding gears and whining engines. The
gun rattle started to die down. Now just crackle and cries.

"You come an' get us, mothafuckas!"

The black guy with the star on his beret jumped off a burning
tank, dropping an empty clip. He snapped in some fresh rounds
and gave Jose a wink as he passed. Jose felt a strange sense of
gratitude and pride. Now Puerto Ricans started to come out from
everywhere—from under cars, trucks, down from fire escapes.
Some even came up from the sewer.

There were prisoners. The three white boys looked lost, one of
them with a wetly fresh jagged cut on his face. The squad of black
men lined them up by a wall just as Jose and the other Puerto
Ricans came out to watch.

The black soldier with the star on his beret drew his pistol and
went up to one of the prisoners.

"Hey James," he said.

James was tall standing on that smoking APC, his AK pointed
up at sky.

"Yeah, what about it, Ronny?"

"Polly wanna cracker?"

Ronny put the pistol to the boy's head. The boy clamped chattering teeth down.

"No," James said. "Polly don't want no fucken cracker."

The gun popped, the head splashed and spackled and splat. The body all sack, the blood-stained fountain.

Jose stood still.

The Puerto Ricans cheered. They laughed they clinked beers and started lighting joints. They even joined in when Ronny inquired about crackers again. *Noooo,* the Puerto Ricans yelled cheerfully, and another body fell cracked and broken.

The last prisoner, he was hip to what was coming. He stood still, defiantly glaring through that bloody face. It angered some of the Puerto Ricans so much they started to pick up bottles. Collected a boxful. By that time the defiant one was sliding down the wall, torn and blasted.

Jose started to pick up on something wicked. He saw all those guns on these black freedom fighters. The Puerto Ricans were not armed. They stood around like civilians. When most of the black troops took off to respond to a series of explosions up the street, the remaining freedom fighters started talking in low whispers. They were staring at the Puerto Ricans.

"Fuck it, man," a black trooper right beside Jose said like he had run out of patience, "just slump the crackers, man."

The black freedom fighters started arguing. One of them said the Puerto Ricans should be spared because they were poor, but another brother calmly pointed out that this was the *Race War Dream Sequence* and not the *Class War Dream Sequence.* By this time, Jose had worked his way to the front of the group of complacent *compatriotas,* who were smoking reefer and slapping hi-fives like they had pulled it off all by themselves. And they partied, while others discussed their fate.

Jose stepped up to the black soldiers, still wrapped up in discussion.

"Wait up," he said. "We're Puerto Rican, man."

James hopped off the now-flaming APC. To get in Jose's face and calmly plant the words.

"You're Puerto Rican." He spit to the side. "So what the fuck is that?"

The black troopers laughed.

Jose fought the pulsing panic, trying to think clearly. What a time for this question on identity! Now the Puerto Ricans wouldn't have a hundred years to putz around with the answer.

"Puerto Ricans," Jose said, "are part white, part black, an' part Taíno Indian."

Jose's words created a hush, even though ammunition ignited by flames in the nearby APC made little pops and fizzes. There was a breathless waiting that was answered by Ronny cocking an AK.

"Well all right then," he said, pulling Jose aside to the wall. "Just don't take this personal. I'm only shooting your white part, brother."

Crackling sky. Fulminate of mercury. The rain poured down. Droplets danced on the windows. The thunder booming him awake. Was it the thunder? The wordless quiet around him made him start, to see every eye in the classroom was on him. There were titters and shivers of laugh, and the buzzing fluorescents above were too bright.

"Mr. Vega. Did you have a nice nap? Don't know if you've noticed that you're next?"

Harriman Berry was sitting at his desk, already making a little red zero in his book. He shushed the laughter and tapped the desktop for quiet.

"You were supposed to read your spring affair short story today. Do you even have it?"

Jose rubbed the sleep from his eyes. He spent all night bouncing from dream to dream, from Lucy to Lucy to Lucy. There was also that sparkle tag sparkle on Anita's wrist and her victory grin. Jose finally crawling from hot bed feverish chill to sit out on the fire escape. Trembling until sun. No more Dinky news. Walking to school hoping to spot him, but nothing. This nap in Harriman Berry's class was his first real sleep since. He could only stare back like the man just had to be kidding, in light of all that's happened. And so Jose gave him an indifferent shrug. The kind teachers see thousands of every day.

Harriman Berry gave him another zero and a brush-off motion. He was the whitest Puerto Rican anyone had ever seen. Tantrums were part of his teaching style. Usually nervous and screechy, Harriman Berry was the best comic relief Jose could hope for.

At the front of the class stood a beat boy in baggy all. Edwin. Harriman Berry motioned to him. "All right, Mr. Burgos. You may begin your narrative."

Edwin nodded all eager and clutched that tattered coil notebook page. Shreds hung from the edges like strands of Parmesan.

And so the thing was that *he* was in *love*. She
waited until he was in bed with her and was about
to, about to put it in right before she stopped him

and told him she had genital herpes. He didn't
have genital herpes, but he felt like he was too in
love to stop so he had sex with her. And then he
got it. All of a sudden she had to get away from
him. She moved and told him to never, ever get in
touch with her again, in any way. The End.

Edwin took two steps back, expecting applause. It was just
starting to bubble up when Harriman Berry slammed his hand
down on desktop.

"*That* was your story?"

Edwin looked insulted. "Yeah. Sure."

"Really? I tell you I want a spring affair, and you give me genital
herpes?"

The laugh bursts were quelled by a few hand slams on desktop.
Berry's eyes were jumping wildly from student to student.

"What the hell kind of people are you!"

Voices rose in protest. His screech drowned them out.

"This is English class, *English!* I can't believe you'd read something like that to the class. You did that on purpose!"

Harriman Berry snatched the paper out of Edwin's hand.

"Hey! I spent all night writing that!"

The rest of the class spoke up. Three girls left their seats to
plead the defendant's case, while boys in the back laughed and
made fart noises.

"Don't you see what you've done?" Harriman Berry headed for
the door with the piece of paper like it was evidence. "You've sexually harassed this entire class!"

And out the door Harriman Berry went. Doors began opening

up and down the hall, teachers and students peering out. Jose rushed up with the others, heading for the doors to peek at the action. Edwin followed Harriman Berry and snatched the paper back. Now students scrambled, grabbing their books to make an escape before someone arrived to pin them down there. Why shouldn't they book if a teacher abandons the class?

"A teacher screaming on the second floor," the security man said into his talkie.

JOSE WENT RIGHT to Pedro. Being loose in the halls without a pass meant getting harassed by hall monitors. A pass from Pedro meant Jose could flash it and walk free. He came into the small office and found him on the phone.

"Well . . . I'm not saying Reyes is a shoe-in for that city council seat, but if he goes, there's a good chance I could end up being principal. That's the best-case scenario, I know. But right now, assistant principal seems pretty snug in the bag."

Pedro glanced up and spotted Jose there. A crease from the dread of trouble, only a slight nod to say hi.

"I don't know if I'm ready, no. But I'm willing to try. Listen, I have to go. Talk later. *Ciao.*"

Pedro hung up the phone. Jose figured to make it quick.

"I need a pass. Make it for the library."

Pedro didn't even ask. Fished out that pad.

"What a relief. For a moment there, I thought you got sent to my office because of some trouble."

"No trouble, pops. Harriman Berry freaked out over some sexual harassment thing."

"What?"

"I'm sayin I'd rather hang in the library than walk the halls with all those suspicious types around, you know wham sayin?"

Pedro looked at him a moment.

"Listen, can you tell me why it is that a Puerto Rican who is articulate and intelligent like you are has to always talk like a black person?"

"What's wrong with talking like a black person?"

"Jose, you're not black."

"I'm one-third black."

"Oh come on, don't give me that. You know what I'm saying. Look, speaking of suspicious types, do you know this kid?"

Pedro passed Jose that series of mug shots on a card. Dinky looked maybe a little sleepy, but otherwise indifferent in the pix.

"What are you doing with these?"

"Reyes passed them out to the staff. Alonzo Robles. He's the son of a drug dealer. Reyes thinks he's also behind that damned comic book. Do you know him?"

"Yeah," Jose said.

Pedro got interested. He came around the desk, handing Jose the library pass.

"Do you think there's anything you can get on him?"

Pedro seemed scared to ask. He backed away right after the words came out, standing by the window to look out. Hands in pockets, he looked almost wistful. "I mean that maybe there's something," Pedro went on, eyes out the window. "Maybe you can find out something about him that we can use."

"Okay," Jose said, hoping to spring the mug shots on Dinky. "Can I take this with me?"

"Sure. Only don't show it around."

Pedro came back to sit behind the desk, his face solemn. "Look, I appreciate that. I won't even bring up the fact that you were late again last night, well after midnight. Instead of asking you about it or going on, why not try something new? I'll just come out now and ask you, Hey, Jose, *como estas?* You planning to come home late tonight, so I can let your mother know?"

Jose wryly grinned. No telling why. It wasn't like he went dancing. He felt like telling him all he did was leave the pizzeria after Dinky's call and wander dark streets some. Then he thought of stopping off at Dinky's house. Just in case the dude ended up there, but nothing. Jose noticed how the apartment was lit better than the last time he had been there, with cute lamps and some track lights over the plants. There were new drapes. His mother looked younger in jeans. He hadn't meant to come in, or to share a can of soda with her. The pointed questions about Dinky's whereabouts finally forced him to flee. She had to ask him from the door, "You don't think he's back in it, do you?" He saw the worry in her eyes, and for a moment, found it hard to say. Then he found a way to say no, it's not that. After that he slipped into school, another late night *Hogan's Heroes* hit.

"I don't want to be a pest all the time about this. I think you already know that. I just want to establish some parameters, limits. Something we can all live with."

For almost a year now, Jose had been slipping into school after dark. Had swiped Pedro's keys, made copies, memorized his security codes so that the little white box wouldn't set off alarms. Would wander around slow—an empty school is like a cathedral. He would go to the office, play with people's mail. Sit in that big Reyes chair and play with the settings. And he and Dinky would light a joint in the principal's office and not activate the ventilator system so that the scent of thick Jamaican herb would cling all morning and maybe make him go, *Just what is that smell?*

But there was none of that this time, because there was no Dinky. Jose did not usually rush when he did his *Hogan's Heroes*, but this night he felt Lucy shadowing his every move. She was behind him in the hallway, she was behind him on the stairs. It was not a good night to go top to bottom and check all the hiding places. For *BUDDHA BOOK #3* they took a week just stocking up the paper. (Jose never used school paper. He knew every ream was accounted for.) Collated stapled and Mylar-bagged each issue, then stored them in special nooks until D day. The new color copiers weren't so fast so it took them three nights to do two hundred copies.

There were still color copies stored on the third floor that maybe he should get and plant around to keep irritating people, but Jose wasn't going up there. He went only as far as the second floor to stash some smoke for tomorrow's sales, then hurried down to the offices on the main floor. Sweaty Mendoza was known to lift things during his petty confiscations. Many students had already lost beepers, cell phones, cassette and CD players, and even a few cameras. He would stick his finds in a back cabinet temporarily until it was cool to retrieve his prize at a more convenient time.

(Not this time.)

Jose found Dinky's armored personnel carrier, wrapped in a fuzzy towel. This was really the reason he went that night, and once he got it, he booked right out of there. Walked fast but still didn't make it home until 12:45 A.M.

Jose wanted to tell Pedro about all of that, about Lucy. A vague plan formed in his mind.

"I'll be home regular time," Jose said.

Just then, one of the office secretaries appeared at the door.

"Pedro. Reyes wants to see you now. He has a problem."

Pedro turned to Jose.

"Why don't you come with me, so I can introduce you to Reyes? This is the perfect opportunity. Just so he knows you're my son. Come on."

"But I din't do nothin!"

Edwin glared at the hall monitors that had brought him in and were still holding him. Reyes puffed on a cigar. The air system hummed and rattled. He read the story while Harriman Berry paced by the big window.

"You said we should keep our eyes peeled," he said. "That we should report anything unusual. Well, just look at that. Everybody looking for art, and here I am, finding the writer."

Reyes stared.

"Yes?"

"The same diseased prose, the emphasis on sex. The decadence parading as realism, temporarily gratifying yet ensuring a perpetual descent into nihilism."

Edwin's mouth fell open. There was no way he did all that, was there? Reyes puffed, not looking won over. Harriman Berry seemed unwilling to repeat himself.

"I'm saying I know he's involved in the comic book."

"No way, I'm not," Edwin said.

Reyes gave Edwin the kind of penetrating stare that works on preschoolers.

"So what do you have to say for yourself, young man?"

Edwin shrugged as if to say, Ahh, whass the point?

"Can you draw?"

"Nope."

"And your street tag? It's not SPIK-EE BOY, is it?"

"Nah. It's Slick. The girls call me that 'cause I go on real smooth."

The pride in his talk made Reyes grimace. He turned sideways with a creak of leather. The paper in his hand centered directly over his gold trim trash can.

"Well, Slick. You want to be a writer, ahh?"

Edwin checked the faces around him like he wasn't too sure it was safe to speak.

"I like doin it, yeah."

"I'm going to give you a little writing lesson. You were told to write about a spring affair. Instead you chose to write ugly, disgusting filth."

"But that stuff is true!"

"True doesn't make it art. This is a Puerto Rican school, no matter how many black kids the school board sends us! We tend to feel differently about such things. We are a highly moral people. We believe writing should edify the community. Otherwise, why read it? Don't the Americans think badly enough of us as it is? Why make us look worse? What's the purpose? I'm not trying to discourage you. But you should think of Gabriel Garcia Marquez when you write. Ask yourself: Would *he* write something like this? I encourage you to read him in the original Spanish, by the way. It's beautiful."

Reyes reached into a drawer. Flicked open a silver lighter. The flame gave that sheet of Edwin writing a good lick.

"I want you to understand," Reyes continued as Edwin's writing shrunk and blackened to *chispas,* "this is what should happen to all bad writing. Anything that is bad for the community does not deserve to be read. Do you understand now?"

Edwin was staring straight ahead. No use trying to read that face. Reyes grimaced, maybe from the stink of burned paper.

"Pedro, I'm glad you came. I think you might want to talk to our little writer here."

"I would love to."

Pedro left Jose by the door, walking right up to Edwin. Grasping his shoulder like he was about to impart grand wisdom.

"Writing is a responsibility. Always make your community look good. Don't forget that. Build your people!"

"Well put." Reyes puffed, his eyes settling on Edwin with new malice. "So tell me. Do you know Alonzo Robles?"

"He doesn't know him," Jose cut in from his spot by the door. All eyes turned to him.

"This is my son," Pedro announced. "Jose. He's been working undercover to find the comic-book culprits."

Edwin squinted, like he didn't get it. Jose rolled his eyes. Couldn't believe Pedro just said that. Why not just draw a bull's-eye on my back, pops?

"Oh yes." Reyes smiled. "Good to know. How's that been going?"

"He's not involved," Jose said. "He doesn't know anything about it."

"And how do you know that?" Reyes tapped ash from his cigar.

It fell into the silver ashtray that said SAN JUAN on it and had a picture of all those white-faced hotels.

"Edwin can't draw. The two students who put out the comic book are both artists. They draw everything."

"Two?" Pedro sounded annoyed. "There are only two?"

"That's right. Two people behind it. Draw it. Print it. Plant it." Jose stared at Reyes, hoping to see a reaction. "Only two students. And Edwin isn't one of them."

"So, just like that," Harriman Berry snorted, "it's all thrown out of court? After this student sexually harassed my class?"

"Harriman, please." Reyes had lost his patience. "Take it easy, okay? Did you just abandon your class again? I hate when you do that."

Sweaty Mendoza, who had been doing his invisible routine, tapped Reyes on the shoulder to say, "I've placed monitors in the room."

"You go back to class," Reyes continued, "and teach what few students you've got left. We'll deal with it later. Ramos, put our young writer in detention until the bell."

"But I din't do anything!"

Edwin was led out.

"Fine," Harriman Berry said. "But I'll be in here to see what's done about this. I expect action."

Reyes seemed relieved to see him go. "Pedro," he said in that tone that Pedro took for brotherhood, "I'll have the kid see you tomorrow. You talk to him."

"All right."

"And you, Jose. What can you tell me then about Alonzo Robles?

Anything on him I can use to put a stop to this sick mess with the comic book?"

Jose exhaled. His father's expression pushed him like an elbow in the back.

"He isn't involved," Jose said.

"What do you mean?"

"He isn't doing the comic book. He isn't dealing drugs. He isn't working for his father."

Reyes leaned cheek on palm and stared at Sweaty Mendoza like there was a problem. He looked at Pedro.

"Okay, Pedro. We'll talk later."

There was a huff of dismissal, the hint of impatience and disappointment. Pedro led Jose back to his office.

"What have you done?" he whispered as they walked. "Why couldn't you just cough up some names or something? This was our chance!"

"That was real smooth in there," Jose said back with disgust. "You just blew my cover in front of Edwin. Why not just go announce it over the school PA?"

They walked fast out that office, down the hall. Pedro cornered Jose right by the firefighting hose that was coiled up in a red box by the stairwell door.

"But can you still do it? Get some information?"

"They're putting out a new issue," Jose said.

"When? Who is it? How do we stop them?"

Again the Jose grin.

"Give me two days," he said.

12

The beaded rain on the windowpane. The early gray sky. How the breeze said it would probably rain more. The weather guy said it was unusual for the city to have so much rain this time of year. Like New York had become Seattle, he said. Like he longed to go back there.

Anita uses her TV as an alarm clock. At five-thirty that big screen clicked to life, weatherman's words snapping them from sleep. She fumbled and bumbled and clicked that remote to shut off the noise. Clung to him, wrapped around him like escape was forbidden. Dinky at that moment was not thinking of escape. It is well known that in the mornings, 98 percent of all males report having a stiff. Dinky too. She seemed to want to doze just a little more before getting up, but when it was time, how she freed herself from his grip was a mystery. (She was all slither like snake, all slippery like eel.) Anita the sleepwalker went from bed to bathroom. The squeak and squeal of faucet handles. The bowels of rusted tenement pipes from 1893 groan and gurgle. The murmur of shower spray.

Dinky sat up. This was the perfect time for him to play Sam Spade. Riffle through her pouches search her drawers. Took a sniff of that roach from last night. What was in that mix? Some tobacco, almost AMSTERDAM style, but it wasn't just smoke and it wasn't just bazuca. He had done that cigarette crack before. (It was his father's trip to line up his brats and give them a toke. "Get to know the shit you're sellin," he said, "an' learn what it does.") Dinky remembered the way it speeded and flashed him, made his heart full zone. This Anita joint had some of that, but also a holding action, a slow and hazy to the edges with that sudden falling business. He went over to where his pants lay on the floor. Tucked that roach in a pocket for later analysis.

A cluttered bedroom. Anita no neat tidy chick. Clothes bunched up on the chair, clinging to the edge of the bed. A bureau cluttered with scores of tiny bottles lipsticks mascara sticks three brushes eye pencils eyeshade a few spritzers one can of mousse some magazines. Panties, panties, how does a woman have so many pairs of panties? Drawer after drawer. A smell of patchouli. On a table by the bed, a stack of newspapers. They were in tatters, clipped and cut. There on the floor was a big black scrapbook. Its thick pages were empty, but under the book was a pile of newspaper clippings.

The latest victim, twenty-eight-year-old Jonathan
Chambers, was shot twice in the head at close
range with the same .22-caliber pistol used in
the other two attacks

She touched him.
Had forgotten that trick of hers, of appearing at will.

Naked, glistening wet. Wordless, like tranced. She took his hand and led him into the bathroom. The shower water radiated on his skin, her slippery slick. The kissing seemed to wake her. She soaped his stiff, making those little female sounds that inspired. He almost drowned doing the munchies because the water would slide down her tits and tummy into his nose and mouth as she pressed him deeper pink lips kiss

under the heat lamp, her hair all squiggly. She told him to get dressed fast. He wasn't ready for her to appear in that black jump-suit, pulling him along out of the apartment, up the stairs to the roof. Up there, the sky was everywhere gray. The sun hardly getting started, making the edges of the frame glow.

The roof made him think of Cesar. His father liked roofs. "Some people think they birds," he said once, after that kid who worked for him "fell" off one. "So I just like to see if they can fly." The roof was wet in places. She brought Dinky right to the edge of the parapet, making him get pensive. He kept seeing that scene between Cesar and Johnny, both of them standing at the edge. Was Cesar out to find out if Johnny could fly, or was it Johnny who would push his father off the top? Was it why he ran off to the marines, because he couldn't do it?

Anita was standing right at the edge, her face concentrated on the below like a diver. And she had brought Dinky right to the edge with her. He did not in any way back off. He was with her.

"Are we gonna jump?"

"No," she said.

Squatted into lotus. Pulled Dinky down with her. The breeze was still saying rain as it lightly brushed hair from her face. Dinky decided that looking at her was good, the way she looked all Puerto Rican Emma Peel.

"Do you ever watch the sun rise?"

Dinky was not into having to pretzel his legs. He sat right on the edge and let them dangle. The rain breeze chilled him.

"Sometimes," he said.

"I do this every morning. I clear my head of everything. I open it up to all the signals floating around out there. I invite them in." She smiled like she hoped to freak him out. "I listen to voices."

"Voices?"

"Yes." She was holding his hand. "Do you ever feel like someone, some force somewhere, is talking to you, telling you things?"

"No."

"Never?"

"Nah." Sadly, like he wished he could say yes.

"I didn't, either. Before I changed everything. Do you believe in something corny, like havin the power to change your life?"

Dinky hadn't expected philosophical questions. Fucking always left him a little stupid afterwards.

"I don't know," he said.

She touched his face, her eyes aglow as if she would now minister unto him.

"I was just like you," she told him soft. "The first time I came up here, I thought that was it. I turned my last trick. I came up here to finish it. I was gonna jump."

Dinky weighed her words. Tree-lined Kelly Street had not risen yet, though there was some guy getting into his Lexus.

"I was alone on the streets for a year after I shot my ex. Therapists kept tellin me I was a victim. I wanted to die. That morning, the sun came up an' it talked to me. So everybody on the streets thought I was small, this victim. But it wasn't no mistake he drew the bullet. Wasn't no game of Russian roulette. Was an execution, Dinky. I was justice. I have power. I make my own life. The sun talked to me."

Dinky saw how she looked tranced, pumping his hand with the importance of her words. The solemn look of her gave him chills.

"I claimed myself. The streets didn't wanna accept that I offed a guy, that I planned it straight an' pulled it off. It's not a woman's place. Tell me, Dinky. In your line of life, do you meet a lotta killers? Gun boys? Blood freaks?"

Dinky nodded grimly. "Yeah."

"They're all guys, aren't they?"

"Yeah."

"Not a single female killer on the streets gettin her props, right?"

"Girls don't get props for doing that," Dinky said, fighting a shiver. "Guys laugh at them."

"If a woman shoots a guy, it must be some accident. It's a man's profession. Guys at the posse house never believed me when I told them I planned my kill down to the last breath. They laugh. You poor thing, they say. An' then they won't fuck me 'cause they all know a man died in my bed."

"Like it's bad luck," Dinky said.

"Yeah. Maybe the guy got hit by lightning or something." A small laugh that died quickly. "No. I killed a man in my bed and it felt good."

The way she looked out over the Bronx. Like she owned it. Like she found a way to beat it.

"Every day I would come here, an' the sun made me stronger. I lost the scabbies an' welts. I stopped givin it away. No more glow pipes. I changed my diet, I worked out. I wasn't gonna be part of the same rip no more. This time when I came back, I would be in control. I would be the posse boy with the biggest gun. I would get notches my way, so special that everybody gonna sit up an' take notice. I've just always wanted to do something nobody else had ever done.

"An' thass how I became a career girl."

Dinky felt mystified. Talk like dreams like drugs like walking into a strange room where you know something is wrong. A smell, the colors, something. But you can't exactly place it. The junkie woman he had known was gone. In her place, a new kind of soldier. Centered, objective, oriented. It made him feel young and incomplete and in need of some soul-satisfying mission. He almost envied her. Had to touch her face. She closed her eyes.

"Dinky. What are you doing to me? Sweet baby."

The sun cut an orange slit through the murky dark.

"I wanna make this whole city, this whole country know who I am. Not just 149th Street."

The kiss was slow motion. Dinky didn't care if he fell.

She was trembling. Rain breeze? The two of them squeezed tight on the edge of parapet. She wiped at her face fast like she didn't want him to see.

"Shh," she said. "Here it comes."

The sun spread across sky. Not strong aggressive but seepage that pushed the inky dark away. It slowly bronzed them. They didn't say anything for a long time, as the city below began to stir. Buses exhaled hoarsely and sewer grilles belched vapor. Cars sputtered to life. People headed down 149th Street toward the subway.

"You know so much about me," she said, like it was a pity.

Dinky thought about that a moment. Running into her just when she popped some stiff, and didn't she talk about already popping two people before she almost plugged him? He knew too much about her. He started to think about what it would feel like to smack into pavement from so up high.

"It's so hard for me to trust people, Dinky."

"You can try."

"But there's my career to consider. I just can't be stopped right now that I'm almost gettin there."

"Gettin where?"

She watched the city, not him.

"I'm the first Puerto Rican female serial killer," she said.

Dinky gripped a bit of parapet for support.

"You what?"

"America's number-one female serial killer is Aileen Wuornos. Seven confirmed kills."

Anita took a deep breath.

"I'm gonna beat her record."

Dinky stared. So pretty, the glow in her eyes. How she went from angry to glorious was a mystery to him. She was looking down on the big city from a great height and it looked like she had already came, saw, conquered.

"So? I ain't no cop."

"But are you my friend?"

Dinky slow-nodded. "Friends don't fink on each other."

"But I can't be stopped now, don't you see that? I still have three more kills to make to beat the record for sure. This Angel thing could get in the way. I mean, the cops sure ain't gonna catch me. Won't it suck that *they* don't get me, but Angel gets me for something I din't even do?"

"Who knows what Angel thinks? Maybe he thinks it was a posse that did it. Thass maybe where he'll go first."

"Besides, I love Angel."

"Yeah, right. An' you love me."

"I do?"

"Yeah. Said so last night."

How did they end up in bed? No way to tell. Naked was an automatic response with them. They obeyed the impulse. Kids with a new toy. And they would play that shit to death.

She didn't need a stocking to strangle him. She had a way of locking her arm around his neck and squeezing that brought the same result. She slipped him inside and strangle-pulsed him with such precision that he tremble-wracked all spasms. "Sweet baby," she cooed to his gurgle twitch, "you're so good to me."

The warm after dozing.

They had run downstairs to pick up the papers, because like any star she had to check the reviews. Boy was she *pissed* when she saw that her last performance hadn't even made the headlines.

"I don't believe this shit!"

Pages flew as she searched. Dinky looked too, not sure what for. She stuck it in his face. The police blotter page, just before the sports:

Bronx
Hispanic male, shot to death,
Beck Street. Identified as
Federico Alvarez, aka Freddie,
27, of 689 Longwood Avenue.

"You see that? I can pop three guys in Manhattan, an' get headlines, did you see?" She held up some of the other clippings that
Dinky had flipped through before. "But lemme pop two dudes in
the Bronx on the same day an' look, not even an inch of copy! An'
they still missed one!"

"Maybe they haven't found him yet."

"Shit. It just don't pay to work my ass off in a borough like this."

They were removing their clothes, to jump back into bed while
the crisp morning cool was still on them, and the sheets felt fresh.
Did she say *three* in Manhattan? Already Dinky was trying to make
sense of all those numbers, doing the math while pulling off his
jockey shorts. The bed felt cold and wonderful, the soft silk of her
on top. Three plus two is five, a voice said, and that makes five
dead people. The thought that she might be lying was exciting. The
thought that she was really a killer excited him. The thought that
she might just fuck him to death was exciting. The touch the feel
the breath of her no matter what, no matter what shape or what
form she took: exciting. Dinky wasn't even arguing with it. The side
of the street he came from didn't truck with the law. The fucking
was cosmic enough. As he tried to slip mind back into throbbing
body, he saw her take out the ANGEL bracelet. He was thinking the
least she could do was give it back after a fuck like that, but she
snapped that shit on her wrist like it was going to stay there for

keeps. They clung to each other in the dizziness, under body-heated sheets.

"I want to see Jose," she said, sending Dinky into a quick set of bad dreams.

The cat clock with the moving eyes said it was already nine-thirty.

13

All that constitutes a person is a series of experiences connected by memory and by certain similarities of the sort we call habit. If therefore we are to believe that a person survives death, we must believe that the memories and habits which constitute the person will continue to be exhibited in a new set of circumstances.

A book on dreams with lots of pictures. Something about dead witches and their ability to appear at will to people they spook. A paperback about drug-induced hallucinations. And that fat book by Dostoevski about crime and punishment.

Jose sat by the windows. Facing the entrance to the school library so he could spot Dinky right away. (The library was always the place they met if they hadn't seen each other in the morning.) He didn't know how he felt about that ANGEL tag being in Anita's hands. No news reports about some dead girl found floating in a tub. (Shivers. The water would be so cold by now. Cloudy soap islands floating on the surface like ice floes. Lucy underneath. How she turned to wink at him.)

"Stop it," Jose said. To her or to himself. Shutting his eyes.

Opening his eyes.

She was over by the Ancient History shelves, looking mousey and meek in her preppie Latina gear—plaid skirt, white anklesox, and white blouse. Plus she had on those little black-rimmed glasses. Made her look intelligent, not vicious. Jose stared at her like he was reliving a memory.

She sat at his table, clutching that big book on Alexander the Great that Jose was already familiar with. A Lucy-scented breeze as she placed the book down and began flipping pages. She knew what she was looking for. Jose noticed her hair looked towel-dried.

"I just wanted to see if they still had this book. I'm not sure if I showed it to you before."

"You showed it to me," Jose said.

"Are you sure? This picture of Alexander the Great?"

Slid the book across so he could see.

"I've always thought this picture looks just like Angel." Absently stroking the page. "It still does look like him, doesn't it?"

"Yeah." He slid the book back to her like he had seen enough.

I'm talking to a ghost, he thought. Couldn't take his eyes off her. Alive or dead. Nothing had changed. She would always have the power to walk into every room every space and make him feel she was out of reach. The feeling that she was escaping him. That he was always chasing after and could never catch up. That she was passing him by, at last leaving him for the little boy he was, the UNman, the UNmade, the ever UNfinished. Like she wanted him to be there to watch her *go* past. This was not new. Only worse now that he had killed her. "The boy who never does anything about anything," she used to call him. "Why don't you take charge?" The feeling bit through him. The boy finally does something, and he does it *wrong.*

Not like Alexander. He rocked out from Pella, the capital of Macedonia, in 334 B.C. Fucked Persia up the ass. Knocked them to shit at Granicus and then his famous appearance at Issus where he sent Darius packing. Twenty-three years old, he was, same as Angel. A major kingpin, a man of the people. The symbol of Puerto Rican ascendance in the inner city. The big world conqueror. Lucy turning pages and seeing nothing but Angel, Angel, Angel. She was looking at those pictures now, same way she had then. Jose fighting off the images, and Lucy smiling vaguely back, as if she pitied him for trying.

They had been in Fifteen. Where they used to go after school, to study, do smoochies, fuck, whatever. Wasn't like they *lived* there. Sure, maybe Lucy dressed it up like it was their place, but it was pretend. He was no posse man and he didn't buy it for her. She was lying in bed with that Alexander book. Caressing that Alexander face on the glossy page.

"Looks just like him," she said.

(Jealousy like a plum pit. Caught in his throat.)

"Did you know that Angel is the same age as Alexander?"

(Jealousy's color red not green. What he saw.)

"It gives me the shakes to think that someday he may just conquer the world."

"He's a fucken drug dealer, man. He ain't no world conqueror. He's a fucken goon."

"Yeah, right. You're just jealous 'cause he's got a life. He's a real man, doin real things. An' you're doin what? Jose schoolboy, sellin some weed?"

Jose took the book from her. Got up from the bed to look out the window. It hurt to look at her.

"Listen. Why don'chu go study with Angel?"

"Why don'chu just grow up? You're such a little boy, I swear. I'm fed up."

She slipped into her shoes. "If I was with Angel, I sure wouldn't be in his bed studyin no history books."

The toss of her hair, like she shook all trace of Jose off. She was making for the exit. He spun her around by the arm. She shoved him. He pushed her up against the wall.

"Why don'chu keep dreaming? There ain't no way a guy like Angel is gonna go for a bratty little snot like you. You're just a wannabe posse chick. You don't have the right bra size."

She pushed past him, then turned like she would smack him.

"You take that back."

(He should've known what was happening by the way she was checking his eyes. Either dying for him to say it again. Or dying for him to take it back.)

"Fuck that. I mean it. You couldn't ever land a guy like that."

(The burn on her face. He *had* to continue.)

"He's way too uptown for you. He'll take one look at you an' think, shit, where'd I put that box of Pampers?"

She picked up her windbreaker, wordless. Face unreadable. Jose felt it. He had gone too far. Couldn't stop.

"You'll never land him," he whispered.

"Just watch me," she said.

He took her tactical retreat as a sign of victory, but it was like that *Tora! Tora! Tora!* movie. "All you have done is awaken a giant and fill it with resolve." Pedro rented it the night that Lucy canceled a study date because she was going out with Angel.

"You gotta be kidding, right?" Whole cities tumbling into the sea. "You call to tell me something like that?"

"I'm just being truthful. I don't gotta lie to you. Do you prefer I lie, an' you hear from somebody at school that I went with Angel to see the new Keanu Reeves movie at the Guild 50th Street Cinema, 33 West 50th? The seven-forty showing? I'm saying it just in case you don't believe me an' think I'm makin it all up. Just come down an' have a look. See for yourself. Just don't thinka doin anything stupid. Three of his boys are comin with us. We're takin the Jag."

"I hope you don't ruin ya night, expectin'na see me."

"I'll try an' keep busy."

Her words clawed through him as he rode the subway. Maybe it was the air conditioner that made him tremble like that? Still had the shakes out in the muggy night, spotting Lucy in a black dress with flared bell sleeves. Black choker. Slick red lips. She was always baggy pants guerrilla fighter with him, never saw her do the feminine like that. Arm hooked to her man. Mouth going, eyes darting round. (Jose too much a shadow to be spotted. Or was he a ghost?) Angel's head tilted toward her as if he was listening but a crooked grin like he really wasn't. Looked young, boyish, quite unlike an Alexander dude. It could've been Jose if he wore Fubu.

The call came that night. Two in the morning. Jose alone in the living room watching TV like he had been waiting.

"I got him," she said. "I got him an' you said I cun't even get him to look."

"You got him. Yeah, right. One date an' she's a fucken posse wife already."

She was breathing hard.

"Angel is the nicest guy. Calm and smooth. After the movie he unhooked from his boys to be alone with me. Took me to City Island. We had champagne and a real good joint. He kisses real good, Jose. Better than you. He really likes that I'm not a posse chick. You hear that? He wants to bracelet me."

"You mean tag you."

"Yeah, whatever."

"He says that to all the girls, stupid."

"I bet'chu a hundred dollars he fucks me."

"You think I should care?"

"You don't dare bet now 'cause you know I can have him. So maybe you're learnin'."

"I don't give a damn who you fuck. Or who gets fucked by you."

She laughed. It was one of her big laughs, like he had really delighted her.

"You'd rather lose a hundred bucks than admit you're wrong?"

Couldn't remember if he made the bet or not. He was telling Dinky he was through with her, especially if he saw her in the hallway at school. She was starting to skip school. A posse wife don't got time for classes. One day Diana came up to him outside science class, after he hadn't seen or heard from Lucy for a week. Handed him an envelope with a note:

YOU OWE ME A HUNDRED DOLLARS.
—LUCY

The silence was just the intake of her breath. She closed that Angel book and slid it back to him.

"You never paid me my hundred bucks," she said.

The library was dead. A few kids clacked away on that pitiful bank of slow, outdated computers. Tables sat empty all around

Jose except for one by the windows, where a cluster of boys made cracks. Laughter roaring out was immediately stifled by the rabbit-faced librarian, who let out a long hiss any time noise made a comeback. Jose thought how cool it would be if Dinky would walk in right now and see Lucy. Or not see Lucy.

"Why am I seeing you?" Jose asked himself.

"Guilt," she said.

"I don't feel guilty," he said. "I feel dumb. Like I should've stopped it."

He pulled the LUCY panels out from his bookbag. Slid the folder across to her like it was proof. Lucy examined each page like she was a copyeditor. Stopped at the panel where Jose swipes the ANGEL tag. Caressed the bright Dinky colors with her fingers.

"So what is it you want?" he asked, tired.

She smiled from a distance. Jose now noticed the dark bruise around her neck. The mark of his hands, holding her under. The sharp stomach twitch.

"What was it I wanted?" she mused, eyes shut like she might dream on it for a while. "What do you think a Puerto Rican girl wants?"

"Please don't ask me that now," he said.

"A girl wants to be taken care of," she said.

"Even if it's by a fucken criminal? A walking scum that dicks his own people?"

"Oh yeah?" The old challenge was in her eyes. "An' who are my people? You gonna tell me that?"

"Shh." The librarian spun to face them from behind her circulation desk, which floated in the middle of the room like an island. Lucy glared for a moment, shutting the folder and sliding it back.

Her eyes went clear turquoise, like the water off a white sand beach. Her chair scraped loud.

"I want my tag back," she said, getting up with a huff.

"What do you need it for?"

"I won't go away until you give it back."

The words through hair, movement. The shivers hit him. That cold breeze. Clammy feel. Why didn't he ask her if she was still in the tub?

Reality waited its turn. There by the entrance, Toothy Barbara with a sad sympathy in her eyes as if she had seen the whole thing. Jose decided he would surrender. Act as if he had been expecting her all along. Tired of the story. Best to end it all now. His glance motioned her into the chair Lucy had filled. Toothy Barbara paused for a second.

"You sure you want me to sit down?"

Jose stared, his table cluttered with his books about death and ghosts and guilt and Alexander the Great. The folder with the panels sat there in plain sight, too. Dinky had told him he shouldn't walk around with any art, but Jose could not part with them. He started to feel like he had nothing to lose and nothing to hide. Toothy Barbara waited breathless, the bated breath, the breathing. Something about the way she was breathing.

"Come on, sit. You came all this way, right?"

Toothy Barbara pulled the chair out some more, then she pushed it to one side and swapped it for another from a nearby table.

"That one's wet," she said.

She was wearing that pleated skirt again and a low-cut blouse that reminded Jose that sometimes females dress strategically. All those open buttons, and the glittery necklace leading down to that valley in between . . . Toothy Barbara let him drift with thoughts, content to sit and watch him watch her. She checked his stack of books, her every fingernail glossy pink. Jose watched her hands sail over by across and land right beside the folder containing the LUCY panels.

"So where's Dezzie?" Jose thought he should say something. Toothy Barbara shrugged.

"See, I have this theory." She was whispering like this was a secret. "There's no such thing as coincidence. Things don't just happen. You sent that note to Dinky through me because deep down, you wanted me to see it. You wanted to show me that you took action. And I think you wanted to involve me in it. Almost as if you already knew I was the one that needed to know."

"I just wanted you to pass it on, man."

"You knew I would read it."

A library assistant struggled with one of the window shades, which squealed as it slowly descended. Sunlight blotted out somewhere.

"You don't have to impress me," she said.

"I wasn't trying."

"Why don'chu give up that Lucy shit now, an' carry on wit'cha life?"

Jose wordlessly slid the folder across the table to her. She opened it.

" 'The fight led them into the bathroom,' " she read. Quietly turning pages. Jose didn't say anything. She shut the folder.

"These are beautiful," she said. "Did it take you an' Dinky long?"

"How did you know it was us, Tooth?"

Toothy Barbara shrugged.

"You know"—ironic laugh—"I really wish you would stop callin me Toothy."

He was the one that started that. Not a big teeth thing, really—just that big smile of hers. Overwhelming, flash sparkle from a toothpaste ad. It had been a joke, a barb, the kind boys and girls send across classrooms all the time. How was he supposed to know it would catch on? It must have mattered to her to be the only girl in school that he bothered to insult on a regular basis. Why did her zany energy, her crazed rabble-rousing biting wit bother him? He was the one arguing with her in the stairwells about Hitchcock and Scorsese. There he was on stage, at the other end of the table, debating her on McCarthyism. That was him standing in cold November rain as she and her small crew shot the running sequence—the teenage heroin mom running down the street by the expressway. She is making a break from the world of men and everything they demand of her. Her condition is so severe that every time a man looks at her, an item of clothing pops off. "She can feel the way men look at her. Every time, she is stripped of something!" (Toothy explained the concept to him, painstakingly detailed on storyboards which she drew herself. No slouch with that pen.) A naked running girl.

Toothy Barbara managed to cheat most of it, but this shot with the bra flying off took choreography and fishing lines and coordination; where was the coordination the working together the organization? "You fucking Puerto Ricans," she screamed after another take fell apart, "why din't I hire me some Cubans?" And Jose shivering in that thin leather jacket with his hair slicked back like fifties—his was the look that sent the girl's bra flying—and twenty-six takes later, Jose sitting with her on a stoop while she fishes out a smoke.

"So what did you think?" she asked him, while they watched "her" boys pick up all that fishing line and gaffer tape.

"You'll be the queen of B-movies yet," he said.

There was a sudden crash snap as a window shade broke free of its cord and shot up clatter squawk. A burst of sunlight stream. Toothy Barbara all eyes sideways, like she was expecting some other shoe to drop.

"I saw you," she said.

"You saw me what?"

"It was a Thursday night. I was doing the wrap-up on this hooker flick for Miss Beetle's class. I was cheating some shots in the yard across from school when I caught these two boys sneaking into the building."

"So? Could've been anybody."

"I caught you on tape, Jose. Both of you. You wanna come to my house sometime an' check out the footage?"

"Why din'chu go to Reyes then?"

She just stared back.

"You got what you wanted now, star reporter for *The Sentinel.* You got all the proof you need to bust the big *BUDDHA BOOK* case. Reyes will give you a medal. You'll be a shining example of Puerto Rican youth. There will not be a fourth issue thanks to you. Why don't you just take these pages now an' walk them over to Reyes?"

She just stared back.

"Go ahead. Do me a favor." He slid the folder to her as far as it would go. "I wanna see what my father's gonna do when Reyes calls him into the office. An' there I am. An' there he goes."

Very slowly and with great precision, Toothy Barbara slid the folder back to him.

"You should keep those to yourself," she said, "until you print them."

Jose stared up at those dull white globes that hung from the ceiling like upside-down mushrooms.

Dinky dropped his bookbag on the table. He pulled a chair over and sat, munching on that licorice twirl while giving them both looks.

"Silly me," she said, not taking her eyes off Jose. "Here I was, thinkin maybe we would get to walk to class together."

"Three's a crowd," Dinky said.

Jose shot him a look that said, You're not being helpful.

"Dink," he said, "I want you to meet Barbara. Barbara, this is my best friend, Dinky."

Barbara relished every ounce of intro. Held out her hand like a debutante. Dinky gave her hand a quick shake.

"Well." She got up, shouldered her bag. Paused reluctant. "I guess I'll see you later. You still comin'na my house?"

"Not me," Dinky said.

"Sure, Barbara."

" 'Barbara'?" Dinky nudged Jose. " 'Barbara'?"

"You still look pale," she said. "Try an' eat something, okay?"

Jose blushed.

"Okay honey," Dinky said.

14

Everybodies: Happening Wall Street strip club. One of a string of new places peddling woman flesh in the year of the backlash. No torn seats no disinfectant stink. Clean bouncers in white shirts. Clientele that carry briefcases. The latest stock figures ticker by over the lounge. A place where a man could relax after a day of business, with a martini. And a lap dance.

Anita hadn't thought she'd land the job. Too many blond girls from Long Island who sun up on Riis Beach for that coffee tan. She didn't need to barbie on the beach—already had that gold Puerto Rican brown. Big round eyes that could blink innocent or blink knowing. Once she got up on stage, every eye was on her. She stood out sharply from the flabby girls who worked the early afternoons with their lazy, noncommittal moves. It gave Anita the chance to dominate, to get all the attention and those crumpled twenty-dollar bills.

She was there, whenever. Anita worked all week, open for sudden calls and emergencies. Gave Manny her beeper number. Proved herself reliable and willing to go the extra mile. Doing four

shows a shift plus time on the walkway time behind the bar pushing drinks, time in the cage by the entrance. (Manny loved her in
the cage. Liked to beam her dance onto all the video screens.)

Manny never had much to say about her work. Stood by the
stage at all times like he was brooding. Watched every girl dance
like he was searching for early signs of wear and tear. Being
Puerto Rican meant the girl couldn't get acne or a bruise without
facing a pink slip. The spick chicks were always suspected of
being crackheads. They had to always be on the double clean and
not gain weight. Manny was strict. He used to have three Puerto
Rican girls. Now there was only Anita.

She was glad he was watching her today, because she had the
moves fluid. Manny could tell when she was distracted. Those
recent nights when she had Angel on the brain, her moves would
go all molasses and Manny would wander away from the stage
(never a good sign). It frustrated her. For almost a year, she had
forgotten him. Avoided the street, found a career. But he came
back to her like something that was still missing from the picture.
One trip to Beck Street was all it took.

Anita found Jose because she found her father. She had always
found him. It was a trick she learned from her mother. By the time
Anita was five, Pedro was a mythic figure, a shadow in a black
Pontiac. The man buying *coquito* on the corner of Tinton and
149th while glancing over his shoulder.

"See him? Thass ya father," her mother would say. Slim, sensual
trigueña named Alicia. Blaming her *arrugas* and loss of her figure
on Pedro. Always on the move, from apartment to apartment. "Your
father doesn't live far from here." (And then he would move. And
then they would move.) Alicia brought Anita with her, every time. To

sit on a stoop and wait until he came out. The moment Pedro showed, Alicia would spring up with Anita. "Porque, Pedro? Porque? Porque no me mandas dinero? No ves que tienes una hija?"

Pedro wouldn't sit still. Soon he moved to another part of the Bronx, maybe another woman to live with. Alicia would walk with Anita up and down Kelly Street, from Longwood to Prospect Avenue, asking every *trigueña* about the man in the picture. "He only likes *trigueñas*," she always said.

It didn't take long for Alicia to figure out maybe the reason Pedro didn't want her was because she had an Anita attached. She started to beat her some and drink too much and not chase after Pedro. That made Anita chase Pedro for her, as if maybe Anita could prove she was useful. Anita always found him. Walked up to whatever *trigueña* he was with at the moment. "Do you know I'm his daughter?" (The woman would stare back into those green eyes, realizing at once where they came from.)

One day, Anita stopped being at home so much. The streets were better. At fifteen, she started to advertise that she was a girl— tight shorts, red toenails and those long legs of hers. She got her pussy popped by three boys she had been drinking with. (Surprise.) And after that it wasn't the same.

She had to have a boyfriend.

Loco was her first. A good reason to leave the nest. He had a car, money, and a place to share. A cute smile and a goatee that tickled. Not so surprised when kisses and hugs turned into slaps kicks and punches. To make her swallow her words he would strangle her and come to her squirming. The Russian roulette game while he was fucking her was his idea—only the gun never ended up pointed at *his* head. When she got ugly from fists, he would fuck her from behind so he wouldn't have to look at her face. She took all that, in the mysterious way women have of taking that from brutal men, but when she found out he was making it with some fish called Wanda, she snapped. ("He's an asshole, but he's *my* asshole.") She got that teeny .22. Got a few spiked joints from a friend. Fed it to him that one night. When his games began, he was too sluggish to climb atop.

And so she was able to tie him up.

Loco laughed at first, making like he would burst out of her knots in no time, if he needed to. He laughed like he was in control. He stopped smiling when she mentioned Wanda.

(She better than me? Hmm?)

click

he rocked he twitched he tried to wriggle her off but all that did was make her wet. Made her want to make it last. If he could only stay soft and cringing for her! He had always said that she belonged to him. Didn't he know that if she was *his,* then he was *hers?*

(New math.)

click

first trip of the hammer made his face turn white. The second squeeze, empty chamber happy shudders. (There's a bullet in there somewhere, honey. You just wait.) Doesn't he remember how much he loved to play this game, pulling his gun on her in midthrust? How he used to spin the chambers on that revolver. How come he doesn't want to play now? What a wet face on him. What a wet pussy. Started to resist, to struggle hard.

"You better kill me after this, bitch," he said, "'cause I'ma fix you good for this shit."

"Okay," she said.

And she saw why he had done all that spooky shit to her. (If that was male, then she was male.) It was thrill, it was power sex. It was control as long as she had that trigger. She cried and laughed at the same time. Slapping his wet face so he would play along.

"Make like a monkey."

Delighted by his screeches.

"Now you're a dog. A dog!"

Barked raspy pit bull.

Twitch twitch twitch. Volcano. She shuddering in lengthy spasms. Why was he screaming so much? Nobody was going to hear him over the Luis Miguel they were blaring upstairs.

"Baby, I don't know why you cry so much. Hmm? Look. No bullets. See?" *Clack* spun those empty chambers. Rummaged in her black bra. A nice shiny bullet into the empty chamber. And her grin as she set the revolver spinning.

"No!" he said.

The prosecutor stumbled to convince a jury that this innocent, scarred little girl had brutally and without remorse executed her former lover. That she planned it, drugged him up, tied him down. Even lay on him while he bled to death. The defense showed that the deceased was a crack-dealing pimp with a record three pages long. Just the look on him on those mug shots was enough to make the jury want to lock him up.

They gave her therapy sessions instead of a sentence. They

wanted her to talk about it because they thought it might help her. She *didn't* want to talk about it because if she did she might start telling the truth.

"Your aunt called my office yesterday," the custodian of the court told her. "She's distressed that you're not staying at home with her."

"I can't stay with her," Anita said. "She drinks like my mother. I can't be around that."

"But you're supposed to tell us where you're staying."

"I'm not staying anywhere."

And that was the most truth she ever spoke to them. She had no boyfriend no crib hardly a place to crash. The streets slammed in her face like a door. Loco was a name, and everybody he was with either shunned her or wanted to pop her. She got no props for offing her ex. Anita got smaller from her kill. The boys avoided her, even though none of them believed she offed Loco—the dumb fuck drew the bullet. The girl was bad luck.

"But I killed him. I planned it," she insisted sometimes after too many drinks, but people only nodded yeah, right, the bitch is cracked. They started calling her "Fruity Pebbles."

The crack thing started how? A new hole to fall into. She was desperately alone and any guy that was nice to her was a daddy. She could do business, but no man would take her in, take care of her. This was because no guy wants to sleep with a chick who might pull a piece once she hits the Sealy. The fact hit her the night Ronson refused to fuck her. Ronson the beautiful black-eyed prince of Cypress. He had a way of listening to a woman that made her think he could really hear her. Her last hope on the street was to slip into bed with him. But he said no, and started to put on his shirt.

"But I thought you said people been sayin I was the victim," she cried, finally getting the reality of her place.

"It don't matter," he said without looking at her. (The jingle of his keys.) "What counts is that a guy died in your bed."

After that, she was selling it. She was selling it wholesale she was selling it free she was giving it away for pennies. She dreamed of a spark a fire that certain look she caught in Loco's eyes the moment bullet slammed into skull, but it was all bear breath and dick stink. She was hitting the streets hard, haunting stoops. It was on one of those many nothing trips that she first spotted him. He was reclining on a milk crate. Watching traffic flow while sucking on that vanilla shake. Rocking that crate. Harassing pigeons with rubber bands. So many jokes for her as she waited for that some-times pickup. Those moments when he even peered into an arriving car.

"He don't look worthy," he would tell her with a wink. And she would ride off glumly into her stinky swamp, backseat condom stink, copper mouth taste. Anita felt sure she wasn't born for this. She had killed a man, but hardly got much press or TV. How could Lorena Bobbitt get worldwide attention for clipping a guy's dick when Anita offed the whole guy?

(Was it because she was Puerto Rican from the South Bronx?)

The guy's name was Bello. It means "gorgeous." A mystery where the tag came from, considering his burnt frying pan face. His clothes were no event, just another spick guy in army pants and dirty sneaks. He invited her to come ply her trade at one of his parties. He was known for throwing mad crazy festivities of the radical sex nature that always ended with a gangbang. He always said ten girls were coming but it was usually three, with maybe twenty or more guys in the house. The girls would get crammed full with pills booze smoke. Acid in the ginger ale. No telling how the girls would take the fun to come—if they were lucky, they would pass out after the first hour. Eyes screwed backwards as male hips thrust grasping legs twitch all spasm no life in those hands the way they lie thwack on the mat, open-palmed, no grip. (Nobody checks for a heartbeat. Those guys inna rush.) And no matter what, Bello always gets it on tape.

Anita was the only girl in the house that night. There were thirty-one guys. At first there had been other girls, but by the time she realized they had vanished, she was already blurry from bazuca blow and that fucking ginger ale

after that   parts missing   blacking out between takes so there was only video flash stroking her tits squeezing too hard fingers fists everything entering her

lights dizzy spin spin the black circle

she sucked every   all inside her
(everywhere)

After, he showed her the tape. So funny when she caught herself staring at that girl on the screen and thinking, Who is that girl and why is she screaming?

"Don't be surprised if you see this on sale someplace," he said. Like she should be honored.

Anita had joined the pantheon of Bello's women, the videotape gallery of crackheaded skeez who ritually got gangBOOMed to live forever on cheesy $19.99 tapes. The stars were pale ghosts that moved from table to table hoping someone *anyone* would buy them a drink, a shot, a puff. Anita tried to wear it like she had planned this all along, but there were no props to that propeller plane, either. One night she sat on a stoop and Angel appeared like it was the movies. He sat beside her and didn't say anything at first. Just looking at traffic. It was almost like they were doing it together.

"I saw the video," he said. Not looking at her. Chomping on a plastic straw. She didn't even try to laugh it off, or act like it was some sort of accomplishment. Her face was burning, and no way to hide it.

"All I wanna know," he said, and then the words stopped. He chomped on straw he watched passing cars.

Anita struggled to find words. The world looked like a glassy wet fishtank. Blinked to make it clear.

"Do you want me to take him out?"

Anita froze. He stared right into her.

"Is that what you want? Do you want me to off that Bello bastid?"

There was anger all over him. Why? She couldn't think. She battled the trembling.

"No," she said.

He tossed down the straw and walked away.

From then on: "He loves me. He just can't admit it."

Sitting on a stoop high humidity high heels candy-colored skirt. Blowing big bubbles through her plastic wand. Floating them over to where Angel was doing his street patrol. Pigeons followed him around as if he played some magic flute. And wasn't he pretty, all boyish energy and curly hair? The fuzz on his face that would never be beard. One moment he was barking orders, the next he was chasing bubbles. He popped them licked them had them burst in his hair all soapy.

"Should give up that shit," he said.

"Bubbles?"

He smirked. Pigeon wings flapping.

"This. What you do in life. Waitin for cars."

"Yeah?" She so catty, but it was pretend. "An' how do I keep payin for my new place?"

Angel had some fingers in his mouth. Serious contemplation.

"You gotta getta manna take care of you."

The sly grin made Anita flow all warm.

"You makin an offer?"

"Nope."

The pigeons took off, scatter. A grinning swindler as he backs away, swinging to avoid an angry stream of bubbles.

From then on: "He's a strong man who doesn't know how to say, 'I love you.' "

Was he going to be like that, look down on her because of her crazy past? Anita got on the case. Set up a network of informers. To track him to know him to find him any time, anywhere. Haunted his favorite Members Only posse clubs where Jags and limos made Hunt's Point look like Rodeo Drive. He treated her like one of the trusted, picked her out of the crowd. Could always cross that velvet rope. She thought she was winning, the closest of all, until the night outside that nothing club where she had expected him to show. Waiting around with the usual group of Angel groupies, when one of them screamed into her cellular and fell into a crying fit.

"Oh God no," she said, "Angel is getting married! Right now, he's gettin married!"

A gaggle of girls ran to their phones like reporters scrambling with a hot lead. Anita just stood, biting her lip until it bled.

Lucy arrived on the scene like fresh milk.

Should've seen her in glossy red lips. The girl had no street creases, but she was loud chatty and arrogant. Anita's sources didn't know shit about her until she was tagged, that was how fast it happened. Freaked out all the Angel groupies, who would talk about how they were going to beat the fuck out of her. Anita went through that too, thinking she might just pop the girl. Reading books on Amy Fisher, Carolyn Warmus, and Jennifer Reali dissuaded her. Killing in order to get the man just didn't work for females, though there were three Amy Fisher movies, and even Pamela Smart got played by Helen Hunt. Did you have to be white to get so much attention? Anita had *offed* her man. Lay on his hot sticky writhing and she came, she came. That's at least a couple of movies right there plus a porno short.

What pissed her off was renting that CNN video about serial killing in America and finding all two hours devoted to men. Aileen Wuornos only got passing mention. The leading female serial killer of note should rate at least twenty minutes with maybe some footage. It was the usual MALEcentric shit. The male serial killer is "fascinating"; the female serial killer is some sort of freak. It made Anita throb. "I don't wanna have to start killin people out here just to make a point," Anita once remarked to Ronson, the only person she bitched about it to. "Maybe I'll get to put Puerto Rico on the map, know wham sayin?"

Ronson had laughed. She sounded like a boastful street player. It was part real, part put-on. His smirk was one she was familiar with. He knew, and she knew. She wanted to be The Beatles of serial murder, but she was Puerto Rican, so the world would always say Menudo.

Lucy getting tagged ended Anita's time on Beck Street. She went up to a roof one day planning to jump off. Instead, she heard a voice with a plan.

She stopped walking the streets. No waiting for cars. No tricks no drugs no hanging out at posse bars.

No following Angel.

Macrobiotic diet. The gym on Fourth Avenue got her that nicely muscled trim figure. Her golden skin free of bumpies.

She was thinking B-movies and Americana. Being a stripper was the perfect vocation for a female serial killer. Not only was it perfect for bagging victims, but it would make a movie deal more likely. (Being Puerto Rican was a hard sell—she was looking to add as many ready-made elements as possible.) When her friend Minnie took her down to Everybodies, she got the job. She saw that as fate making the path clear. From that point on, not a face she could come across or a moment she could live now that didn't have significance.

Anita thought long and hard about the kind of tag she would

leave. It had to be something she could pace out, that wouldn't give her away too quick. She didn't want to get too heavy with the message thing, but a statement would be nice. (Hollywood says keep it simple.) It just happened to be Bello's tape because it captured a moment, immortalized her. The idea she got was to cut it into segments and leave an "episode" with each body. To do it exactly right, she bought eight five-minute tapes at Malik's on Broadway and duped them all herself on two VCRs. Skipping the opening part just a little, she cut eight scenes at four minutes each. Aileen Wuornos killed seven, which meant Anita had to pop at least eight to be safe. This was because the bastards who did the scorekeeping might not include Loco as one of her kills.

Except for a shot of her ass in Tape 4, she does not become truly visible in the series until Tape 6. She was possessive about her kills, and hoped the tapes would mark them as hers. The tapes sat in her closet for weeks. Then, one morning, she took one with her in her bag. Primed and loaded Carlotta. Safe and snug walking with her. Expectations in the air. She let instinct guide her. It was like channeling.

First was Steve. A fine sloppy mess that was, but she pulled it off. Parked off the West Side Highway. Purple evening skies. Nice tinted windows. Tape 1 and some lipstick on a napkin, sure, but Carlotta had to take two quick bites because he was so strong—almost got out of the car. Why didn't she bring a towel? Lucky she had a big hat, and that puddle to rinse in. She thought that everyone on the subway could tell something was up with her. She pretended to be on drugs.

Second was Dave. He talked a lot, too much, and boy was he ever insecure! He suspected her all the way—too many TV movies. It made Carlotta's bite all the sweeter. He snapped brittle like a twig, made pretty sounds, but she could not stay. Strolling couple with dog. Never do Riverside Park again. Hasty Tape 2 and sloppy lipstick smudge on napkin. She was lucky to get out. Wore ugly knit cap.

Third took weeks. Why did she wait? Felt unready, like maybe she was pushing it. The newspaper coverage spooked her at first. Stomachaches, cramps. It was that line in the *New York Post* that pissed her off the most: "*He* may strike again." Set off Carlotta shivers. Her finger in the Bible coughed up Matthew 26:39.

Jonathan wanted a date. Appeared like magic, inserting himself like fate. She tried her best to talk him out of it, but he squeezed and squeezed. This time it was the FDR Drive. She decided she liked it on rainy days. Tape 3, and a bloody red kiss. Another breathless escape, another long subway ride where she felt tranced and drugged out. The comedown after good sex.

Why was she so inept? The idea was to give clues, not give it away! The night the cops came to her building, she squatted on the floor with Carlotta drawn, naked trembling. The tears were from feeling cheated—but it was only some domestic scene downstairs. Watching the cops leave, it occurred to her she had already made a big mistake. How could she have not thought of offing the one link from her past that knew the tapes intimately? The guy even appeared on the first and second tape. Anita hadn't wanted to strike in the South Bronx, where a murder did not often make the papers. Manhattan was definitely more of a showcase-style arena. She hit the Bronx streets, taking it slow, hoping fate would grin and open a door.

Fourth.

Smelly doorway stink. Where she found Bello slinking like in days of old. The supreme alley rat. Cigarette always lit so lips acrid dry. She didn't plan on kissing him much.

She could tell he hadn't thought of her in a long time. When he saw her approach under dingy vestibule glow, she could see the dream spread in his eyes like he thought he was tripping. How regal how *royal* the teeny crack baby he once knew. Laughed when he asked what she was doing for money these days, like maybe he had an eye for peddling her flesh again, maybe making a new tape. (A couple more of Bello's parties and she would've been just skin and holes.)

She passed him the little promo card featuring pix of lethal tall blond California babes with tits erected full of hormones glassine packets silicone chips packing foam and those tiny plastic peanuts that kill turtles when they swallow them.

The purple shimmer of dress sliding down her thighs.

He leaned back in bed with the bottle, the memory of how they used to fuck swirling in his eyes. (Hers too.)

She tied him to the bed. Relaxed the man so groggy he didn't notice until. Then she was climbing off him after giving him a quick hit off her silky tits, a toke of smooth belly skin.

Bello's life hadn't changed a stitch. It was the same place, and the same cabinet where he kept all the master tapes. They lay there in drawers, spines up like books, numbered and in sequence. Her hand stroked them like she wished she could take them all, but she only took hers—No. 42 of 106. It seemed Bello had been very busy while she was gone.

He was protesting. Wasn't into kink. Tied up, and not even sprung! Whassup with that?

"What the fuck you get all naked for if you ain't gonna fuck me?"

She put that salsa CD on. Dithered with the volume.

"You ever see that movie about Lizzie Borden? It had Elizabeth Montgomery in it. She kills her mother an' her father with an ax. When she does it, she gets all naked an' the blood splashes all over her."

Something gave her shivers. Made her grip herself.

"I like the splash."

so

she turned the music low enough to be romantic.

(Devorame otra vez.)

Carlotta stroked him slow. Past his lips spitting so much gibber-ish. The little boy whimpering body buckling under so useless.

"Please," he said.

And she popped that stupid Freddie bastid, it was just like a dare. She couldn't miss the opportunity. Didn't even leave a tape or any shit like that. It was an impulse. The urge almost made her pop Dinky. It was a good thing she managed to hold Carlotta back. The memory of his smell was still on her body.

Tonight she would make No. 6. She would have Dinky bring her Jose on a silver platter. And she wouldn't tell him about the phone call she was making, just before hitting the stage.

"We're not home right now," Lucy's happy voice announced, "so leave a message. Maybe we'll get back."

(The beep cut off her laughter.)

"Angel."

She so breathless, feeling teenage. "It's Anita. I know you're underground right now, but I hope you can beep me. I really need to talk to you about everything that happened."

She hung up, and went out to dance in her cage.

15

R ecess on the Bruckner Expressway.

South Bronx fire escapes rule. They are deck, den, balcony. A spick porch. Jose was three the first time he stepped out on one. Was the closest thing to flying. Standing on thin metal strips all scary like he might fall between to down there so far below. At first it terrified him, but later he liked it so much they had to keep him from sticking his head through the bars out to where there were no more rails. The best place from which to sight fire engines, big buses, and the train. There was that time the tractor trailer got stuck under the el, top peeling back silver like sardine can—but there is nothing in the world like the Number 2 train storming past the window all rush all vigor with that steel feel of New York people and a city so machine. Made Jose long to be a part of it, to make a dent. The best he could do back then was drop water balloons and snipe passersby with batteries.

Jose was sitting up against the rail, slowly turning pages. It was Dinky's turn now to fill up the rest of the twenty-eight-page issue. He had shown Jose six pages about Cesar and some short pieces for the back cover, but nothing ever like this. Thirteen pages of well-paneled artwork, walking you from one side of Anita to the other. Jose flipped the pages back and forth, first stunned by the quality of the artwork, the panels, the unusual layout. Then he was hit by what the story was saying. Words and pictures assaulting him. Almost like LUCY pages.

"These are amazing," Jose said.

Dinky was busy rolling. They had said they would smoke that entire ANGEL bag. Thick spongy green. No brown no twigs hardly any seeds. Smelled like dreams and rain forests and the slowing of time. Dinky looked like he really didn't want to talk about it.

"Has to be your best ever."

No response from Dinky. He dutifully rolled two fat joints. Amsterdam style. Filter rolled from a matchbook. Gas compression lighter, with Angel's compliments. The first toke was his.

"Yeah," he said.

"I'm just thinkin like this: I'm thinkin, yeah, okay, we said it was gonna be only real stories, real life. But you know, these panels are so good. There's just no way we can't print them, man."

"Yeah."

"I'm sayin even though it's a true story, true life issue."

"But thass what it is," Dinky said, calm and accepting, passing the joint like even life's injustices made sense. Jose paused before his toke, trying to figure if maybe . . .

"For a moment there, you got me thinkin like maybe this story about Anita is true. But it's not, right?" Dinky was looking off into distance.

"Of course not," he said.

After that, they had to walk the streets. Everything was in segments. Snapshots. The rainy gray sidewalk skies. Kaleidoscope
slow, strange.

There were words. Dinky words about what a fuck he was to still
be carrying those panels around. Jose didn't tell him he showed them
to Barbara. He was starting to think that even though he and Dinky
were two parts of the same nation, they had separate futures coming
up. Jose was having his first thoughts about jail. He was thinking
about what Pedro would do when he found out. He'd want to keep it
quiet, cover it up. Where did Dinky get that third joint? (Dinky could
roll pretty fast.) This one was straight and true with no tobacco to
weaken the knees. It floated them right across Southern Boulevard.
They were smoking it out in the open like the reggae song, and then
Dinky got all spiritual like Puerto Ricans sometimes do.

"Do you think this stuff will give us bad dreams? I mean 'cause
of how you got it?"

And then they saw. The red pulsing flash of cop car lights off
the Dedication Wall. The small crowd of people, the blank-faced
cops. A body in a garbage bag.

Jose ran. Across the street blind, making cars honk. Up Avenue
St. John with Dinky behind, breathless. They crested a hill of rubble
that flanked the lot. Only then, slow.

"It could be Lucy," he said to Dinky.

"Maybe not," Dinky said back.

The lot was a boundary. Three different posses shared a border
there. Didn't matter if they had the same boss, boys will be boys.
The people in the neighborhood were used to bodies cropping up.
The lot was a dumping ground. It was a wonder the cops didn't
post a watch on the place and catch somebody. Maybe it was their

dumping ground, too. Jose had heard of cops sometimes offing drug dealers that got snotty. (Or just black kids.) Sometimes the cops were a posse.

The body was lying beside an unruly patch of tall grass. They had peeled back the garbage bag. A cop with a camera was taking snaps. Jose didn't know what he felt when he saw it wasn't Lucy. It was relief. It was despair.

"What happened?" he whispered to Dinky as they stared down on the body. "What's Angel doing with her?"

"Maybe there won't be a body," Dinky said. "Maybe Angel will just dispose of it some way."

"You think he would disappear his own wife?"

Dinky shrugged. A fresh licorice twirl to munch.

"It happens," he said.

The body in a bag. A young guy. Ratty face of a street vet. His throat a ragged bloody wound.

"That happens to finks, traitors, and fuckups," Dinky said. "He looks like a hundred guys I seen."

The Dedication Wall stood like a bulletin board. Could express the state between rival posses. But except for the dark blotch where Anita had blotted out Angel and Lucy's heart, all was calm. Posse tags coexisted side by side with no overlap, no insult. The two of them stood watching cop lights flash wicked off posse tags.

"I'm sicka this posse shit," Dinky said.

Maybe that was why he had trashed those pages, the ones he had shown Jose about Cesar and his brother Johnny, where his mother said, "I want my family back." Dinky tore the pages to shreds and Jose couldn't stop him.

How was it subway so sudden? Tunnel lights in the windows

like flashbulbs. (Those fucking paparazzi.) The local train slogs from station to station. The roll and toss, New York speed. The decision was they would blow that fifteen-hundred-dollar Angel grant. They did not want to be holding onto that. The first place to go was just off Sixth Avenue. A narrow staircase, up and up. Jose always hit the Three for a Buck box because he loved the old stuff, while Dinky scanned the new releases along the wall.

"You won't end up in jail," he said, bringing over that new Jim Woodring book. "You got a clean slate, a clean face, put on a good suit. Ya pop's a guidance counselor. You get a good liar—I mean *lawyer*—an' after they see what a good kid you are, they'll probably wanna stick you in the Golf Ball. Thass that detention center in Brooklyn. Small-time juvies go there. I did some time there when I was fifteen. It ain't so bad. They got a good library."

Rows and rows of comic books, in boxes on tables spilling over in piles, hanging on the walls like precious artifacts. The smell of printed paper bright colors plastic bags those big posters of Superheroes springing into action. Jose thought none of them could help him now. He didn't know which way to turn on it. It was just that going back to a regular life with Pedro and the moms seemed impossible after Lucy. It was a two-faced life. It would be pretend, never-say, slide along and don't speak. It was keeping it under his hat. It was shame, surrender, a lie. It should change everything. Why should he act like nothing happened?

"Ya pops can get'chu a lawyer," Dinky said.

"Don't call him my pops."

"Well he is, ain't he?" Dinky added another *Justice League of America* to his pile. "You rather have a drug dealer for a dad? What you think my father gonna do for me?"

"Pedro ain't gonna do shit. He'll run out. He won't want nothin'na do with this mess. He's gonna book on my mother. An' you know what? I'm fine with that. My mother will be hurt for a little while, but she'll be okay. He'll be gone. It'll be worth it. Just to get rid of him. I know he'll disappear when he finds out. Didn't he book on Anita when she got in trouble?"

Dinky bit his lip. Dug his fingers into those ranks of plastic-covered comic books. The search continued with almost frantic angry trembling. The *DNAgents* surprisingly good first series. *Alien Worlds* eye-popping surprises—seeking out old Charlton *Fightin Army*s and *Army War Heroes*—how did Dinky dig up that old Gold Key Classic version of *Crime and Punishment?* (Now Jose could skip reading the book.) *Sgt. Fury* not so good on story but they had John Severin for a while, and that Baron Strucker was always a kick. Jose never got over the disappearance of Russ Heath—the best for Tiger Tanks and the look of sweat on battle-weary men. Sam Glanzman should've got a Pulitzer for *USS Stevens* and his knack for searching humanity that always made war look noble, and stupid.

Used to get one hundred pages for a quarter back when. Jose was pulling those old Joe Kubert covers while Dinky went from Elaine Lee's lady vampires to Tim Vigil—plus that new stuff from Buichi Terasawa. Dinky had been more into gore than science fiction, but when Jose laid those issues of Don Simpson's *Border Worlds* on him, it changed his concepts. Who remembers Doug Moench's *Planet of the Apes?* Those rare issues of *Starstream?* It seemed nobody wanted those old issues of *Warlord,* the way Jose grabbed them up at fifty cents a pop. He was digesting war stories, pulp comics, reprints of *Modern Romance.* There was something about past meeting present that thrilled him, yet now there was a hollow feel. Comic-book panels had always been a place to run to, away from life. Now with his LUCY panels, he felt he had violated something. Panels were too real now. He kept seeing those Dinky panels, all worded, sequenced, toned. Gothic lettering. Sort of Tim Vigil, sort of Howard Chaykin. Real life, pretend? Jose wasn't sure but right now these comic books were looking a little silly.

Still, he had his stack, and Dinky had his. The ritual same as always. Reconnection through habit. A sense that things stay the same no matter what. So what if it really wasn't their money? The least Angel could do was buy them $123.09 worth of comic books. They were in an electronics store looking at video games when Jose really saw there was a weight on Dinky. It made him think of those Cesar pages he had torn up.

"Your mom asked me if I thought you were slippin back into the business," he said as they checked out the new *SIM* titles.

"Well, what did you say?"

"I said nah. I know you ain't in that. But something's got you all fucked up today, huh."

Dinky passed him a new Lara Croft game.

"She wants me to do something about my brothers. My father's hidden them away someplace. She wants me to find them. You see how different we are? You complainin about your father—"

"Stepfather, Dinky."

"Yeah. You complainin about him an' the worst thing he might do when he finds out all this shit is help you. The worst thing my father can do is probably off me."

"Your father wun't off you."

"Oh yeah? You know better than me? He wants me to get to

work for the firm already. He needs me. Can you believe that? He told me that shit. He wants I should make a choice. My mother wants I should make a choice."

"An' what do you want, Dinky?"

"I want *out*," he said.

FROM THE FIRST there was something possessive about the way he crammed those fifties in her G. Three a night since he first spotted her. Visited her cage first. Was always in front for her stage show, and she always spoiled him. There were many men, but only a few that triggered Carlotta. She couldn't say why. It was a look, a tone, a certain touch. She always tried to talk them out of it. For example, why pick me from all these girls? He loved Cubans, he said. Wasn't she Cuban? (She smiled. The white man's concern with origins. Didn't have the heart to tell him.) He seemed to be giving orders, and took it for granted that he had already bought her with all those fifties. "We're not allowed to go on dates, it ain't that kinda place." But some men do not take no for an answer no matter how much screaming, and that's the way it should be if Carlotta was going to wake, baby, wake. All she needed to know now was what kind of car he had. When he said Mercedes 380, there were stirrings all over her.

His name was Alan. He wanted a date.

THE BIG TABLE. Cleared of old work, new pages laid out. The LUCY side by side with ANITA. The colored pencils, the Magic Markers. Jose was spitting panels out fast, two, three pages.

Dinky started coloring them right away, a couple of intro pages and a back page they both designed full of teaser notes, innuendoes, in jokes. Jose threw in those last panels of BARBARA to add a twist of suspense. "I'm doing a movie," she says in that last panel, "about a boy who kills his girlfriend. An' how he gets away with it."

"I don't know if I would trust her," Dinky said.

"She could've turned us in, Dink."

"But why should we let her in on it? Why should anybody be in on this? Wasn't this just ours?"

Dinky went over to the window. Dug into that ANGEL bag for more weed. Was rolling absently, not even looking. Jose watched his fingers work blind.

"Dink. We ain't gonna have this after this issue. We just ain't gonna have this, are we?"

There was rain. It crept up quiet like a thief. It poured down sudden and hard like a tantrum. The wind beat it against the window, wet against their faces.

Dinky licked the joint shut.

"No more Haunt either. How am I supposed to keep the place if I don't work for my pops?"

Jose didn't say anything. He was thinking about how he had started out as a nice boy, Dinky's "straight" friend. Now he was a murderer. Almost felt like the old Jose schoolboy was a lie, couldn't go back to that. Had to take a new road, face it. But what did that mean? Jose lost himself in pages, rolling from him until the issue was completed. (Dinky always did the masthead.) He was looking at that page where Jose is asking, where, where is Lucy's body? What has Angel done?

"I can't believe he hasn't done anything about this," Jose had to say. "That he could be sittin on that body."

"But why should he come right out with it, dude? You forget this guy is a drug dealer?" Dinky's voice sounded a little annoyed as he lit that joint. (The snap hiss of that gas compression lighter.) "He has every reason to shut up. What if it was a rival posse that did it? You think he'd want word to get out on the street that somebody walked in an' iced his lady? So he keep it small until he finds out. What about the cops? Should he invite them into his crib to check her out in the tub?"

"Dink. What would you do? I mean if it was you?"

Dinky handed him the joint. For some reason he picked up that goofy photo of Angel and Lucy that was sitting on a window ledge. Stared at it for a moment.

"I would garbage-bag the body for a few days until I find out who. If I can't, maybe I'll dump the body and spread the word that some posse I don't like popped my bitch. Then I would make a war and use that poor stupid bitch to expand my turf."

"You think there'll be trouble over that tag Anita blotted out?"

Dinky grinned. "Yeah. I'm sure Angel's gonna pick on somebody to pay for it. But the tag is gone at the same time Lucy's gone. So how's he not gonna think it was a move by another posse?"

Dinky got in his face, stabbing him with a finger.

"You're off the hook, don'chu read that? You think goin'na jail is easy? You know that even doin Golf Ball time can be rough. I just wanna prepare you. You don't gotta do any noble shit here. Why even thinka goin'na the cops?"

Jose held up a fist. Giving Dinky his knuckles.

" 'Cause it's the one thing my stepfather doesn't want me to do."

Dinky tapped knuckles with knuckles, slow.

WORK WAS A snap.

So psyched she forgot her tips in the dressing room. Didn't doll up. Very casual in baggies, ponytail, no makeup. That big shoulder bag. (She had learned to make sure and bring stuff on these jobs.) Only waited three minutes on a Park Avenue corner before his Mercedes showed. A pretty gray gleam.

She jumped in like a bubblegum-clacking teen. Chit chat chat. "I've only done this four times before," she said.

Twenty-third Street. Right by the water. He was tense, too tense, so she had to give him something to calm him down. Unzipped his pants right there. The windshield started to splatter with rain just as he came into that peppermint-flavored condom. He wriggled like death throes.

"Thass for free, honey," she said. "Now we can do the real thing." (And that was her excuse to go rummage in her bag. Then she slipped her arm around to squeeze the pretty gurgles out of him while Carlotta pressed against his temple.)

"Hey! What is this shit!"

Her grip on him solid. Learned those holds from Loco's old copy of *Stalking and Immobilization Techniques*.

He wriggled like a man should. Who knows from birth that he can shake off a woman like some bothersome flea. (Not this one. Her time at the gym came in handy.) Can't take a girl serious no matter what size gun because God already decreed that man hath the upper body strength and that male ability to over*power* her, any *her.* Like some written guarantee. (And men go down believing that shit.)

"You get off me, bitch."

"Baby. Thass no way to talk."

"I ain't gettin rolled by no stupid bitch!"

She squeezed the squawkings out of him until his hand reached up blind. Beat against the wheel, useless. His face a darker color than white now.

A good time for rain heavy pattering against the car like a hundred stamping hands. The world all blurry beyond glass. A quiet parking space facing dark turbulent river. The other parking spaces along the cement wall were empty except for that one car parked maybe thirty feet away, along the entrance to the East River Parkway.

All of a sudden, Alan lunged, knocking her against the window. Swung her sideways with a fierce man noise. An ugly blue flash through her head.

And that's when Carlotta bit him.

It was an underwater sound, a coconut shell burst. A tiny round hole. He looked real surprised. There was just a mark, a crack across his face. Then blood splashed and he was making sounds. She punched and smacked him. It was too quick, too fast, her timing got all thrown off like she had wanted to prolong it, had come all this way and got robbed

(his bloody hands scrabbling at the door to try and open it. She hitting him with Carlotta and all that sticky splash)

and then

everything just stopped.

(wasn't it just like a guy to roll over and play dead?)

She was listening to the sound of the wet gush, as if rain was seeping in, drip-dripping on the leather seats. The bastid was bleeding on everything. She had it on her. A slick sticky feeling that pissed her off.

She cried. It was instant, it was quick. Just the weight of her life, of her mission, of the things she had to do. Her punches against the glass, an anguished cry that soon just stopped.

Not a car not a person in sight through red splash on the windshield. Was she supposed to bring a hose with her now? She had three bottles of seltzer. Shaking them made a jet stream that scrubbed and bubbled those stains clear (the tint on the windshield helped). Used that rearview mirror, wetting her face her hair her arms her hands. Stepping out of the car to change in the rain. Smiled at two joggers who did not see much past their hoods. Traded plaid shirt for big orange T. Lost the bloody baggies right off. Better the British army shorts. (Her legs wobbly like she had just had sex.)

The towels good for wiping down surfaces because Anita touches too much. The bloody clothes went into the garbage bag she brought. Even changed the sneaks for those cheap red sandals (the girls call them jellies).

Freshened that lip color with an extra coat, then pressed her lips against paper napkin (compliments of McDonald's). A kiss red and final that she left sticking from Alan's pocket like a tip.

Planted Tape 5. Gave everything a last look like she wanted to make sure she didn't forget anything. Feeling warm and flushed as she slammed the car door. Legs weakly pulsating. Raindrops cool, ticklish. Walking the rain-quiet streets. (New Yorkers hate the rain. See how they run.) An orange juice from a deli to replenish her liquids. It was only at the moment when she took her change that she noticed the blood spirals dotting those ten diamond stones six carats each, almost like grease stains. Made her suck in a breath and head outside to pocket that shit for now. In the subway, there was still this vague sticky feel to her hands.

The Parkchester local rocked her. Baby in a crib. A clattery sleepy high. Killing made her so horny. Her body craved Dinky, writhing underneath her. Her body still craving Angel. Writhing under her, finally.

And she thought, Aw, fuck. Like she woke from a good dream. And cursing the idea that there was still yet another decision to make.

"BUT WE SHOULD at least talk about it," Dinky said.

"But we been workin on it like we're gonna print it," Jose said, exasperated. "We did the whole issue. Why we gotta talk about it? I thought you knew we gonna publish this."

"So thass it, thass how it is?"

Jose and Dinky stared at each other. It took a long time. Maybe it was the smoke slowing them down. Maybe it was something else.

"Yeah," Jose said, seeing Pedro and Lucy and Angel all in the same picture.

"Okay," Dinky said, and he put the finishing touches on that cover masthead.

16

A slow speed to everything from all those Dinky joints.

Going downtown on the 6 train had fuck-all to do with Jennifer Lopez. They bought comic books and video games and some sneaks. Then after five joints they realized they were not going to smoke that whole ANGEL bag, so Dinky got the idea of selling it. They knew just the perfect dude too, so they headed toward St. Marks Place.

Walking Eighth Street reminded Jose of the many times he had walked those streets with Dinky and Lucy, sniffing out a jam a rave a secret undercave where beats thumped lights flashed and all the white kids hugged everybody. Dinky had noticed that whenever Lucy hit the party, she would act like she wasn't "with" Jose. Still available, like Jose was just an escort, a place to hang her arm while in transit.

"Nah," Jose said. "It wasn't like that."

Okay, how about that time, Dinky said, all animated like he had a big point to make—that time they went to that party and Jose stepped out for a moment to get some smoke and when he came back he found Lucy sitting in a love seat with this guy who had his leg up on her lap? She was touching him. Her hands worked their way up and down his thigh in an absent caress and grasp, moving in circles upwards downwards while her lips dropped words into the guy's face so close it was almost kisses. And Jose standing right there and she went on with her private dialogue, her moment away, like she didn't belong to anybody and everybody could see that shit plain. When she finally acknowledged Jose's glare, she unhooked from the guy with a comic jerkiness like somehow it was all funny. Jose didn't even know the guy. He had stared back at Jose like he was a chump.

"He's an old friend of mine," Lucy said as they walked to the subway, "a real old friend. I known him longer than you."

"What the fuck do I care? You were feeling him up right in front of me! It was like I wasn't even there! How is it you could do that right in front of me?"

Lucy stared at him a moment.

"I just forgot you were there," she said.

"You what?"

"Sometimes I'll forget you're there. It happens."

And Dinky had been there, like he had been many times before. Watching Jose's anguish come spilling out. Lucy and Jose. Fighting all during that express train ride. Dinky quietly chewing on his licorice twirl, like he was now. Crossing Fourth Avenue past the big black cube, where a small tribe of skate punks and mohawk brats smoked cigarettes and squatted.

"How quick you forget," he said.

"Forget what?"

"That you hated her. That you two were always fighting an' calling it love. That you should've just let that shit go."

Dinky sounded mad, as if it made him sick that Jose had killed her.

"I mean that you're doin all this talk like you wanna go to the cops or hand yourself in or some shitty noble crap like that. An' I'm thinkin, whatta you so sorry for? I'm almost glad you plastered that selfish bitch. What the fuck do you owe her after all the shit she did to you?"

They were sitting at a sidewalk table outside Dojo's, under the green and gray awning, picking at their tofu-hijiki platters.

"On top of which, you wanna print the comic. You wanna put out the LUCY pages. An' I'm feelin like I don't wanna be in on it."

"Why not, man?"

" 'Cause it all started out fun, like fantasy and makin funna the old fogeys. An' now it's this dead Lucy in a tub and this Anita thing. It's all too real, man. It was all fun an' underground war an' kickin the Nazis in the ass. It's too real. Something's gonna happen, gonna come from it."

"You sayin you wanna drop out?"

Something in Jose was trembling. It was strange to hear that tone from Dinky, disapproving, almost contempt. It made Jose feel rejected almost.

"I'm sayin I don't wanna be fightin the Lucy wars. I'm sayin thass got nothin'na do with why we been doin the comic book. An' if you just chuck that shit an' don't print it, then nothin has to happen. Lucy stays dead an' you stay free an' nobody knows nothin because there ain't no way Angel is gonna dump that body anyplace. He gonna disappear that girl, you see that? He gets to keep her anyway. So what makes you wanna go to the cops?"

That stopped the words for a while. Good thing they were sitting outside at Dojo's. Not only was the food cheap but you could look out at the people strolling down St. Marks. For a while, they just watched the procession. Of hippie longhairs with their incense stink. The leftover unshaven grunge kids who still wore flannel and Nirvana T-shirts. The black leather Goth girls in black lipstick. The green-hair punks plaid pants leather jackets combat boots and those busted-up straight-leg jeans. (Puerto Rican guys don't wear tight pants. Baggies give those big *cojones* more room. Why everybody has questions about Ricky Martin.) The Japanese girls with Picachu backpacks and thigh-high elevator boots. Puerto Rican boys in buzzcuts and hip chinos laughing loud with their even louder girlfriends chatting high and bossy and watching sharp when their boys pause to talk to white girls. Black dudes that look like Jimi Hendrix or Sly Stone. Why afros, but not black power? That new version of *Shaft* and how it sucked.

Jose couldn't answer the question, but talk about cops reminded him. And so he slid those mug shots across the table to Dinky.

"I got these from my stepfather. They're passing them out to the staff. I just don't think they do you justice, bro."

"I'd like to see one of you under similar circumstances," Dinky said.

"I'll make sure an' send you some of mine," Jose said back.

That stopped the words again.

Those tourists from Wisconsin always stand out, the way they stand at the curb and wait for the light to change before crossing, even if there are no cars. Jose and Dinky smoking down that roach, sitting on the steps of Sounds, the CD store. Spotted Buggy, trying to unload some sheets of acid to a pair of white kids. Not only was he willing to purchase that fat ANGEL bag, but he took them to his place where there was always music and people and a bright-eyed dog named Brownie that chewed on linoleum. Air toasty with buddha, incense, and *costillas fritas*.

The three of them lay splayed on the couch in Buggy's living room, talking out some memories. Buggy was a big *trigueño* from Avenue A who once lived in the Bronx and used to run for Johnny. He was a regular at Dinky's DJ parties and bothered to ask if Dinky was still doing them. It took Dinky a long time to answer and when he did, it was just a shrug.

"That basement scene you had at The Haunt was dope. You should do another party, bro. For old times' sake. I bring all my people."

When they left Buggy's, four hundred dollars richer, Jose said it: "Listen, man. Why don't we use this money an' Angel's money an' just throw a real kick-ass party?"

Dinky stopped in his tracks. He looked north, he looked south. He even tried to look east.

"You talkin'na me?"

"Yeah, dude. Throw a DJ party. We got the money for it."

"Why the fuck should I do that?"

Jose stuck the wad of bills in Dinky's jacket pocket.

"Old times' sake," he said.

Dinky took a few steps before turning around. To face Jose still sitting on the stoop.

"It'll be the last one," Dinky said.

And wouldn't it be the last issue of *BUDDHA BOOK* for them? Jose blathered about how much he wanted *BUDDHA BOOK* to continue on way past them like some legacy, something for the next generation. If he had to pick the most unique quirky crazy talented person in the entire student body of Luis Muñoz Marín, then it would have to be Barbara. She'd be just the one to keep it going. That was why Jose was going to her house, to see if he could get her to come do *Hogan's Heroes* tonight. Dinky begged off. He had something he had to do.

"My ma said she really wants me there tonight. Something she gotta say." Dinky seemed visibly bugged. "I gotta bad feeling."

Jose dragged him into trance and techno record stores, where vinyl lined the Day-Glo walls and DJs of all sizes colors and shapes examined twelve-inchers and played them on earphones for a taste. Once Dinky started picking out records, Jose knew he had him.

"Okay, one last party," Dinky said, the local train moving slow through the black.

And they connected their fists, the gradual knuckle to knuckle taps like they were signing this in blood.

St. Mary's Park. The stink of kettledrum fire.

They call him Arecibo; he is beyond town drunk. Amazing how he don't ignite, he reek so. There he was as always, building his nightly fire for his wandering woman, Joanna. She was a jaded beauty cum crack whore who worked the projects across from the park. Arecibo built his fire every night so that she'd see it while she fucked some *ratón* in some *cueva*. And so she would see him, feeding that fire and waiting for her to come back.

"Twice she's come back," he said. "But when I talk to her, she runs away."

Arecibo's fires could really light up the night, but at this time of evening (when the sky is a linty purple blanket) he was just getting it cranked, feeding that fire hunger like a good tease. Five times Anita had come to him. This sixth time she brought a pint of violet in flame light and he really liked that vintage.

"Good grapes," he said with a grimace.

She held up the garbage bag.

"Look what else I brought'chu. Flammables!"

Arecibo's eyes moistened.

"You are going to make some man very happy some day," he said. (Fat chance, she mumbled.) Busy with his bottle, he allowed her to take the stick and poke to make sure the pretty fire got every morsel.

And then there was that tinny sound. The electronic song of her cellular. "La tierra de Borinquen, donde he nacido yo . . ."

Anita flipped the phone up and ready with the same desperation every stupid jerk with a cellular shows when that shit goes off irrespective of company.

"This is Anita," she said.

"Guess who," Angel said back.

THE SAME LINTY purple blanket sky. Breezes sultry through the kitchen window. Like fire, or something burning.

Dinky was sitting at the dining table, watching his mother nail those teeny beads with her needle. Down they flowed along the string to join other colors. Another necklace. Her bead designs seemed very Taíno. Maybe something that might be sold on a reservation in New Mexico, some Indian strain. She kept looking them over like she couldn't figure out why.

"I never thought of myself as Indian," she said.

Dinky hadn't thought much about being Taíno. All he knew was that reading about "his people" getting conquered all the time really pissed him off. Would've been cool to pass Agueybana and his tribe a few submachine pistols. The bastid Spaniards would've been in for a nasty surprise then.

"I wanna ask you something," his mother said, breaking Dinky's sci-fi channel. The small TV on the counter was on, just background noise flashing black and white. "Lonnie, what do you think of Brooklyn?"

Dinky shrugged. "They should bring back the Dodgers. Why you ask?"

"What do you think it would take to pull the kids out of the posse?"

Dinky exhaled and stared at the TV flash.

"Lonnie, a cousin of mine from Puerto Rico just moved to Park Slope. I went to see him. It's a nice area. There's a yuppie part and a more . . . working-class part. We'd be right in the middle."

The grin was like that of a field commander explaining how they would successfully infiltrate enemy turf.

"I've been working on this, Lonnie."

Yeah, he picked that up. She had cut down on the drinking, and some nights he could hear her on the phone, talking in Spanish like some secret agent.

"He bought this renovated three-family house, and he's looking for people to come in with him on it."

She grabbed Dinky's hands.

"We can have the whole upstairs! Three bedrooms. The boys can share the big one. You get a room of your own. My cousin will give us a break on the rent until we do better."

Dinky was shaking his head.

"What, what!"

"I don't think Cesar's gonna take this shit lyin down."

"Cesar has his ass in the joint. The end."

"That don't mean nothin, Mom. He can still hit back, an' who knows if maybe he'll get out? Would he know where to start lookin for us?"

Dinky's mother stared. A streak of pain crossed her face just for a moment.

"Your father never really got to know my family. It wasn't like they really wanted to know him, either. He has no reason to go looking for us in Park Slope. He never met my cousin. He's a computer programmer. He'd be a better influence on the kids, don't you think?"

"It might be too late for that."

"What does that mean?"

"It means Luis an' Junior aren't like normal kids. They've lived on their own an' had their own cash flow. They might not wanna come runnin home 'ta Mommy. They might be real happy right where they are. Then what?"

"Pssh. Ridiculous."

"Mom! They're used to it. They might not wanna leave."

"You sayin it's not worth it to try?"

"I din't say that."

"Your own brothers? You tellin me I don't know that you think about them, too? Who you think you tryin'na kid?"

Dinky rubbed his eyes like an old man. "I don't know. They might be dyin'na leave. With Pop in the joint, they don't got nobody."

"What do you mean, 'nobody'? Where are they? Who's takin care of them?"

This was exactly the emotional shit that Dinky wanted to avoid, getting his mother's maternal instincts in a panic. She was hooking those beads so fast the colors blurred.

"I been lookin for them. Cesar hid them. I found out where they are, with this creep named Stitches. I don't know how they'll react when they see me. It was a long time ago when I saw them. They might follow me right outta there. Or they might tell me to get fucked."

For a moment, Dinky felt hopeless. Like he was caught between two warring nations and he wasn't even armed. She mirrored that with her look.

"Listen. How much money you got?" he asked.

"Money?"

"Yeah, you know, green? They got those kids that don't wanna learn, an' they pay them to go to school. You hearda that, right?"

"You mean like a stipend," she said.

"Yeah. Thum kids makin money, Ma. How much we gonna pay Luis an' Junior to come back home an' become like normal kids? What if they don't wanna leave the Cesar life an' go live in Brooklyn?"

His mother's eyes crossed with the thought.

"Oh, damn." The needle dipped, a mass of beads made a break for it across the table. "You're telling me I have to pay them to be my kids again?"

"Cesar pays them," Dinky said reluctantly. "An' he keeps them scared. What have we got?"

An answer wasn't coming right away. She blinked away the wet and started scooping up those beads. Dinky watched, impressed with the need for battle in her. Determined to win back her family, to find some way to make the impossible happen. It flooded Dinky with a feverish inspiration. It was *not* the feeling he got looking at Cesar through that plastic partition. It was *not* the feeling he got downing eightballs with his brother. It made it pretty clear what side he was on.

"You don't have to pay *me*," he said.

She squeezed his hand.

Barbara's was a tidy house.

Potpourri smell everywhere, potted plants and many petal yellows dangling from baskets. Here was a net twisted filled with seashells starfish and some sort of crab. There was a matchstick boat, sails puffed with that heavy cross of *España*.

"My father was in the navy," she said.

The clean living room the blue carpeting the shiny coffee table. African masks in the bookcase. Thirty-two refrigerator magnets. Pictures of the family tree, a parade of clutch and hold. There was even a dog. A sunny-eyed beagle so happy the smile made his tongue go lopsided.

She called him "Stretchy" and her "little side of beef," her face going sad.

"He died last year," she said.

Her father a big strapping Latino, mustache 'natch, like all dads then. A hard rough heroic pensive type as he stared out from the deck of that aircraft carrier. The woman he bunks with, a real Ava Gardner. Something very toothy about her smile (sorry)

something very Barbara about her smile, youthful. Like she always laughs.

"My parents are in Aruba," she said.

The big family portrait. There was a tall leggy girl with curlier hair but that same hint of Barbara. Hofstra sweatshirt. And there was that fat boy, making a face.

"My brother lives in Puerto Rico," she said.

Her room was no pink fluffy affair. It was cogs and sprockets and that TERMINATOR poster. A table to edit super-8 film (those tiny strips dangling from nails in the wall). Two VCRs and a small video monitor beside the twenty-seven-inch. A video effects processor. A computer?

"I use it to write scripts," she said.

The rows of empty tenements. The old boarded-ups, passing in parade. The South Bronx that used to be. A bombed-out Chechnya with none of the liberation talk. The slow pans across fields of rubble.

"I shot this when I was eleven," she said

as if something had to account for those jittery jump cuts, those messy pans. "One of my first." Fast-forwarded the dull parts, only wanted to show her best. Her first video production was about a girl who got raped and didn't tell anyone. She shot it with some friends. (She had to get them drunk first.) A teacher got trans- ferred from her junior high because of that film.

"Miss Turner was nice. She encouraged me. She was the first teacher that said I was talented enough to become the first Puerto Rican female filmmaker. Reminds me of Ms. Arroyo."

Barbara was all tour guide, highly adorable in overalls. She seemed a little breathless. She reached into a cabinet and with no words at all put a tape into the VCR that showed two boys sneak- ing into the school building. The camera zooms in just as Jose gets the door open with his coded keys.

"Wow," Jose said, deeply impressed. "I wish I could show this to Pedro. Just play it for him. Watch his jaw drop."

"Who's Pedro?" she asked, seeming thrilled by his response to her footage.

"My stepfather. Guidance counselor Vega. You tellin me you don't know he's my stepdad? I thought you knew everything."

"I do. I just don't know him as Pedro."

Barbara rewound the short clip, playing it slow mode so he could really get a look at himself.

"So why didn't you take this to Reyes then?"

Barbara exhaled like she was dealing with an idiot.

"I'm a player, not a fink. So maybe I'm a double agent. It's just, how can there be an underground resistance movement that I'm not a part of?"

Jose waited. It occurred to him that a pitch was coming, some sort of deal. Barbara waited, too. She pulled the tape out of the VCR and held it. Just held it like she might give it to him—if. Jose dug into his bag and pulled out the folder. Handed it over. Inside was the master for *BUDDHA BOOK #4,* ready to be printed up.

"This is too much," she whispered, examining every page as if she were proofing them.

The *tick-tock* of some big clock. Her fingers caressing those LUCY panels, running over those ANITA pictures as if she were reading Braille. Touching the images like she longed to get inside them. She lit that joint like a housewife reaching for a Valium, sitting up against a stereo speaker.

"So that's why you passed the note," she said. "About Lucy being dead. About you killin her."

Jose felt strange. More real than dreaming, yet there was a pretend quality to the scene. Something he was imagining. The smell of that joint. The first taste, still warm from her lips.

"That's how you killed her," Barbara said.

"That's right," Jose said back.

"An' you plan to put this out even though some of Angel's boys in school might get mad an' fuck you up?"

"Yeah."

"Thass brave," she said. "Dumb and brave."

Jose passed the joint back. The sense that he didn't want to stop smoking, didn't want to get real.

"This second part," she said. "The Dinky story with the first official Puerto Rican female serial killer. It ends right when she goes to take the tag to Angel. It's not finished."

"It's a continuing story. Only we need somebody else to finish it. We need somebody else to keep it goin. Thass why I want you to come with me to the school tonight."

Barbara was relighting the joint. She stopped in midtoke.

"The way we do it is we print up the issue in two nights. We store them first until we have the number we want. Then we spring them on everybody. I want to go tonight and get started printing it. Dinky has someplace he gotta be. So I need you to come with me. I want you in on *BUDDHA BOOK*."

Barbara was wide-eyed. There was a skepticism still clinging to her face, as if she feared being played.

"You're funnin me, right?"

The living-room carpet blue and furry. Her bare feet scraping through the fluff. Her toenail color was called "Meridian," which was like a silver blue. It matched her fingernails.

"I've seen your storyboards. You draw good, an' you write. You're perfect for *BUDDHA BOOK*. Why don't we tip over to the school?"

"I can't now. I have to wait for Dezzie."

"Dezzie?"

"Yeah. She's stayin here with me."

"What about ya parents?"

"They travel a lot. I'm here alone until Friday when they come back from Aruba."

"They just leave you alone?"

A careless shrug. "Sure. I got enough stuff here to keep me busy. Mom, Mom, I wanna be a filmmaker! Okay, dear, sure. Mom, Mom, I need a video-effects processor! It just goes on and on, man. I got them well trained. I mostly get the place to myself. A bothersome aunt stops by every now an' then. I got Dezzie stayin with me." There was a pause. "I gotta have Dezzie come in with me on this, right? You know I don't do nothin without her."

Jose grinned. Slow like he was getting dirty thoughts. She read those thoughts and punched him.

"It's not like that."

"You mean about people callin her Lezzie instead of Dezzie?"

Barbara toked on that joint with a half smile.

"So would it bother you if I was only into girls?"

Jose watched her magic eye go from hazel to green glimmer.

"I don't mind that you like girls," he said.

"But I like boys, too."

Jose felt like something was happening but he didn't know what it was.

"I gotta tell you that right now, I don't believe in any of this. Like it's not happening. But I'll go along anyway, in true Puerto Rican fashion."

The click scrape of keys. Dezzie came in, wearing that checkerboard dress. She found them sitting on the floor. Barbara gave her a kiss. Dezzie settled down beside her, grabbing that joint. Grinning at Jose as if she already knew all about it.

"So," she said, "when do we start?"

The *tick-tock* of some clock.

uzzed from her kill. Horny as hell. Looking for someone to fuck to death. Starved. Desperate. Longing to swallow. How she hated that word "symbiotic." How she loved that last, startled gasp. Walking the streets in a dizzy daze. Just like the movie right after the vampire fed. Walking with glazed eyes after gorging on fresh blood.

She was back at the newsstand. The kiosk on the corner opposite Anthony's Pizza. Carlos the newspaper guy thought maybe she was an actress or a theater person, the way she always seemed to be looking for reviews. (This is the story he would tell the TV cameras after.) What was she looking for, those early mornings? Would buy three or four papers. Would search page after page and curse, then pick up another and search page after page until sheets were fluttering down onto street corner, careless. Go through the papers and then leave them, which in a way was good for Carlos. He could gather up the sheets and reform the papers. (And resell them. Fuck that.)

The television stations ran with it: "THE LIPSTICK KILLER." News reports where they seemingly trace her steps from one kill to the other. An illustrated map. A criminologist who said the police must know by now if it's a woman or not. DNA tests on the lipstick traces could tell them, he asserted, but the police say the lipstick does not necessarily have to belong to the serial killer. The chances of the serial killer being a woman are small. Serial killers are more likely to be men than women.

"If it were a single serial killer, then why hasn't this person left a note anywhere? Serial killers have a tendency to announce themselves, to tease the police and create a current of popular interest. They are fully aware of the world's eyes upon them. And yet this particular killer has not even left a note." (Pick pick pick. Maybe Anita should look this guy up.)

"It seems to me," Greta Van Susteren said on the CNN show *Burden of Proof,* "the New York City Police Department are going a long way to deny that this serial killer might be a woman. Why is that? What's the purpose to getting so tight-lipped when speculation heads that way?" (Okay, Anita had to admit, Greta was a personal heroine. Smart, poised, unstoppable with her words when she got going—Anita hoped to have her interview her someday.)

There was nothing about Bello. That evening, she walked over to Intervale Avenue and cased out the neighborhood. She fought off the urge to head up to his crib and have a look. Maybe she would have to call the cops herself and tell them there was a body up there.

But no. If they find Bello, they might find her quicker. His being undiscovered meant she had more time to pile up bodies. More newspaper clippings for her scrapbook. The TV pissed her off, no matter what channel. The bastids were behind by three bodies. The mayor kept popping up by the police chief, making it sound like they would soon crack the case. "This is just media hysteria," the mayor said. "It gives sick people too much attention."

She lay down on the bed with her *New York Post*, where resided the investigative reporter she liked the best. He had been covering her work and asking a lot of the right questions. She picked him as the means to correct the record. She would include Loco as one of her kills, give the stats, make it clear she was down to one more murder to claim the record. She pulled out the box where she kept her "souvenirs," picking a few choice morsels. She decided to include that Loco clipping—they might start looking for her quick after that but she still had only one more murder to go.

This serial killer thing wasn't a forever job with her. The whole show is supposed to begin with the ending. She planned on the afterwards just as much as the during. The first Puerto Rican female serial killer planned on at least a movie deal. Interview with Greta Susteren. Two TV movies like Amy Fisher. A book. It would all start with the note and that little packet. She slow-grinned, imagining the scene:

The award-winning *New York Post* columnist was in his office when he received a call from a woman identifying herself as "the Lipstick Killer." She also left a manila envelope in a phone booth with a note, and items from each of her victims, including two that the police so far had not accounted for.

The buzz still on her. Thinking about Dinky made her so wet, but she didn't have time to look him up now. There was Angel on the horizon. He had always been the dream, and now the pulse for him was coming back, that moist pussy throb that told her she wanted him.

His voice on the cellular.

"Guess who," he said.

"Angel."

"Anita. Like I was almost expectin you."

"Why's that?"

"Because whenever I was down or in trouble, you'd pop up. You was always like that. An' here you are again."

"I want to help you, Angel. I know what happened with Lucy."

There was a silence, a pause.

"Come see me," he said.

That Dinky voice was strong in her head, him telling her *not* to see Angel. That it could be dangerous for her. That he might think she offed Lucy. And yet Anita could not stop herself. There was clearly a link between her and Angel that she had to explore to the core. He had been waiting to hear from her, was this true? That made her pulse, but again, Dinky inserted himself: "Of course he's been waitin. He thinks you did it. You gonna walk into a trap."

She thought about the last time she had seen Angel. He had just fought with Lucy. Sources reported it was a big one, with screaming and broken glass. When Anita chanced to spot them, they looked tired and unhooked. Later that night, Angel was alone at Derio's, where he drank quietly in the back alley. A phalanx of his boys headed off all bothersome groupies. Anita passed through. Anita always passed through.

"Angel."

Softly petting his thigh awake.

He patted her thigh back.

"Those stockings, or pantyhoses?"

She lifted her fluttery skirt a little so he could see where it all ended. His eyes glassy. The smell of bubblegum and beer.

"It's not that I don't like girls," he said.

He wasn't looking at her, like his words were all aimed away.

"It's just, how come they gotta get pregnant?"

Angel had the look of someone eager to break out of a spell. She knew he was going to sleep with someone. She wondered if he was the kind who would pick a strange woman to fuck rather than someone known, close.

"I shoulda known better. What made her go pull that shit? Why did she think she would be any different?"

Then they were walking, she silent behind his brooding. A parked car. Sitting on the hood, under clattering elevated train. The passing roar. The deep quiet after.

"I can't have no hooks," he said.

"No hooks," she said, kissing him.

"You sure?"

She grinning through sad, through loss. "Yeah. Free trial offer. For a limited time only, so order now."

His lips were warm but would not part. Resisted her salty kiss. (Tears do not help the flavor.)

A summer seemed to have passed. He disconnected. Turned away. Took a long swig of beer.

"Nah," he said.

SITTING AT THE counter of the Quality Donuts on Prospect Avenue. Nursing that coffee. A cigarette. Calls on her cellular. She strolled over to Fox Street just to get a look at where they found the body. Boy's name was Tacho. He worked security for Angel. He was on post the night Lucy got tubbed. Evidently he had cut out for a milkshake and a blow job. Angel offed him as a signpost to his boys, who weren't so happy with the deed. Now the talk was starting to go round that somebody offed Lucy, and that Angel was trying to cover it up. It sure sucks when your own boys start to talk about you. Is somebody after him? A lot of talk about his tag getting sprayed over, speculation about who. (Anita grinned all through this talk.) Did Anita inadvertently start a turf war? She thought that was cute, pretty spick boys wasting each other because of her. She felt like she was that Helena of Troy chick. Maybe it was better *not* to clear things up right off, *not* to risk herself at this stage of her career. Wouldn't it suck for her to have gone this far with her plan, only to get offed at the last moment by Angel for a kill she didn't commit?

Anita fingered those ten diamond stones six carats each. They brought Dinky to mind so strong. Jose with him, the three of them connected. Yet what did she know about family? Anita had always been a solo act. It was all animal instinct with her.

It began to rain. Thunder first, then a few flashes. The first *patter-patter* tapping against storefront glass. Then it was like thousands of fingers thumping on that sleek Jaguar.

Anita might be psychotic, but she wasn't crazy. She spotted the Jaguar sitting on 156th Street, just like he said. Spotted his boys taking up positions up and down the street. Spotted Angel sitting in the car, waiting and breathing that cigarette smoke.

Anita stood in a nearby vestibule. She waited, too.

A FEW QUICK clicks. Red lights turning to green. Jose pressing buttons on the keypad.

Something about an empty school that is a lot like church. Touch the hallway tiles like they were Byzantine frescoes. Barbara and Jose brought window shades down over windows so that the flash of copy machines would not attract. Dezzie brought the 8mm Palmcorder to capture the whole trip. Jose showed them all the ropes, from how to disable to alarms with key codes to all the little storage cubbies where they hid *BUDDHA BOOK* until launch time. The bathroom on the third floor was where they kept the reams of copy paper and the completed issues. He showed them the whole underground other life of that Stalag 13. Then they worked in the office, Jose showing them how he laid out the pages for quick copying on the three color machines. Maybe it was the flashing copier lights, or the 8mm camera—Jose couldn't say why the girls began to strip. That was Dezzie, running down halls in bra and panties, letting out shrieks like an Indian brave on the attack. That was Barbara, parking her bare ass on the copy glass (FLASH!) for that sudden photo of her Puerto Rican moon, her tits pressed against the glass, the side of her face and the side of Dezzie's face squashed against glass (their tongues in mid-flight barely touching in open-mouth kiss). And then they were pulling down Jose's pants, parking him up on that copier glass for his ass photo.

"Hey, we're supposed to be working," he said, but who heard him? Never before had times been so zany crazy in Stalag 13. He and Dinky had fun all right, but it was small and private and laid back. It might mean cranking some Li'l Kim on the boombox while toking mellow, but it was never all this laughter and foreplay. Barbara's lips pressing against his, Dezzie's hands around his waist. Her fingers were drawing little circles as they headed down his jutting hip bone. He was between them, pressed against soft girl skin front to back. Barbara face to face, lips against lips. Her arms around his neck. Dezzie, from behind. Her pussy pressing into his ass, her hands running up and down his chest, his hips. And then she was touching his stiff.

"I think it's time you give up this Lucy shit," Barbara said.

"Thass right," Dezzie seconded, kissing his ear.

"You ever hear 'un tornillo saca a un tornillo'?"

"No," Jose lied.

"Two tornillos," Dezzie said.

Barbara's tongue entering his mouth just as those LUCY pages started to roll off the copy machines, Dezzie's hand gripping his dick. Was there a reason for him not to flow, to lose himself in bodies? He reached behind. His hand found Dezzie's pussy, warm and moist through her leggings. And how she pressed against his fingers. Barbara laughed. How many hands were on his dick? Right there on the office floor, with copier light strobing from one machine to the other to the other, the slap click of paper, the stink of ink of wet pussy of dick his lips on tits. Four pretty nipples all in a row. Like a good Puerto Rican, Jose got on his knees and kissed ass, times two. What a wicked joint, maybe a little spicy.

Dezzie always carried condoms. It was her idea to head over to the gym. The lights were low and made little circles on the waxy floor. There were mats there they could lie on. The girls wasted no time in sitting on him. The copy machines were still humming, click and clatter.

Barbara tried to explain. The thing with Dezzie was that she needed it all the time. She was into anal sex and orgies. When she had seen Jose at the apartment and asked, "When do we start?" she meant the threesome. Barbara shared everything with her.

And then a gasp. Jose inside her. Snug and hot. The two of them sucked in a breath.

"Jesus, Jose."

"Yeah," Dezzie said, fingering herself. Climbing on his face. Jose not thinking. Not about Lucy not about cops not about anything other than that pussy in his face, that pussy riding his dick. Where did Dezzie get that bottle of water? Splashed them, splash and run, back down the empty halls past empty classrooms. War cries, like they were Apaches. Jose, wearing Barbara's panties on his head like a kerchief. Cutting up those pages. Reinserting them for back-to-back action. Showing the girls how it's done. Dezzie with that camera light caressing Barbara's tits.

"To collate them, staple them, bag them." A boxful of comic bags that was kept in a wash closet on the second floor. "Then we hide them until splash day."

Dezzie and Barbara were both watching the issue take shape with round, wondering eyes. They were all three on the floor, passing pages to each other, with Barbara at the end stapling them.

"It looks great," she said.

"Yeah," Dezzie added.

"So what do you think Lucy's gonna thinka ya comic book?"

Barbara's question hung in the air a moment. It brought back more Lucy than Jose could bear. A sudden sense of despair. Didn't he even want her there, still? Even after all the shit she had done to him? Didn't he want her to see the issue, to see him even now, with his new lovers? She wasn't there to see him grow, change, become.

"But she's dead," he said.

The tone went right past Barbara, who nudged Dezzie.

"Yeah, right! Talk about the artist losing himself in his work!"

For that second, Jose felt more alone than if he had been by himself.

THERE WAS SELF-PRESERVATION and fear and all those instincts that kept her alive. There was also that need she had that his eyes look at her, that they look at her and everything stops. He would not be able to resist her this time. She had to trust in that, put it to the test. He had been marked a long time ago, for her bed. He was the one everything pointed to. The smell of her wet pussy was driving her crazy. Sense or no sense. Dinky or no Dinky. She had to take the risk.

So she walked past Angel's boys all up and down the street. She had Carlotta with her. Seeing him waiting for her in the car almost warmed her heart. He had the same pretty boy looks, except for that sleepless but *not* in Seattle about him. They sat there listening to the rain's drumming as if neither of them knew where to start.

Anita could see the movie version clear as day. If she directed it, then she wouldn't bother with a lot of dialogue. Film is good that way. All that he said she said gets in the way of the action. If Anita shot the movie, then she would show the two of them sitting there. She would show her getting mad and then he was mad. He pulled a .45. She pulled Carlotta. For a moment they sat like that, and then Angel put his gun away. A soft laugh place. There was some talk, and then Anita pulled out those ten diamond stones six carats each. Dropping it in his palm like glittery *gusano*. Saying those words that started it and ended it, leading him to her bed.

"The fight led them into the bathroom," she didn't say.

18

Like a series of slides.

Class silent. Heads bowed. Mr. Taylor grimly handing out quiz. Jose gave the rexograph a good sniff.

Dinky's empty chair. Barbara giving him long peeks under tumbling hair.

1. Define the following: Epicycle

Deferent

Ptolemaic Universe

Krebs Cycle

Kepler's Universe

There was no Lucy.

Not a hint of her on dark streets, no appearance in his bathtub last night. No Lucy dreams, no tossing and turning through feverish heat and that night of cold sweat, where he had to sit out on the fire escape. She was gone and he missed her. She had threatened to keep coming back unless he brought her the tag. What happened? If it had all been in his mind, then he could make her come back. He just had to get that tag back. He should've told Dinky yesterday. Only how was he supposed to tell him he needed it back so Lucy would go away? So Lucy would come back?

    2. Explain Lindblad's theory of the formulation and development of spiral arms.

    3. Brief bios on each: Lindblad

                          Oort

                          Hubble

                          Seyfert

                          Herschel

    4. Who is closer to religion than science?

                          Swedenborg

                          Newton

The sketch started all by itself, between questions 5 and 6. It was Jose's answer to the drag and pull of having to be a teenager three days after becoming a murderer. He was in a different place, and the world couldn't tell. Grades and report cards and little round zeros in red ink. How does a teacher penalize a kid who has killed?

Ocean wave. It was the pen squiggles that did it, making the ocean appear like that. Jose wasn't even aware of drawing. Girl by the water, crying. Water splashing her thighs. Where she fell from sob. Sky Crayola purple. Round Linus Van Pelt moon. Coney Island beach. Roller coaster a plunging diamond necklace on velvet. The screams and howls, carried by breeze. The stink of New York sea-water.

He had never hit her before. That was the first time.

The blow had shocked him, how good it felt just for a second. To have her shrink, though she regained her former size and defiant like stone, grinned after. And that made him feel like she had his emotions on a string.

They had gone back to Coney Island on one of the last red sun-light days. It was just the two of them this time, no Dinky double date, just to make up for that last Cyclone incident. And it should've been beautiful. Instead, every step was a stereo rebroad-cast. When she made that crack about finding someone to sit with her on the roller coaster, he flipped. Dropped his orange drink CRASH right on the spot.

"Look, I was jokin, okay? We don't gotta go on no fucken Cyclone, okay?"

"Oh yes we do," he said, pulling her over to the ticket window. Wasn't even looking at her when they sat. The steel bar came down to lock them both in place. Side by side.

She fought the laugh. Kissed him petted his dick her tongue poking at his closed lips the sudden tip and swerve and that ugly   drop   that made him yell something

made her laugh   and laughter   was all he could hear through the heaving. When they got back down to Earth she was still laughing he was walking the sand as it got dark   to fight the dizzy. Lemon drop streetlamps blinking to life. The remains of two hot dogs with onions sauerkraut mustard ketchup fries and vanilla milkshake all staining the blanket of beach.

"You shun'ta eaten so much," she said, biting down on the laugh.

He swung. Instinct from where? Knocked her hair loose.

She walked along the water's edge, searching for her barette in the sand. She wouldn't cry, such a tough soldier and

then she fell. Fell where the water could sweep over her legs. Not so tough now, huh?

She was quiet on the trip back. No matter how much he cuddled her.

Fingers tapping the desk. (Real.) Taste of pencil. (Real.) Nothing fake about the quiz. No dream, no Dinky. Rain crashing against the windows. Pen went dry on him as he pressed in some curves. Lucy crying in the water.

"Come back," he whispered into her tumbling hair.

"No," she said.

7. Name the street in the South Bronx that is named after Luis Muñoz Marín.

> **(a)** Colonial Avenue
>
> **(b)** Hoe Avenue
>
> **(c)** There is none

8. Bazuca is

    (a) a kind of bubblegum

    (b) a smokable mixture of crack cocaine

    (c) a hollow-pipe item used by U.S.
        troops to fire anti-tank projectiles

Barbara sent glances from her seat. She was in dark blue tunic, silver buttons, a real military girl. Big contrast with Dezzie's happy polka dot dress.

"That's it. Pass your papers to the front."

Mr. Taylor's voice rode the bell. Sheets rustling. Jose put the finishing touches on his beach sketch. Most kids just getting up with their paper to deposit it on the way out.

Jose and Barbara brought their papers up at the same time. They walked out into the hallway slowly together while around them everything ran blur. Dezzie was on his other side. Unbidden, she pecked him on the cheek. Barbara was just staring at him. Before she and Dezzie walked into their math class, she handed Jose a clump of paper. When he opened it, he saw it was the head of a rose. Petals fluttered down over his pants like wet drops.

CESAR'S PALACE IS on Southern Boulevard, on the third floor of that other building that Dinky's pop owned. The Palace was the flagship crackhouse. Not just anybody could get in there. It wasn't just a hole to sink into, it was a private club scene with a guy outside holding a clipboard. The riffraff could stream into the other crackhouse on the first floor, but the elite climbed the stairs.

Dinky didn't need to be on the list. The moment the door guy spotted him, he gave him that long-lasting handclasp. "The man come back from the dead! You *in* again?"

Dinky answered no questions, wore that tight-lipped look that implies duty. He was just floating around, maybe hoping to find Samson or Duke, two guys who might have an idea where his brothers were. Walked those sparse rooms. A few lounging bodies. Sunlight blocked out. Music and soft talk. The glazed, lazy look to eyes. There were a lot of people that Dinky didn't know. Some of them grinned, said hello. In the living room, couples snuggled on the couch while a woman named Tita mixed her special crack brew in a series of fingerbowls and rocked to jazzy trip-hop. Condoms dental dams finger thingies jellies. Enough supplies for a sex club. Crackheads tended to get naked very fast. Dinky remembered that his father had hired those two young hookers to ply their trade in-house. The girls were clean, efficient, and happened to be twins. (The Suarez Twins had survived all the bad effects of three years of street life and still looked like movie stars.)

Whoah, a bowl of joints, virtually ignored in the world of quick puffs and heart rushes (Dinky dipped his hand in. A few for the road). He kept his eyes peeled. No need to bump into Stitches in here. He was walking through another fishtank blue room when he noticed a curly-haired munchkin of a brat heading for the free joints in a bowl. Recognized him at once. And he caught that tiny hand before it could dig into the freebies.

"Yo! Get off, Stupid."

"Don't be like that with me, Dinky man!"

How did Stupid get up here? Normally he was shooed right out because the curly hair was a born thief, picked pockets snatched stashes and one time even broke into some of Cesar's loaves. The kid was usually doing post downstairs, on the stoop. Stupid, they called him.

"Hey. You supposed to be up here?"

Stupid stared up at him.

"Man. It's like lookin at a dead guy! Jeez, Dink. They told me you was gone!"

"Gone?"

"Yeah. Like ya big brother. Poof!"

Stupid gave him a sudden embrace, a hard little kid number that was difficult to untangle. Dinky pulled him into the small hall between rooms where maybe he wouldn't be seen.

"So what are you doin here?"

Stupid rolled his eyes.

"You should know better, runt," Dinky reprimanded. "Just thinka what happened the last time they caught you up here."

Dinky hadn't been there to see it, but he heard. Cesar hung Stupid from the parapet by his ankles. Taped his mouth shut. By sunrise they had to take him down because the high-pitched whimper made dogs in the area go apeshit. Stupid seemed to think about that for a moment.

"Forget it, man. Let's not thinka the past, right? Look, I'm just stoppin in. Just wanted to hear some sounds, grab some smokes, an' okay okay. You forced it outta me. Don't tell anybody."

He looked around, pulled Dinky closer.

"There's a woman, Dink."

"What?"

"Shh. A woman. She hangs out here, in the backroom."

The urgency in his voice made Dinky laugh.

"Who is it? You mean one of the Suarez Twins?"

Stupid pulled him close again like he didn't want to risk being overheard.

"Nah, man! I ain't talkin about somebody who sells it. I'm talkin about a woman. She's nineteen. Her name is Eva. She ain't no crackhead neither. She's just checkin out life, takin from this bowl, from that. You know her? I got to make out with her. She kisses like nobody on the face of the earth, bro."

Dinky let the laugh ripple out slow.

"But you're ten," he said.

"I'll be eleven next month, shut up. Look, can you just cover me with ya body for a sec? Thass it, walk around, don't be stayin in one place, it's conspicubus."

"What?"

Stupid pushed him into the living room, where he maneuvered him over to a coffee table. From behind Dink, he reached over and grabbed a handful of joints. Dinky knocked them out of his hand.

"Stop that shit! You gonna get caught again!"

"What are you, the Psychic Friends Network? Get the fuck off! If they don't wan'chu to take joints then why they put them out? Hah?"

There was a yell.

Stupid jumped, pushing then pulling Dinky back like a shield when hands appeared to grab him. Dinky pushed the grabber back. Jumper was his name, a scarecrow face brat. He recognized Dinky, and hung back for a moment like he was looking at a ghost.

"Don't worry, man." Dinky grabbed Stupid by the T. "I'll take care of the runt."

Jumper stood watching as Dinky pulled the wriggling Stupid right on out of Cesar's Palace. All the way down stairs to stoop.

"All right, all right, get off." Stupid sat on the steps like the war was lost. "I din't even get to see Eva again."

He pulled out a roach the size of a fingernail, clipped to a hairpin. Stupid was trying to light it when Dinky offered him one of the loose joints he had grabbed.

"Shh, keep it to yourself," he said, but Stupid jumped into the air with a yell as if he had scored the winning run. He did a Snoopy dance on each of the five steps, then jumped on the balustrade, his tattered sneakers clomping with every dance move. He lit the joint.

"Ah man. You gonna get in trouble." Dinky settled down on the steps.

"Who can help it these days? Let's say I'm on a break."

Dinky watched the boy, thinking it was a break stumbling into him. The kid was connected, fast-talking, and could thief real good. He was in with his little brothers. Best of all, it was almost guaranteed the kid would never spring a leak and go running to Cesar.

"So listen. How you feel about Stitches?"

Stupid gave him a careful look over as smoke puffed out his nostrils.

"You workin for him now?"

"Nah."

Stupid watched the street. "He treats me worse than ya pops."

"Oh yeah?"

"Yup. All the juniors on the scene wanna poppim. An' my friend Mikey says the guy touched him."

"Wha'chu mean?"

"You know. He's a prevert. Mikey told me the guy grabbed his balls (I mean Mikey's balls, right?) an' he said, 'Thass mines.' It made me talk to my friend Jacky about gettin a piece. Ain't no Stitch face touchin my balls. Shit."

Dinky grabbed him. Shook him like he better be on the prudential.

"You serious, or just mouthin off?"

"I wun't lie to you, man! You an' ya brother were my favorite COs. You should come back, put that Stitches outta business. 'Cause once ya back, whass he gonna do? Step outta the way! I mean, you the boss man son! He gotta respeck that. Man, you guys never used to hire me so much. But we had good times, right? Is he comin back too, ya brother?"

Dinky grimaced, attacked by past. "Nah." A cluster of posse boys across the street were staring at him like they were comparing notes.

"Well? How about it? You gonna let my arm fall off?"

Dinky took the joint. Toked light. Those looks he was getting from that crew on the corner was making him paranoid. All one of them had to do was get on the cellular and tell Stitches. The guy was not necessarily the enemy, but maybe he might get the idea to bump off the second in line to preserve his place—things like that happen in the business. Stupid was looking at him like it was some big moment, to be sharing a toke with the next in line. Like rocking with royalty. Dinky pulled Stupid into the vestibule, away from eyes.

"Listen." Gripped the kid like this was no time for jokes. "You seen my little brothers?"

"Sure," Stupid replied without pause. "But nobody sees them. You read that? They in The Factory, bro."

"What the fuck is that?"

Stupid squinted at him. "Where you been, bro? It's a new place off Longwood. Stitches opened it. It's like his own scam. He gets the kids workin in there, an' they never come out. But I'm in touch, know wham sayin? The junior underground, right here! I know my way in. I bring the shifts snacks an' shit. Let's face it, man. All us kids are in the shit here. We gotta stick together an' maybe form a union. They wearin us to death, dude."

"Is it hard to get in that place?"

Stupid stepped back like he needed more room to brag.

"For anybody else, yeah. I mean *nobody* goes there. But me, you know I'm slick! I got so many of my homies stuck in there, so me an' some boys, we slip an' slide a pipeline so we can take care of each other. You know me, man. I can fit in that sewer hole an' sneak that kilo right out'cha ass!"

The excitement dropped from Stupid's face. He could read the heavy on Dinky, some weight that was bending him a little less tall than when he remembered him.

"Yo. Wha'chu got in mind? Tell me."

Dinky went over to that little diamond of a window in the door so he could spy out the street. The tone of Stupid's voice had changed so much now that Dinky almost felt he wasn't in there with a kid.

"I wanna get my brothers out."

Dinky didn't believe that he had said it that it came out from his mouth words words saying it saying what he wanted to do and that this was what he wanted to do this just wasn't right, something was off, this couldn't possibly be Dinky talking making the decision taking the step picking a side finding a solution. (Say that again.)

"I wanna get my brothers out."

It was Dinky talking all right.

Stupid's face slowly brightened as if it was only dawning on him now that he might be involved.

"You? Makin a move? Wait...I get it. You're movin against Stitches! But wait a minute. Stitches works for ya pop...you're movin against ya pop!"

Dinky grabbed him by the shirt.

"You don't tell anybody, you got that? I find out you opened your trap just once, an' I'll—"

"I won't, Dinky!"

Dinky let go of him. Stupid stared at the wall like he was tranced.

"I'm so sicka doin stoop. Takin shit from that ripface, Stitches... You gotta put me on the squad, Dinky. I'm ya man. I'll do commando for you." He wiped his eyes. "I can get'chu in. I'll get'chu out, too."

Dinky's eyes were on those boys on the corner. First there were three and now there were five. Stupid got on tippytoe so he could look through the glass diamond.

"Stitches people," he said. Dinky grimaced, like that was all he needed.

Stupid pulled him away from the door.

"I know another way out," he said.

WALKING THE HALLS. Why am I here? The shuffle of papers. The *Niña* the *Pinta* the *Santa Maria*. The big cross on billowing sails. The picture of that Spaniard bastid who got an arrow in the chest while looking for the Fountain of Youth.

Mr. Martinez was a huffy bitch when mad, waving his arms around. Made everybody laugh with his girly tantrums. He was rattling again like a runaway train about how hardly anybody bothered to do the essay on what it means to be Puerto Rican. So what does that say about Puerto Ricans right there? The Puerto Ricans battled the Spaniards for close to four hundred years and were glad to see them go; but when the Americans came, the Puerto Ricans dusted off those Spaniard flags and spoke lovingly of *"la madre patria."* So what does that say about Puerto Ricans right there?

The history teacher wasn't saying. His name was MacMillan. Probably would have preferred to talk about the massacre of Glencoe than 1898, which is maybe why he went from the sinking of the *Maine* to the film footage of German tanks. From one holy cross to the other, painted on Panzers that stomped through Europe in record time. Mr. MacMillan had ordered a film on the Spanish Civil War, but got World War II instead. "It's just about empire building," he said, to tie it all together, leaving the students to figure out how to go from U.S. Marines landing in San Juan to German troops entering Warsaw.

"The Jones Act of 1917 ensured, among other things, that Puerto Ricans would have instant United States citizenship," Mr. MacMillan said while the Luftwaffe flattened Poland. It was all shmooshed up in Jose's head—the *Maine* blowing up, the ruse the Germans used as a pretext to start the war—"This makes you all Americans," Mr. MacMillan said, or was trying to say, no way to tell over the screech of those Stuka dive-bombers. American. As American as? Just as? Less than? Is there some fine print at the bottom of the contract? The tumbling dark. The sense of floating, a body separated from soul.

The cop that came to speak to Mr. Marrero's social studies class was Puerto Rican, of course. This was because the police department had started a massive recruitment drive in the inner city. They put up posters of a cop, splayed out on the sidewalk like he had just gotten shot. "Some people wouldn't do this job for a million dollars." Facedown, hands reaching. "A cop does it for a whole lot less." Of course, the cop on the poster was black. Making the guy white was no way to get inner-city sympathy. It might even give people ideas.

The Puerto Rican cop was nice. He talked about the dangers of drugs, the lure of posse life, and the reasons why students should report any suspicious behavior right away. When he asked if there were any questions, Barbara got up right away, giving Jose a wink.

"I just wanted to ask you, I mean about you sayin the police aren't racist. Amadou Diallo, a black guy, got shot twenty-one times while standin on a stoop. Abner Louima, a black guy, got sodomized by cops in a stationhouse because he was gay. Anthony Baez, a Puerto Rican, was killed by a cop when his football hit a cop car."

"Well, yes," the Puerto Rican cop smiling while he cut in before the question, "but really, those are just three people out of millions. How many days a year go by without incidents? That should be the question."

"But that wasn't *my* question," Barbara said.

"But we'll go on to another question now," Mr. Marrero cut in.

"THE POLICE ARE here," Pedro said.

Jose had gone to his office to get another pass so he could feel free to wander. He thought he would drop by the library during lunch to see if maybe Dinky would pop up, and then he got a good look at Pedro. He looked sweaty and his eyes wouldn't stop blinking.

"It's not enough that we're getting all this negative press. Now it looks like another dead body for Reyes."

"What?"

Pedro went out the door like a shot, Jose right behind him. The busy hall bustle. The two of them plowing through students. There, not far from the bust of Luis Muñoz Marín, stood Reyes with a uniformed cop and a detective in plainclothes.

"No," Reyes said. "Not at all."

"But she was a student here, wasn't she?" The detective looked a little annoyed. "She's registered in this school."

"I told you already. This student hadn't been coming to classes for quite a while. We pulled her records and, as far as I can see, this doesn't involve the school at all."

Reyes. His white-striped suit and hat made him look like an old-style *patron*. He was wagging his finger a lot like he always did when he was losing control.

"Besides, what are we supposed to do? We're educators, not criminologists."

"We just want to talk to some students who might've known her," the detective said, his creased face colorless. "We want to maybe make an announcement. Let the students know we'll be available to talk."

"Why can't I just give you the class number she was in, and you can go there and talk to the students? Why an announcement? Why upset the whole student body with news of another casualty?"

Pedro nodded to Reyes, rubbing his palms together nervous. Jose felt an odd tremor, a sense of something bad happening.

"An announcement isn't going to hurt," the detective said with a wry smile.

Reyes pulled Pedro close.

"This is Pedro Vega, the guidance counselor and assistant principal of the school." Reyes seemed upset, was talking fast. "I'm sure he'll be more than willing and able to assist you in whatever you need, gentlemen. I have some pressing business."

Reyes swiftly departed. Pedro shook hands, first with the detective and then the officer. Jose just stood there, staring at them as if he was dreaming. They didn't seem to notice him.

"We need you to make an announcement," the detective went on, taking out a small pad. Flipping to the page. "The dead girl was a student here. We need to see if maybe we can talk to some students who knew her..."

"Yes, yes, sure." Pedro's voice sounded all echoey, underwater. The throb in Jose's stomach was getting worse. Falling into a cave. Somebody turned up the reverb. The detective was showing Pedro the facts all written down in the little pad.

"Lucy Maldonado," Pedro said. "I think I remember her." He looked at Jose. "Didn't you know a Lucy Maldonado?"

Jose felt himself falling into black.

19

The cold water compress on his face woke him.

He was lying in that couch that Pedro had in his office, one of those leather things that therapists use. Pedro was right on him with that wet towelette. This close, he looked almost caring.

Jose sat up.

"Whoa, not so fast. You fainted out there."

"Yeah," Jose said.

"Here. Have a sip of this."

Pedro passed him an orange juice. It was hot and a little bland.

"Why did you faint?"

"I don't know."

"I hope it hasn't been me putting pressure on you about the comic-book thing. I mean, let's face it. That comic book looks pretty small and insignificant right now. Did you hear Reyes call me the assistant principal? I couldn't believe it! So much worrying I did for nothing. It looks like a shoe-in."

"Long Island," Jose said.

"Who wants to be living in a place like this where kids keep turning up dead? This girl just now. They found her in a garbage bag, just a few blocks from here. Of course, Reyes gets mad when the cops end up here, almost as if everything begins with this place! Is the press going to find another way to drag us into this? Why are we responsible if somebody else gets killed? Why are we to blame for this neighborhood? Aren't we trying?"

Jose fought the urge to say, It was just not the right moment. He had waited a long time for the body. Now the body was here. The reality had arrived. It was no comic book.

"I have to make an announcement," Pedro said, like he was excusing himself.

"But give me a pass first."

Pedro took out his pad and scribbled. Tore off a sheet.

"I can't wait for us to move," he said.

THE LIBRARY. THE tightly packed rows of books in Spanish always fascinated him, drew him. Something impenetrable about them, the hidden secrets. Jose could *read* Spanish, but after a while he would get a headache. It was like work. Didn't feel like his language. Yet he knelt there by the shelves, running his fingers over the names: Pedro Juan Soto. Jose Luis Gonzalez. Luis Rafael Sanchez. Puerto Rican names proudly on book spines. He felt they should mean something to him. Why didn't they? What was he missing? Were they writing about him?

It was Dinky sitting by the windows this time, chewing on that droopy licorice twirl. His face wasn't showing anything as Pedro Vega's voice came over the PA system:

To all the students. Something very sad has
happened. Lucy Maldonado, a student in Miss
Fuentes's class, was found dead last night.

"This is my last day of school," Dinky said as Jose sat down at
his table. "I ain't comin back here."

"Tomorrow is splash day." Jose accepted the licorice twirl Dinky
proffered.

"How did it go with Barbara last night?"

"It was good."

"Oh yeah?"

A slow grin from Jose. All he could manage. The stiff, strange
feel. Part sick, part elation. Something was happening for real this
time. Confirmation. The two of them listened to more Pedro words
about how she would be missed, about the special pain her friends
must feel. About how he would be available for counseling.

Dinky spilled out the plan, the whole great escape. Sounded
better than Steve McQueen on a motorcycle, jumping over barbed
wire. Running to free his brothers meant the basement of The
Haunt was no place for a party. He had already picked out another
joint, called Macondo. It was a cheap-ass dance hall on 139th
Street that was now a private club. It already had its own sound
system and DJ outfit, plus lights and strobes and all that disco shit.
Dinky planned a party like the old days, had even called a few
other rappers and DJs. (Good thing that big wad of Angel cash.) It
was going to be a real Dinky blowout. The kids at school would
remember DJ Dinky's parties. No big deal to print up flyers and put
them all over the school. Jose could do that tonight.

"You *are* comin tonight, right? To the last *Hogan's Heroes?*"

"I don't know." Dinky grimaced. "I ain't into that whole group scene."

"But it's the last one, Dinky."

"Fuck, we gotta see Anita tonight. She called on my cellular. I can't bring that shit to school! Do you know I got searched twice already today?"

Jose was not listening to Pedro's words. It was a background noise. He was thinking about Anita having the tag and wondering how to bring it up. He could tell Dinky he needed it back because Lucy had been haunting him and he had to make her stop. Or he could tell him he needed it because Lucy had been haunting him and she stopped. And he wanted her to come back.

"I need that tag back, Dinky." That was all that came out. Dinky nodded slowly, as if he had known all along.

"Yeah," he said. "Let's see if we get it back from her."

"Why does she wanna get together?"

"She wants to see you." The Pedro words suddenly stopped. For a moment, Dinky and Jose waited.

"She really know I killed Lucy?"

Dinky nodded.

"She found out just like it says in your panels?"

"Yeah. I guess I didn't tell you that the story is true. Did I tell you that?"

"Dinky! No fucken way."

"Yeah, man. It's true. Just like Lucy is true. It's all real, bro."

"Even that stuff about her being a serial killer?"

"Shh!" The librarian tapped on her circulation desk for emphasis.

"Whass she shushing us for?" Jose nearly yelled. "Din't Pedro just talk our ears off? Why didn't she shush him?"

"I can't explain about Anita," Dinky continued quietly. "She said she was gonna prove it to you or some shit. But I'm tellin you, man, that shit is true. I believe her."

Jose waited. Maybe it was a joke and Dinky was holding out, but his face was as sincere as truth itself. It was only dawning on him now that all these things they were in, all these major events, were going to split them up. He didn't know if it was permanent. He didn't know the same way humans never know when death separates them from loved ones.

"I'm thinkin that after tomorrow, everything is different. I'll end up livin in Brooklyn if it works. If it doesn't, who knows what happens? But The Haunt's gotta go. There's no reason for it. I can't just walk away from it, an' I can't just leave it there for somebody else to come an' play. I can't take it with me an' I can't leave it behind."

"Why not burn it?" Jose said.

"Ain't that been done before?"

Jose shrugged. The South Bronx was once a landscape of burned-out buildings.

"My father was always sayin the worst thing that could happen would be to have a fire. It invites the cops to come in an' snoop around the buildings, an' they'll see what's goin on."

"All we need is some gasoline," Jose said.

Dinky's eyes went glassy.

"She's really dead, ain't she?"

Jose wondered if maybe Dinky had been hoping this was some sort of hoax. Pedro's words came back, but only in chunks. Jose hadn't heard much of it.

"I wonder what he said."

"The usual shit," Dinky muttered. They both had no reason to be in school anymore. Jose was just about to say maybe they should go hang at The Haunt and smoke something, when he noticed Barbara and Dezzie standing up against the library doors. They were right in front of the electronic gate that beeped if you tried to swipe books. They were both staring at Jose. Something about how they were looking at him made him nervous. He looked at Dinky and saw that his face was a little disturbed as well.

Barbara and Dezzie came right over to their table. The contrast between them could not be more striking. Barbara in her blue tunic looked like a navy cadet, while Dezzie in her wild polka dots and pointy shades looked like something out of *American Graffiti.*

"Hey, killer," Barbara said, giving him a peck on the cheek.

"Hey, killer," Dezzie said, giving him a peck on the other cheek.

Dinky smirked. "So, 'killer.' Anything you wanna tell me about last night?"

Jose smirked back. "They're on the team."

"They do good last night?"

"Yeah. We got about half the splash done. We finish the rest tonight. You in on that action?"

Dinky looked at all of them. Like maybe he couldn't talk in front of the girls.

"Four's a crowd," he said.

"Four is two couples," Dezzie said. Correcting him. There was a weird silence.

"So Lucy's dead." Barbara's eyes right on Jose. "A heavy sigh. The camera pans the faces at the table and finds them blank."

Jose stared back. There was something on Barbara's face. He was trying to identify it. He had known that face for his entire high school life. Knew it well enough to feel he could read it sometimes.

Only this time, it was different. This time he had touched that face, kissed those lips, those eyes. Her face seemed open to him in a new way, someplace way more personal than before. It made him almost feel he knew her. And that was only from sex!

Dezzie sat beside Dinky. "You bother me," she said.

"Oh yeah?"

"Yeah. You get under my skin. Jose said you drew that whole Anita shit yourself."

"Thass right."

"This Anita thing," Barbara said. "Evidently some masochistic male fantasy-type deal? You often dream of bein fucked to death by your girlfriend?"

Dezzie laughed. "Mmm. I'd like some of that action myself."

"All girls are psycho," Dinky said.

"No, not enough of them," Dezzie shot back.

Barbara's eyes on Jose. "Splash day tomorrow," she whispered. "I can't wait."

"I won't be here," Dinky said.

Dezzie scowled. "I'll try an' get over it."

Dinky got closer. To drop the words in her face.

"Hey. You got a problem with me?"

"Yeah," Dezzie said. "I wanna fuck you to within an inch of your life."

Dinky burst into laughter.

"She's coming out," Barbara said, her tone still light and casual. But Jose identified what was on her face. In between moments of toothy smile, there was tribulation on those lips.

"I'm sayin you bother me. I don't think you're normal." Dezzie removed her shades. "That really attracts me."

The first bell. Sounded muffled in the library through those thick doors. The scurry of kids through the big windows.

"We should run out now if we gonna go," Dinky said to Jose. "You know they lock the doors after the second bell."

Dinky was already up, his drawstring bookbag over his shoulder. He was already walking past Dezzie, who pulled on his arm.

"You don't dare fuck me," she said. "You know you won't survive it."

Dinky burst into laugh again. It made Dezzie bop him.

"Stop laughing," she said.

Jose was taking longer to leave. Barbara got up with him, facing him, turning with him, facing him. Waiting. Her eyes were asking questions. Maybe the girls were going to class. Maybe they were coming with them to The Haunt. Maybe they would just go along.

Out into the hallway. Dinky and Dezzie in front, Barbara and Jose bringing up the rear. By the stairwell doors they stopped. Dinky looked at Jose and Dinky looked at Barbara and Barbara looked at Dezzie and Dezzie looked at Dinky and Dinky looked back to Jose before he went through the doors and down the stairs and Dezzie was with him.

Jose looked at Barbara.

"You look like you were crying," he said.

"I want you to fuck me. I want you touch me with those hands. I want that so bad. An' then tomorrow we make a splash."

Her eyes looked moist.

"I'm with you," she said.

THE MAIN HAUNT. The big maze and the big slash Dinky had painted through it. (There would be no solution, no one true path.)

The TV going and no one watching. Dinky had cued up the Playstation. Lara Croft just stood there, waiting, her big tits rising and falling with every breath. Nobody was playing with her. When Jose and Barbara left him, he was lying on the floor trying to roll a joint. Dezzie was on top of him. She pulled off his T, and slid her hand under his pants. Into his crotch.

"I'm just holdin it," she said.

That Jay-Z was pumping the room nervous. Dinky preferred his hip-hop just a little more thuggish, but that's what happens when you hang with girls. Nonetheless. He winked at Jose. The girl was holding his stiff, and that was never bad.

Jose took Barbara to Fifteen. Lucy's old place. Lucy's old curtains. Lucy's stuffed animals. Lucy had spent time in that bed with him. They had fucked there. Watching Barbara undress, Jose thought that his sex with Lucy was frantic, rushed, always on her terms. If he most times wanted it, she would say no. Whenever she wanted it, he always said yes. Lucy was always in charge. She was a speed demon, distracted like a frolicking puppy, obsessed with missing out. She wanted to be in on everything, to get the attention, to receive the praise the prestige. Jose was just there. She never had to work hard with him. Angel made her work. She gave up those baggy pants, those big shirts. She became blouses and tight skirts, open-toe high heels with straps snaking up her calves. Jose watched her become a woman for somebody else.

(Barbara pulled him down into bed.)

It wasn't enough for her. That he didn't make money that he wasn't a posse man, and what can poor spick boy do when he doesn't happen to be "bad"? How do you score pussy when you're not doing crimes? The street pecking order says you're either a player or you're being played, and no girl gives it away to a chump. This is the training, this is what you feel what you know when you sit on the stoop and watch some teenager your same age driving by in a car that makes every girl nearby say, "Wish I could get a ride in that." And you're not a gold chain boy and you're not into selling drugs. Breaking the law just doesn't thrill you or make you feel complete. And you come to hate posse, and hate that soon people think of that when they think of Puerto Rican. As if there was nothing else to put in that picture frame.

(Barbara removed his T. Touched his chest. She had on a black frilly bra. It unhooked right in the middle for easy removal.)

"Jose," she said. "Stop thinkin so much."

"Why are you here?" he asked, fingers trying to open her lips.

"Because I'm horny," she said.

All those beautiful Puerto Rican girls, following after chasing giving their hearts their souls to these criminal fucks. Watching their lovers kill people rob people rip people off, and there she is, trying to bring up a family. Trying to fall in love in the middle of urban warfare time. A real sick life. Everybody scrambling for money. The older people sure screwed that one up, and so the fucking teenagers had to make their own way in the world. Form teams, accrue funds, find mates. Make their own rules, carve out a life.

(She was ripping that condom packet with her teeth. Gripping his hard dick. Giving him a lick before putting on the gym hat.)

Lip to lip, eye to eye.

"Don't think about her while we're fucking," Barbara said. Putting him inside, and how their bodies both *spasmed.* A flow, a connection of no Lucy. No ghost, no girl with a tag. No drug dealers, no posse boys, no need for cash flow. Jose wasn't thinking of anything. It was as if fucking her cleared up his mind. Afterwards, lying together. Afterwards, finger games and some tickle. She kept trying to put her hair in his mouth. Then, still naked, she just got up and walked right on out of Lucy's room. Jose followed her, out to the Main Haunt. There they found Dezzie, lying on a gym mat, smoking a cigarette with glazed, satisfied eyes.

Dinky walked in at that moment, naked from the waist up, carrying two gasoline cans.

TAG: You're it.

Blasting loud frenzy. Colored lights spinning flash. Anita wrapping colors around her like a scarf. A stripper has a way of giving music a physical form. Hands, hips, legs. She was a painter with music. Her body was the brush.

They had had time. Time to lie around and get stoked with smoke. Time to play video games time for another quick fuck. Time to go do *Hogan's Heroes*. All four of them because that way they could work faster, get it done. Collated, stapled, bagged three hundred copies of *BUDDHA BOOK #4*. There was a somehow sense that it wasn't so important anymore. There had been no Reyes proclamations, no rounding up of hostages, no one had been shot. Maybe Reyes had better things to do. Maybe this was the moment to drop it.

"I don't think so," Barbara said as she bagged another complete issue. "I think it's quiet now because there hasn't been a new issue. The moment this shit hits, it's gonna be the bomb."

"Yeah," Dezzie said. She was bagging too.

But Dinky acted like he didn't care too much. He had gone

beyond school and a student comic book. Reyes was small potatoes. It was his father he was fighting now. It was maybe the same for Jose, who couldn't stop thinking about what Pedro would do.

"I still say you should shut up about the whole thing," Barbara said. "Even if you put out the comic book, who's gonna know it was you that did it, much less tha'chu offed Lucy?"

"I mean, who's gonna know?" Dezzie put in.

"I want Pedro to know."

Jose said it with such calm finality that they just dropped that shit and went on bagging. The fun part was running around the building, dropping issues every place. In desks, lockers, tabletops, bookcases, teacher mailboxes, even in Reyes's office. It was everywhere, again. Once they were placed and some of the remaining issues hidden, they ran the fuck out of there as if they didn't want to be anywhere near now that the deed was done.

"So," Barbara said, as they stood by her stoop. "Later, right?"

"Yeah," Jose said, giving her a peck.

Dezzie didn't say anything to Dinky. And Dinky didn't say anything to her. Somehow, watching them go into the building made them feel better. The air felt lighter.

THEY WENT SHOPPING. "Make sure an' look grown-up," Anita had said, because who knew if Manny was in a cranky mood and wouldn't let them in? When they entered Everybodies, they heard that pulsating techno screech Chemical Brothers acid mix, and Dinky knew right away that she was on. She was center stage, ringed by lights, hips thrusting. Her G-string had all those twenty-dollar bow ties. She was wearing a black sparkly bra. The black stockings would take time. Lying down, on her back, her legs doing that V for Victory. Turning over, poking her ass up to the audience.

She crawled over to the edge of the stage right by the cage, and there was Dinky. In gray slacks and white shirt like she had never seen him. She wiggled over to where he was by the lights that rimmed the stage, by the press of man hands in gabardine suits, and took his twenty dollars.

"Did you have any trouble getting in?" she yelled over the music, knowing Manny would roll his eyes if he caught her talking while doing a strip.

"Nah."

"Where's Jose?"

Dinky didn't say. A few feet away behind, Jose was leaning against a railing that circled the walkway. He was wearing a black blazer and tie. It almost made Anita lose the rhythm. Jose was looking right at her like he was memorizing her. She gave him a small wave, those ANGEL diamonds doing a shimmer dance. When they all sat together at a table after her strip, Candida had hit the stage. Curvy and lithe like kitten, she writhed to some old Erykah Badu in her sequined kitten gear. And those little black-rimmed glasses.

"Isn't she amazing?" Anita seemed really taken with her. She stood by their table with the three beers she had brought, glinty sparkle of sweat on her skin. "She's really got something."

"I can see fuckin her," Dinky said. Eyes roving her.

"I can see you fuckin her too," Jose said.

"Too bad I feel taken," Dinky said.

Anita smiled. She passed the beers around like a waitress before she sat between them. Giving Jose a nudge.

"Hey. Does this mean Jose doesn't fuck?"

Jose watched Candida hump the pole.

"It just means I can see him fuckin her."

The music shifted to fast speed. Guitar squeal and crunch. The girl's name was Passion and she liked metal.

Dinky gave Anita a kiss hello that seemed to startle her. There was a look of sweet surprise on her face, as if nobody ever did that before. Then Jose leaned over and pecked her cheek and that made her look surprised too.

"So. What do you think?"

Anita happily held up her arm to display those dazzling ANGEL stones.

"They look better on you," Jose said.

Anita stared at him. Her face was unreadable. She raised her bottle toast-style.

"Here's to you, killer," she said.

Dinky looked at Jose.

Jose clinked bottles.

They all clinked bottles.

Passion was squirming along the stage in waves of twitch and thrust.

"So what did you guys think of my show?"

"You have great moves," Dinky said.

"You have the same eyes as him," Jose said.

Anita with the beer bottle to her lips, paused everything.

"I do not," she said.

"You do. Any time Pedro wants something, I can tell just by lookin at his eyes."

Anita took a long swallow of beer.

"You sayin I want something?"

Then Dinky put his hand on her thigh, slow and sure. It was almost possessive, like he knew what was his and he was impressed he could have it.

"You wanted me to bring him," he said. "Here he is."

"I don't have that much time," she said. "I just wanted to let you know something." Her eyes went from Jose to Dinky, and back again. And then it looked like she didn't have the nerve to say it.

"Does he know about me?" she asked Dinky. Without taking her eyes off Jose.

Dinky shook his head.

"Show her the comic," Jose said.

Dinky pulled the comic from his shoulder bag and passed it over to her. The moment she saw the cover, she let out a yell like a little girl who got a present. She tore it from its bag and yelled out about Lucy and then she was seeing her in the tub and asking questions so fast and the metal music was too loud for them to register what she was saying until she got to the ANITA pages. Then her face changed. She looked around her like she feared being seen.

"Jesus, Dinky." She rolled up the comic, pressed to her sparkly chest. "What have you done?"

Before either of them could answer, she got up. "Come on, we gotta talk." And she led them around the stage, telling Manny a few words before she took Jose and Dinky to the back alley, where the music was a faint echoey throb and they could sit by chain link and stare at Dumpsters. There was a small stoop there, and that's where they sat. Anita was standing, her high heels making sharp rifle sounds as she paced.

"I can't believe you did this," she said. "You both did this? This is something you both did?"

"Yeah," Jose said.

"But you killed her."

"Yeah."

"You killed her an' you drew it. You turned it into this." She held the comic book up like it was exhibit A.

"Yeah. I did the LUCY pages. Dink did the ANITA pages."

"This is my story," she said, her eyes going liquid. "Dinky, do you see what you've done? You've immortalized me. It's like I can never die now. I've been in a comic book. Just like Aileen Wuornos. Just like Amy Fisher."

Jose and Dinky looked at each other.

"You gotta let me have this, okay? I can't believe how you did this. You really did something big for me. Imagine it, Dink." She sat on the stoop beside them, lighting a cigarette. "After I get caught, I'm makin all the papers. People get wind there's a comic book. Some little guy goes an' finds a copy an' prints it up. Before you know it, it's on TV it's in magazines it's runnin around like an underground cult classic. I mean, thass the joint. Thass Americana. Thass just what I want. To live forever. I cun'ta done better myself. Man, just what is it with us?"

Jose shrugged. Dinky was lacing a sneaker. She pecked them both on the cheek. And then she started to cry. It was silent, the way the tears sped down her face.

"I'm tired. I can't keep this up. I thought I could, but at this rate I'm gonna clock forty stiffs before the cops find me. I can't go on like this. I wanna get to the meat. I'm only tryin'na make a point. I was gonna do two more but I can't. I'm tired. Angel is back. Angel is my one sweet love. I have to take him with me, do you see? It was just always meant to be."

Dinky pulled out a joint and lit it. A toke, and he passed it to Jose.

"With him, I'll make seven. That ties the record. An' with Loco, my first, that should make eight. Then somebody will just have to beat the first official Puerto Rican female serial killer."

"But wait," Jose said. "You mean that you really . . . ?"

Anita laughed, almost like relief, wiping at her wet face. Exhaled for calm.

"I'm sayin tha'chu don't gotta worry about Angel, little brother. He ain't never gonna bother you after tomorrow. Can you imagine men, the way they are? I show him the tag an' give it to him. I tell him some posse offed his wife, an' he gets so grateful he wanna tag me. So guess what?" The sob came out like a cough. She exhaled for calm again, puffed on that cigarette. Then she tossed it, and grabbed the joint from Jose, giving the doorway back into the strip club a look. The music was still pumping. A few girls lingered by the entrance like they needed some air. "He gave it to me. He gave the tag to me. Like, how come men are so stupid? Cun't he think that maybe it belonged to somebody else, that maybe I woulda liked my own?"

She bit her lip, sniffle.

"Fuck that. I don't wanna be tagged anyway."

"I want it back," Jose said.

Anita rolled it down to the edge of her wrist, making it jingle.

"Why?"

"Because after I offed Lucy, she kept coming to me. She kept coming in dreams, on the street. I could hear her laughing, walking around, she was just bothering me. She would pop up an' talk to me. Finally she told me the only way she'd go away was if I gave her the tag."

Anita and Dinky looked at each other.

"But now she's gone, you see? She's really gone. I'm thinkin maybe if I get the tag back, she'll come back an' I can give it to her."

Anita nodded slow like it made perfect sense. She unclasped the tag.

"Yeah," she said. "It belongs to her."

She dropped the tag into Jose's hand.

"Sweet dreams," she said.

"We're havin a party tomorrow," Dinky said. "It starts at eight. It should last all night." And he handed her a copy of the flyer they had printed up and left at school. Barbara said she would pass them out.

"A party," she said, like she had no time for such shit. She folded it up though, and put it in her purse. A girl came into the alley all clattery in heels walking fast.

"Hey. Manny wants you to sub for Johanna," she said.

Anita got up like she had to go right away. She walked some steps, leaving them there. Then she turned back and gave them each a peck.

"Thank you for the comic," she said. "Call me on my cell."

She was heading out, and then she turned back, to clasp Jose's hands and look him in the eye.

"You don't gotta tell nobody," she said. "You can keep quiet about it."

"I'm gonna tell Pedro," he said.

"But you can get away with it," she whispered.

"So can you."

"No, baby. My story begins when I get caught."

"Me too," he said.

Dinky shrugged.

"You're wastin ya time," he said. "He's goin'na the cops. Thass what he said."

Anita frowned. Slowly let go of his hands. Then she motioned for them to follow her out of the alley, back into the teeming pulsating strip club, where they lost her in the throbbing mass of Americana.

21

Then, they separated.

"So. You sure you wanna do this?"

His mother was making coffee even though it was late night. Like they had a lot to go over. She wanted to be sure about the plan. Too bad they couldn't do like in the war movies, and have a mock-up of the location, the perfect setup rehearsed to a fine edge. Could do it in his sleep. Take that M-16 apart and put it back together. Blindfolded.

"Sure I wanna do this," Dinky said back. Almost like he was offended. "I already set up my connection. I set the ball rolling. I even paid the kid, for Chrissake."

She grabbed his hands. "But it's dangerous, Lonnie."

"So whass new about that? Please, come on. Don't start playin the concerned mother. You wan'cha family back, don'chu?"

There was a hardness in his tone that his mother would proba- bly think is bitterness. But Dinky couldn't say that. When they ask him someday, Hey, *what are you?* he will say, *Awake.* Awake and breathing like never. Aware of heart, rhythm, pulse. But there was something else he was trying to figure out.

Was he gifted, lucky, cursed? His life was peopled with murderers, psychos, thieves. A father that could kill him as quick as kiss him, a mangled childhood all streets and twisted temporary loyalties. What to believe in? He had a deep need to align himself to something bigger, some noble cause. To wear a uniform, fly a flag. The idea of joining his father's NATIONless army sickened him—but to fight to make a family, that was corny beyond words. It was a perfect comic-book story, where there is always a villain to overcome. There was no posse to give him support, no nation with which to claim kin. It was just him, jumping in. His father called it "being slick." "You gonna get a spike up ya ass, sittin on the fence like that." So, from frying pan to fire.

School. What about it? He thought he could maybe become a normal clean kid, all straight and narrow. Like Jose. Jose was his straight friend. His only real link to something outside posse. Only Jose joined the world. He murdered Lucy and became like all his old friends, the busted and broken lizard-eyed troops. And all Dinky wanted was to maybe just be a teenager.

The point was, he would give it up. He would lose The Haunt. His own private domain, his separate world. He didn't belong there. He had always shared it, first with Johnny, then with Jose. Maybe it inspired him in some sick way, to see Jose so bent on losing freedom, even though he could slide, get away with it. So it was that Dinky would just lose The Haunt. It would not be true freedom anyway, with his father attached. He would let it all go—

the DJ equipment, the Hubcap Room, even the Dinky Toys. (Okay, he might keep one.) It was all from a past life. Needed no reminders no baggage for the new one.

When Johnny left, he took nothing. A complete fade-out. Dinky spent weeks agonizing over his brother's things, finally storing the stuff in the basement after he stopped doing DJ parties there. It didn't surprise him how it all disappeared one day, after Cesar mentioned doing "spring cleaning" down there. The point was well taken. Who was it said let the dead bury the dead? Some shit like that. Dinky thought there was no need to burn the place. He had read a book once where people used to watch buildings go up in flames the way some people watch baseball games. Park themselves on a car and munch on popcorn and just watch. He figured that wasn't his bag. Been done before. No flames this time.

Abandonment. A recurring theme. A family trait. Dinky thought about genes. Was he breaking the chain, or living up to type?

"What I'm saying is that I don't want to risk losing you. I mean if it's that dangerous." His mother served up that hot cup of coffee. "I'm not out to trade you in for anybody else."

"It'll be fine," Dinky said. "We'll do this."

"YOU SURE YOU wanna do this?"

The TV screen showed white ladies in bathing suits, promenading. It was a beauty contest called "Nuestra Belleza." Here were ladies from nearly every Latino country on the planet. Places like Mexico, Spain, Argentina, Honduras, Santo Domingo, even Puerto Rico (which isn't a country at all). Jose noticed there was no black, no gold, none of the rich textures that make up the Latino fabric.

No slant eyes, no African feel to the hair. It was all white. "Nuestra Belleza." What does that say to all the lovely *trigueñas* out there, watching? Jose was on the couch, thinking of all the Rican girls he knew who were "of color." It disgusted him not to see them represented. He searched for the remote, but it was Pedro holding the power.

"You did say tomorrow you'd spill the beans about that Robles kid. I for one don't care that much. You know that, right? You don't have to feel anybody's forcing you. I just felt that it would be a feather in our cap."

"Sure, pops. Pedro."

"I also feel a lot more at ease, having heard Reyes say to that cop, Oh hey, here's the assistant principal. Lots of responsibility already being put in my hands."

There was a tall white blonde strolling down the runway in a pink bikini.

"Miss Puerto Rico likes to skate, dance, and go to the beach."

"Let's face it. That Robles kid has already got a record with Reyes a mile long. It won't make any difference what you say. Just go in there and tell him he's behind the comic book. Just please, for Chrissake, don't tell him the kid is selling drugs. The last thing we need is to be responsible for some embarrassing drug bust. Some lockerful of crack. Ugh, I can see it in the papers already."

There was a tall white blonde strolling down the runway in a black bikini.

"Miss Dominican Republic likes to skate, dance, and go to the movies."

"Pops, do we gotta watch this crap?"

"The thing is that, well, *esto es una tonteria*. What's the worst that Reyes can do? Suspend the kid. He's out on the streets and really, wouldn't that make him happy anyway? I mean, what kind of system do we have when we punish a kid by throwing him out on the street? A kid like Robles will see that like a reward."

"But Pedro, if it's not Robles, you can expel him all you want. The comic book will keep comin out."

"The point is to try."

"The point is to lie?"

Pedro pulled out a cigar. Jose hadn't seen him smoke those before. He lit it with one of those turbo gas lighters that fizz, spinning the cigar slowly to ensure even flame distribution. The same Reyes stink began to fill the living room. A white brunette, promenading, doing those little turns. Miss Honduras?

"The question is, do you really know who it is that's behind the comic book? And do you want to reveal that or not. I guess I'll have to understand if you feel more of an affiliation to your peers than you do to family. I was suggesting you hand over the Robles kid because that's an easy kill. And Reyes would eat that up."

"An easy kill?"

"Do you know who it is behind the comic book?"

"Yes."

"Who is it?"

"I'll tell you tomorrow. What difference does it make now?"

"I'm just curious."

"Be curious tomorrow."

Jose headed toward the bedroom just as his mother came in from the kitchen with a tray of edibles for the hubby. Jose gave her a peck on the cheek, thinking for sure that Pedro would book on his mother after the chips fall. And how could that be bad for her?

"Be strong," he told her.

"Okay," she said, making a face.

"I just wonder how they did it, that's all," Pedro said, puffing on that cigar. "How they pulled it off all this time."

"Did it ever occur to you grown-ups that maybe these kids were sneaking into the school at night, maybe using a set of keys and swiped codes to defeat the security? That they used the copy machines in the office? That maybe all you had to do was plant somebody in the school to catch them at it?"

Pedro stared at Jose. His face broke into a big smile.

"Fuck no! Are you serious? How could that not have occurred to us?"

"*Oye,* watch your language, Pedro." Dolores pinched him.

"It's just wow. You have to tell Reyes tomorrow. Why didn't that occur to us?"

"Maybe because you're all a pack of idiots," Jose muttered, walking off into his dark bedroom. Where he crashed into bed without even removing his clothes. To sink into black without even thinking.

And to sleep, without even dreaming.

22

The Factory was a squat ugly building that stood between two boarded-ups. It had an alley in the back that was easy to guard. The junkies would head back there where they couldn't be seen from the street. They would put their money in the fake brick. The stuff itself was actually coming from one of the abandoned buildings, where kids were holed up, sometimes for days, with only an occasional Happy Meal for solace. The crew that worked the joint belonged to Stitches. Since local posses started shooting up the alley in drive-bys, Stitches added three more "doorways" so people could come inside, knock on a door, and get some. The source of the stuff was hidden in the bowels of one of the buildings. If the cops came, it would be a shell game. No raid, no ATF squad would ever be quick enough to catch them, to snatch the works. The stuff would go up in smoke, the crews would vanish through rat holes, and the cops would only find a bunch of kids who couldn't find their way out through the maze. (The youngest kids were usually not taught escape routes.)

The kids were brought in by the crews, who spent their time

doing security. They carried the TECs and were too important to be captured. The supervisors got the orders for product to the kids through an intricate system of pulleys and buckets, holes punched through ceilings and floors. It was up to the kiddies to fill the orders and send the goods to the appropriate doorway or the next handling station. Sometimes the kids themselves would have to run goods from building to building, floor to floor. It was tricky. Some floors were sealed. They would squeeze themselves into dumbwaiters that were pulled up and down. There weren't so many ways to get in and out, but Stupid swore he knew ways the crews didn't suspect.

After some beeps on the cell, Stupid and Dinky met up three blocks away. Stupid gave him another deep kiddie hug, then took him inside a vestibule that faced the complex.

"Thass it right there," he said, an early morning jumpiness to him. He lit a small roach but Dinky took it away.

"Are you kiddin me?" Dinky was almost yelling. "Not before an action. No way!"

"It makes ya eyes sharp!"

"I don't need you all sluggish. Put it away."

Stupid tucked the roach away. "Ya the boss."

He led Dinky around the block, down the side of a building where he left Dinky to wait while he disappeared behind a mound of rubble. Dinky thought only for a second about what he would do if *he* were the one getting set up. He blew the idea off. Stupid came back, walking with a strut.

"You got twenty bucks?"

Dinky hesitated. Stupid stomped his foot impatiently.

"Yo man, come on! Freedom ain't cheap. I gotta take care of my people."

Dinky forked over a crisp one. Stupid vanished again behind the big mound. Before he could get those thoughts about maybe getting taken, his cell went off. What made him pick "LADY OF SPAIN" for a theme?

"Dink here."

"Yo." It was Jose. "You on the move?"

"Yeah. It's happenin right now. Where are you? School?"

"Nah. I'm goin in late. I'm just walkin streets right now. I wanted to tell you good luck."

Jose sounded small in the cellular, a real munchkin dude.

"Same to you," Dink said back.

Stupid appeared, making his way along the rubble wall with this other little kid.

"This is Mego," he said. The kid had a scar from his ear to the edge of his mouth. That shit looked nasty. Mego looked Dinky over carefully, with a face so worn it could've belonged to a forty-year-old midget. The kid was not at all awed and maybe still suspicious.

"You sure?" he asked Stupid.

"Yeah, man. I'm tellin you, he's straight."

"All right. But in twenty minutes, I'm not even here. Got it?"

Stupid didn't answer. The pair did a strange handshake together. Dinky felt weird, very on the outside. Almost a "Herb."

Mego led them along the rubble wall, into a basement window where there was nothing but more rubble and plaster stink. Up into a stairwell where they were told to wait. Mego listened, then they floated past a half-open door where there was radio noise—maybe

Guy or Bobby Brown, with static. Now up a landing in the half-dark, across a hall, then two more landings.

"Gimme a little time to get up on the roof," Mego said, and then he vanished into the dark.

Stupid led Dinky over to a large space where it seemed the walls had been knocked down. No apartments, just plaster and chunks of wall, cracked beams and torn wiring. There was a dumb-waiter, one of those old ones you see in South Bronx apartments that never work. This door was open. Inside, a black shaft with cool air and ropes going up and down.

Stupid stuck his head in. Looked up, looked down. Spit into the shaft. Dinky watched with a strange mixture of admiration and regret, as the kid grabbed a pipe that was sitting by the door. Tapped out a sequence. There was silence. Regret, why regret? What was it that made Dinky feel bad about this brat, who should be home someplace playing video games instead of being guerrilla fighter? What was this war all these kiddies were fighting? Dinky felt almost guilt that he would be leaving the runt behind.

"Whassup?" Dinky asked.

"Shh." Stupid looked up and down the shaft again. The ropes did not move. Stupid tapped out a sequence again with the pipe, then dumped the pipe and pulled out that roach clip again. Dinky was feeling pretty jumpy, what with all those little sounds and voices from someplace above or below to keep him tense.

"What happens now?" he asked.

"We gotta wait."

Stupid's lighter only made sparks.

"You paid me good money, man. You see my new sneaks? I'm

gettin me some new pants tomorrow. My friend Spoons, he spent all his money on a bagga smoke. See me, I'm not like that. I pick up smoke all around. I rather save my money for college an' shit."

"College? But you're ten, man."

"Yeah. But that shit's expensive."

"Wha'chu gonna do in college?"

"I wanna work with animals, man. Like people on those nature shows, where they hang out in the woods an' follow monkeys around an' shit? Thass what I wanna do. I like animals. I wanna have alotta dogs. I prefer dogs to people. I hate people, man. I'd rather kill people."

"You mean for a living?"

Stupid was still trying to light the roach. Wasn't working. He looked at Dinky like he had just heard what he said.

"Hey, man, is it real? You really gonna come back now?"

Dinky's stomach pounded. Guilt dry GUILT taste—he spit. Lucky thing Dink was a Gemini. Could lie like a pro, on his back on his feet any time any place, and quick. Stupid was sitting on that mound of plaster like it was break time. Dink sat beside and lit the roach for him.

"Yeah," he said, as Stupid toked deep.

"Hey, man, you think maybe we be a team now? I can't wait to get off that stoop, bro. Ya pop just don't got it. Hey, when he gonna get out the joint?"

"They tryin'na book him on three to five. But he might get out. He always do. Last time he was up for a nickel too, but he got loose."

"I don't want he should get out. You think you be in trouble with him if you spring ya brothers? It gonna be like a shootin war between you an' ya pops?"

Dinky smirked. This was going too far.

"Nah," he lied. "It ain't like that."

"See, this the kinda work I like. Commando. I ain't into that stoop shit. I got fast eyes an' fast hands. Stoop is a real waste of my talents. Crews see us like little kids, they make us do shit work. Maybe you be different. I got me some fine boys, like Mego, an' Spoons. We can all work for you, man. Teach them nasty crews whass what. I'd like to drive by thum mothafucks an' just poppum. Start with Stitches an' work my way down. Teenagers, man. I'm glad you different." He passed the roach, like brotherhood. His eyes had that warm toasty look to them. "Hey, man, you know? I tell all my little brose that work around here. We'll form a real forever legion, bro. Like *The Justice League!* You ever read that?"

Dinky toked only a little.

"Yeah."

"But I think, you know, if we gonna crew like that, I gotta change my tag. 'Cause you know, 'Stupid,' that don't work. So I thought about it last night? An' I came up with Tico."

"Tico?"

"Yeah, man. Thass short for TKO, read that?"

"Yeah. I got it." Dinky nodded with smile. "Slap me some, Tico."

They did a hand slap and double fist.

"But if I can ask you," Tico whispered, "how come you got a name like Dinky? Do that mean you got a small dick?"

"What makes you go there? What makes you go there?"

There was a funny scrabbling sound. They both froze. The ropes were moving. The dumbwaiter was a little box that slid right into place. Tico got inside it, taking the pipe with him.

"You wait here. I'm gonna send it back up. Then you get in, okay?"

"Inside *that?*" Looked like a real tight fit for one so tall slinky like he was. Tico grinned, taking that last toke. He tapped his code with that pipe, and started to descend.

There was a nervous energy to the room—all the wrong kind. Something would soon go wrong.

"Get it right, bro! You want that bastid Montego to come up here again?"

It was Luis who was yelling at Junior. They had a pair of buckets before them. The buckets were attached to ropes. Junior was tossing the bags of vials in. Some bags had two vials, some had three. He tossed, he paused, he changed his mind.

"Ah shit," he said, clutching his curly head. "I don't remember!"

Luis shook his head. "You little jerk. Now what?"

The two boys were responsible for three doorways. The other bucket was done and had been sent down its hole, but these two were still on the prep table. Luis got on the cell.

"Hey. Can you repeat fifteen again?"

Luis held the cell away from his ear. Yelling could be heard coming through the earpiece. Junior made a motion that sent one of the buckets tumbling over. At that moment, Tico appeared in the dumbwaiter.

"If that fuck comes up here to slap us up again," Luis yelled at his brother, "I'll kick ya ass!" He was glaring at Tico as he hopped down, slapping dirt off his baggies.

"Yo, Stupid." Luis sounded angry. "You come up here an' you don't bring us no eats? Whassup with that?"

Tico poked Luis in the chest.

"Two things. First, I do you a favor when I bring eats. I don't owe you shit. Second, it's not no Stupid no more. It's Tico. You got that? Too much for you? Should I write it down?"

"Ya name is *Bicho?*" Junior's laugh all shaky cackle, some happy bird. Luis slapped the side of his head but the laugh did not die so easy. It was Luis with the serious face, with the anger painted on at least three coats thick. Tico stared at Junior like he was too little for him to take serious.

"Tico, man. It's Tico." He looked around, seeing the overturned bucket. Made a face like what else is new? That poor little Junior was getting slapped so much he was lucky to still have teeth.

"Why din'chu bring us nothin?" Junior asked weakly from the buckets.

"Don'chu worry," Tico replied, tapping the code. "I brought'chu somethin you might like."

The dumbwaiter disappeared upwards.

TO STUDENTS OF LMM-HS!
THE LAST BLOWOUT

A party of TITANIC proportions
        featuring

        DJ DINKY
        THE CHAOS BROTHERS
        STICKI & SLICK
            live live live

PLUS special guests

when: FRIDAY NIGHT
where: MACONDO/617 139th Street

NO Posse NO 5-0! ONLY ready-to-wear YOUTH!

MORNING. SUNLIGHT. WINDOWS.

South Bronx makes pretty in the morning. Sun lights tenements all bronze. Trees shiver breeze. Around 6:00 A.M., seagulls skim roofs and cry. Almost like being by the ocean. Jose would've missed all that if he had been sleeping, but once he woke from black nada he had to get up. He is up to see the sun crayon the skies, to watch newspapers arrive in a bundle at the corner newsstand. The headlines screech about another man plugged, another body in a car. A busy serial killer. Police stumped. Jose felt involved.

The sight of Pedro in the morning. Freshly suited, cologned. Dolores made scrambled eggs with little red and green peppers. Talked about last night's *novela*. Of course the guy killed her, how couldn't he? Especially after she moved in with that rich skunk on the hill and ran around town flaunting her new life! So maybe his hands just slipped, and she went tumbling off the balcony. What's new about that? Latinos are passionate—besides, Dolores pointed out, women have ways of making men crack. Pedro laughed, saying that a woman can't make a man do anything.

Jose wondered how he would take the news—not the comic book, the murder. Would maybe end up trying to "take care of it," hush it up, under the rug. Maybe he would want to ship Jose off to Puerto Rico, get him out of the way. After all, what about his career at Luis Muñoz Marín? He might be angrier about the effect of it on his life than the fact a girl was killed. He would pull that old card— "What about your mother? Did you bother to think about her?" Jose had already thought it through. He loved her, but her relationship with a man he couldn't respect meant she could easily become a casualty. That she even fell for a man like Pedro seemed a weakness, some sickness from her generation, and maybe there was a price to pay for that. Jose could only take responsibility for *his* actions; theirs would have to run the course.

The eggs made his stomach throb. He wanted to see Lucy again. Knew he wouldn't. Why did that make him cry? (Private time in the bathroom.) He blew it. He killed her when he should've just let her live. Now, no lesson for her. *Big* lesson for him.

He was walking school halls. Sunlight. Windows. The burnt toast taste. Bells. How did Jose skip his homeroom? Walking into school was slow motion. An underwater sound to the film. Kids were turning to look at him. As if all the sound were sucked out. *BUDDHA BOOK 4*—those girls there, they were holding copies. "Oh shit," they said when they saw him. Staring. More faces to turn around, to stare. Talk that stopped in midstep because he was passing by.

What was it on the kid faces, what was happening to them? To have seen Jose commit murder. A hall monitor happened to see an issue of the comic book clutched in girl hands—most students already knew to keep those issues hid when in the hall, but that monitor swooped down and *snatch,* right there. Turned to look at Jose. A look of recognition on the tall broad dude with the rocky face as he looked at Jose, and the kids in the hall did not move, just watching. The hallway monitor put a hand on Jose's shoulder, gruff.

"You're comin with me," he said.

Jose did not even wriggle. They walked about three feet past faces still staring, when there was shouting. A pair of school safety folks ran past. The hall monitor let go of Jose, his talkie spitting out words. Melee on the second floor. Fists and punches and the crackle of a bottle. Sweaty Mendoza barked into his talkie while security goons tried to clear the hall.

Jose shivered—it was Shakes and two of his boys in some blood-all with who? TTG, the kids were saying. War coming down, for some slight, or maybe it was deeper. Some disrespect, some sprayed-over tag, nobody had the details yet but the proof was in the air. Turf war, a boy with a bloody face on the floor, and he wasn't getting up. Who was it used the bottle on him?

"Get the fuck off me," Shakes yelled, trying to break free, but three security goons were on him. They pushed him up against the wall, and that got the girls to start yelling.

"Hey, man! Police brutality!"

The real police arrived. The goons were trying to clear the hall. Teachers were leaving classrooms to see what was up. The late bell rang, and nobody heard.

"I think thass Alex from TTG. He look dead."

"Look. He ain't moving."

"Oh shit. It's between Angel an' TTG. It's gonna get sick around here."

A girl was screaming. It was her boyfriend lying against school tile, not moving. She pushed past security goons, on her knees to cradle his head. Not sure if the cops noticed the glittery diamond tag on her wrist that sparkled ALEX. Jose watched the cops cuff Shakes.

IT TOOK SOME struggle. For Dinky to force his way out of that teeny box that was the dumbwaiter.

Luis had always been the fatter one. Used to have cheeks, and was always laughing. That high-pitched giggle of his could bubble for a long time. His eyes were brighter than Dink's, almost hazel. Curly hair like Johnny's. He stared hard at Dink. The baby fat was gone. At fourteen, the kid had the hollow eyes of an alcoholic. A fine film of dirt all over him like he hadn't bathed in a month. Junior, the hoppiest of all, still had the crazy energy, only now there was nervousness. Bugged-out eyes that jumped, and that shaved head that made Dinky think of prison. Solitary confinement. Bread and water. Was this the high life Cesar had promised them?

He stared.

They stared back. Strangers. The buckets on the prep table were forgotten. What was Dinky doing? He hardly knew them. For a moment he couldn't even remember being related. What the fuck was he doing?

"This is ya brother," Tico said, into the silence, because he didn't get what all the pause and stare was about.

Junior approached. Luis extended an arm like he was going to hold him back. Junior knocked it away. Came right up to Dink, eyes locked. Reached out to touch like it was some mirage. Small filthy hand, right on Dinky's chest.

"Did Pop send'ju?"

Luis sounded like he was making a challenge.

"Nah."

"Why the fuck he put us here?"

The hostility on Luis's face actually gave off heat. Dinky recognized it. It was a lot like the old Johnny. They had all felt that, asked that, at one time or another. They were all Cesar's sons. It took a moment for Dinky to find his voice.

"You're here 'cause he don't give a fuck about'chu. Why you think?"

"I had a dream like this," Junior said, and then he hugged Dinky hard, a little-kid hug that Tico was so good at. (And who was watching Tico? The kid was dipping his hands into all those buckets.)

"So wha'chu doin here?" Luis sounded like, get it over with and step, we got work to do here. Dinky looked at those hard eyes, at the way Luis hadn't moved a muscle.

"I came to get'chu the fuck outta here."

Everything froze. Why hadn't Johnny said that to them, taken them all with him? How could he desert them, jump ship? Dinky felt it now, rabid angry churning. It made him say it again— "I came to get'chu out."

A strange torment fought it out on Luis's face. It seemed they were going to stand there staring at each other all day, when suddenly a bucket tipped over from a violent yank on one of the ropes.

"Hey!" The yell came right through the floor. "What the fuck is goin on up there?"

Tico yanked on Dinky's T.

"We gotta move, now! I got Mego on the rope. If he jets, we don't get outta here!"

Junior's eyes were jumping, but Luis stood stock-still, the battle still being fought on his face.

"It's up to you, man. But I came all this way."

The mad pounding on the wall.

"Fuck it, man, you guys better rock!" Tico was getting antsy, though he was still stuffing product into his cargo pants.

Junior was first. He darted past all of them, squeezing into the dumbwaiter. Tico woke from trance and banged that code out frantic with his pipe. Junior floated upwards.

Luis made a sound—choked. He looked at the prep table, and then at Dinky. The dumbwaiter slid back into place. Luis bit down on his lip like he didn't want to be seen trembling like that.

"Fuck him," he said, just like Johnny said it. And then he was scrambling, right past Dinky, into the dumbwaiter that had returned empty. Tico again pounded out that code. The wall was all angry thumps. Luis slid out of view with a frantic jerk.

"What the *fuck* is goin on up there? You better send that shit down *now,* mothafuckas, or I'm comin up!"

"It's comin down," Tico yelled, grabbing the bucket that had tipped over. With a hand motion, his pants slid down to the floor. In no time, he was directing a yellow stream into the bucket. He looked at Dinky.

"You gonna just stand there? Come on, man! There's another bucket!"

Dinky rushed over. Without a thought. Side by side, grinning like a team, they did their part to keep the business flowing.

The dumbwaiter returned, empty.

The thumps on the wall got louder.

TIME PASSED. LATE bells. Jose thought he would find Barbara. What class was it she would be in now? Math class, second floor.

Mr. Davis with the Mark Twain mustache. Jose stood by the open door, looking in. Student heads were all bowed, pencils scribbling. Must be a quiz. Even Mr. Davis was busy at his desk, didn't spot him. There was Barbara in the back, with Dezzie beside her. They hadn't seen him either, like he was a ghost. What made that kid in the front start clapping? He was looking right at Jose, and he began to clap—slow, rhythmic, pounding. The other kids looked up, saw Jose there. And they began to clap, too.

Mr. Davis at first put up his hands, to try and stem the tide of clapping, but the entire class was clapping now, faster and faster like fury was building up. Like something angry was pouring out of them.

And they began to stand. Some kids in the back first. Then Barbara, whose eyes glistened wet. Then Dezzie, whose eyes seemed to glare. And Mr. Davis, being cooler than most, didn't even try to stop it. Just watched like he was a sociologist. All thirty-two kids in the class, a clapping ovation, and then feet stamping to the beat. A slow protest song.

"Class," Mr. Davis yelled, "stop it!" He walked toward Jose, grabbed him by the arm.

"You have some explaining to do," he said.

"No," Jose said. Shaking his hand loose, walking away drastic, down the stairs. First floor, and heading right to his father's office.

23

B ucketsful of piss, going down the ropes.

"No, *you* go," Tico said, desperately pushing Dinky into the dumbwaiter, tucking in his arms and legs to make sure he got in snug.

"You're right behind me, okay?"

(The pounding was shaking the walls.)

Tico picked up that pipe. Paused for just a second.

"Thanks for gettin me off the stoop," he said, like it was goodbye. Dink was just about to say something when the pipe beat its story and he was yanked upward, the wall scraping his arm. He caught a quick glimpse of the floor he had been on. Going higher. Another floor flashed by like a snapshot, and a throbbing panic seized him.

Bright sunlight. Flash so he was blind. Hands pulling him out frantic.

"He's still down there," Dinky yelled at Mego, who didn't take the time to talk about it. He was working that dumbwaiter, the clatter of springs and squawk of pulley. Where does a little kid get so much strength? He looked down that shaft.

There was no movement. Luis and Junior were looking around just like cornerboys, ready to spring for an exit. They didn't know where to go or what. There was nothing up on that roof. They looked at Dinky.

He pulled Mego away from the shaft.

"Tico!"

Mego shoved him away. "What are you, crazy? You tryin'na get us all killed? Come on, we gotta step!"

"But Tico's still down there!"

Mego again pulled him away from the shaft.

"We gotta jet *now,* or we don't get out! Now you wanna stay here, thass your problem! Tico's been in scrapes before. He always gets out. Now come on, you big ugly fuck, or you gonna stay! Alla youse!"

Mego started running across the roof. Jumped over a parapet to the next roof. Luis and Junior looked at Dinky, then ran after Mego. Dinky reluctantly began to step, thinking he could hear Tico playing that pipe signal on brick. Seeing Junior stop to wait for him reminded him of the mission, made him hustle. Had he come all this way to blow it? So he ran, trying not to think he left Tico in the lurch, fighting off the ugly pictures. The ugliest thing or the prettiest thing was how open his eyes were—maybe it was stupid to think it but he had to say it at least once—*I hate adults.* Hated them for every fucking little Mego and Tico and his brothers. It had been life to him, playing along to follow in Daddy's footsteps. It made him sick.

How did they get back to street, to that alley? Dinky wasn't even aware. Mego led them to the edge of that path, then pointed the way to freedom as if he wasn't able to make the trip. They had barely hit the street before Dinky noticed Mego had disappeared, making him hope that somehow Tico could pull the same trick.

His mother drives like a nut. Lucky thing that Honda Civic is a teeny car that can scoot between, picks up like a bug skittering across carpet to escape that descending *chancleta.* Dinky, Luis, and Junior were all talking at once. The two boys hadn't seen their mother in half a year. Was that why Junior's face was wet, why Luis was filled with bragging, as if he himself had thought up the whole escape? Her face was wet too, but she was chattering away the loudest, riding the high of getting it over while speeding past cars on the expressway. She was talking so fast that she didn't even hear Dinky say, stop, he had to get off, had to go back to The Haunt.

All at once, New York City slipping by. The floating skyline, the Triborough Bridge. She knew what she was doing, down to the sandwiches and ice cream pops she brought. (The kids devoured them like they hadn't seen treats.) She took them right into Brooklyn, down Fifth Avenue—there was even a St. Marks Place that wasn't East Village. The house was big. Hardwood floors, creaky steps going up. There was a deck in the back, a balcony upstairs. Dinky and brothers walked through open-mouthed, like there was Michelangelo on the ceiling.

There were beds in the bedrooms, a big couch. Like Dinky's mom had been prepping the hideout for a long time. There were even fresh toothbrushes in the bathroom.

There was a woman named Lila. She lived on the top floor with Jimmy. Dinky had never met his mother's cousin. The woman was nice, spoke Spanish the way people from the island do. When she spoke English, she sounded like a foreigner.

"In a couple of days I'll move everything out of the apartment," his mom said, carefully, as if she feared Dinky might switch sides. "But the boys can stay here, I've worked that out with Lila." A deep breath. "You can stay too, Dinky. You don't have to go back there."

"I gotta go back," he said, not looking her in the eyes.

"You're not gonna go see your father, are you?"

The leaves were rustling as they stood on that deck. It was strange, like a dream or drug trip. Dinky didn't want to look at her because he knew she was happy. And he did not want to shatter all that fine crystal.

"What trains are near here?" he asked.

He could sense something sag in her.

"I'll drive you back," she said.

24

He found him standing in his office like one of those animals in the zoo that never got used to four walls all cement round and cold food in a dish. Jose stood in the doorway. Pedro motioned to the chair.

The late bell. Kid voices in the halls faded to nada. Up and down everywhere, doors closed. Now the sound of phones, a pen tapped against legal pad. Fingers tapping fast on plaster computer keys. The fax machine whirred click whined. Jose sensed the feel to the air, the sense that something had just happened.

BUDDHA BOOK 4 was sitting on the desk. There were a few copies on a shelf nearby, probably confiscated from students. There was another pile on the funny leather couch.

Pedro sat so slowly that Jose thought he was dreaming. It was the same dream feel like when Lucy came back.

(Jose tweaked an ear. Nada.)

"If you came here," Pedro said in that calm even tone he always used as the official guidance counselor, "to tell me that they, they did this to you because they know you are a fink, then fine. We can tell Reyes that."

"Pops...Pedro..."

"It's a good thing he's not here. Had to go talk to the cops about this kid, some kid just got half beaten to death...I was able to confiscate a *trulla de copias*...there are still some out there."

"Pops."

"Don't call me that! It's Pedro. It's fucking Pedro!"

His hands fluttered around aimless.

"I can fix it. You understand? I can fix this. Reyes isn't going to care about this. It's filth, it's got nothing to do with this school. It's got nothing to do with him, or the staff. It's me, isn't it? It's got to do with me..."

Jose didn't say anything. He undid his bag and pulled out the *BUDDHA BOOK 4* master copy.

"I mean Anita's in there. Who knows she's my daughter, who? Who could've even—? I'm in there, Jose, I'm in the book."

Jose dropped the masters on the desk. They spilled across all showcase style, right to Pedro so he could see. Pedro stared past without touching the pages. He nailed Jose with his glare.

"It was done to get you in trouble, to make you look foolish," he said like it was well rehearsed. "We'll see Reyes when he gets back. You'll give him a few names, and..."

Pedro got up from his chair. Out the window there wasn't much, just courtyard, windows, dingy unkempt grounds. Yet Pedro stared out like he could make out the turrets of El Morro.

"It was me," Jose said.

"You and Robles. Why don't you finish the sentence?"

Pedro shut the door. Stood there holding the knob for a moment.

"You're a victim in this. You were hanging with Robles because you were doing this undercover thing. They got back at you by doing that story about you, about your father, about his twisted, sick daughter."

"I want you to call the cops," Jose said.

"The police. What the hell for, just tell me that."

The quivering rage that Pedro fought to hold in surprised Jose, who felt completely calm. It was almost as if he was watching Pedro from some great height, and pitying him.

"I killed somebody. In cold blood I killed somebody." Jose's voice caught on something. "Thass what's in the book."

Pedro came in for a close-up. Jose waited for the yelling. No yelling.

"You're not telling me that's true. You're not. I don't need to deal with that. I read that thing, you understand? I know the story. I don't need you to mind-fuck me now, Jose. I know you don't like me, I know that, but you don't have to go this far. You're hurting your mother, you realize this."

"I killed that girl, Pedro."

"Shut up with that."

Pacing. Sweeping hand through hair to get a fix, to think, to calm down.

"See, I know you're full of shit because you're not crazy. I don't believe you're crazy. You're a smart kid. How could you make me think you could kill somebody and then draw a comic book about it?"

"How else could I tell you?"

"Don't make this about me."

Jose reached into pocket. Dropped the icy-cold ANGEL stones on the desk. Motioned with his chin as if to say, There. Pick it up.

"No," Pedro said, not going near them. "You're making this up."

"You read the story," Jose said. "You know what it means for me to have that. You know."

"I don't. I don't even see it. I don't believe in comic books."

"You know she's dead. I killed her, Pedro. I shoved her under the water. I held her under until she—"

"Liar!"

The shout stopped everything. Like subway roaring into station with a sound-wave windburst.

"Take it, just take it off my desk."

Pedro pushed it shoved it off. It fell in Jose's lap with a tiny chime sound.

"I'm goin to the cops," Jose said, pocketing the tag.

"How could you do this to your mother?"

"It's not her I did it to."

"Don't you care about her, how she's going to suffer?"

"Don'chu dare talk about my mother." Jose stood up, face to face. "It ain't like you gonna be around to stick it out. I know you. When things get tough, you go." Jose looked like he would spit. "So, go."

"I'm sorry you don't know me."

"I *do* know you. Anita told me all about you. You'll find another little *trigueña*. You couldn't possibly stick it out. I'll be countin the days."

Pedro's eyes quietly filled with tears. He went back to the window like he needed air.

"You don't know me," he said soft.

"I know you gonna leave. You ain't got the guts to be anybody's father."

"But I love your mother. She's the first. You hear? I love your mother."

The silence after his words was like the moment right after the M-80 goes off, and all is still with aftershock.

"If you don't call the cops, I'm gonna turn myself in."

"Can't you just wait? Can't you listen to what I'm saying? Can't you just do things my way?"

"Not this time," Jose said.

He had never seen Pedro so pleading so lost so powerless. A day when the slogans couldn't save him.

"Can you just wait? Can we talk about it?"

But Jose couldn't wait anymore.

25

The comforting sound of bullets slapping pavement. Spitting up dirt. At long last, South Bronx streets again erupting in a childish turf war. Some words some looks, a slighted lover a disrespectful word, or maybe a tag that got sprayed over—drive-bys came back to Southern Boulevard and Anita laughed. She laughed at how stupidly easy it was to inflame old wounds. She laughed at how God-like she could be to start wars, to pile up bodies. The thought of all those young boys bleeding their last twitches on sidewalks through the South Bronx made her wet, made her touch herself. TTG, Angel's boys, SGF, who gave a damn what posse was where? They weren't armies or nations or even families. They should just kill each other off, she thought. It was old, passé. And she would be remembered. They wouldn't. They would disappear overnight. The empty lot they used to dump bodies would soon be paved over. Prefab three-family houses would sprout up all over, cute manicured lawns, and Puerto Rican politicians would talk about a new Bronx that never looked back, never buried its dead, never even mentioned the brats the street chumps the losers that shot at each other for tiny vials of white shit. Anita could see into the future. It was all plain.

She had gotten a room at the Paramount, one of the bigger ones that had a round tub and furniture that was all metallic and geometric like some weird Chuck Jones landscape. It would be better to do No. 7 in Manhattan. She could leave the body there with the last tape while she disappeared back to home turf. A woman that promises a man a great victory has to at least get laid in return. It's the least a fucking street king warlord drug fuck can do for a lady. And Angel said, yeah, no problem. He had just lost a wife, remember? He wouldn't mind some pussy, either. And he promised her a new tag. A new apartment, a fine rig like a warlord drug fuck can always offer. Too bad Anita thought that was all chump shit. Maybe a year ago she would've died for it. Now she looked down upon the ghetto druglord world and saw it for what it was: a dying animal.

She would snack on the carcass.

Popped that cork. Poured bubbly. Right by the round tub with that hot water bubbling all jetstream. Placed those three white cigarettes on the stone rim, her unique blend of bazuca hash speed. Poor boy wouldn't know he was cumming or going.

(Don't laugh. This is serious. Touch yourself.)

"Do that again," Angel said. Sitting in the churning waters, puffing on her smoke.

Anita sat on the stone rim, opening her legs wide, one foot gripping his shoulder. Wetting her fingers with her tongue before touching her pussy, round and round to make that clit poke up pretty pink. Glistening wet.

"Why don't we get this over with," Anita said, breathless and trembling.

26

He didn't mind being alone to rock with ghosts and all that past that came rushing in. Even playing that old Ice Cube that used to be his sound track, the mad Predator days with he and Johnny running the streets in that swift sleek buggy (the girls calling, *Johnny, Johnny, we got something for you,* and Dinky was always into the leftovers). In a way, wouldn't they all be together again? Johnny couldn't stay in the marines forever, was sooner or later to return, and then what? No drugs to run, but maybe life, or what passes for it. Dinky didn't know what that was yet. The sky would not fall because there would be no more Haunt. Jose on the floor in the Hubcap Room, rolling around those Dinky cars like he was twelve, making engine sounds and motor roars and *crash!*, the Citroën smashed into that Mercedes truck. And Dinky rolled a joint and they didn't even smoke it. The sky would not fall. No more spick kids with guns in cars no fast deals no need to express the crime life. The story was no longer the shit that was around him. The story was *him.* That fallen got paved over. There would be no Holocaust Museum on Brook Avenue.

Jose went with him to that spot on 125th Street where the bus stopped. It was a special bus to Riker's Island. Could see all the prison families lining up waiting. The hard faces the sad faces the confused anxious faces the ones that were used to it. The families of people who stumbled and tripped, who made a life out of crime or who just got caught. It was a big crowd. Jose and Dinky leaned against a brick wall across the street. Munching on some warm bread from the bakery nearby. The two of them waiting.

"I'm not goin home," Jose said.

"But shun't you at least see ya moms?"

"Nah."

"Wha'chu think Pedro gonna do?"

"I don't know." Jose talking about the wild vibe at school, the standing ovation, the kid from TTG that got the shit kicked out of him. Strange times. They would miss them all.

"I just go an' drop this shit on my dad. Tell him whassup." Dinky didn't seem sure, the way he scanned that crowd waiting for the bus.

"You think thass where I'll end up?"

Dink didn't get the question at first. Jose seemed pretty calm and centered for a dude getting ready to take a murder rap.

"I really think you should find another way outta this," Dinky said.

"You do?"

Dinky watched the crowd. The bus slowly approached from down the block.

"You know what? Fuck it. Fuck it an' fuckim. I ain't goin'na no

Riker's. He can eat shit an' die. Lettim read about it in the papers. I ain't gonna waste our last day together goin'na see his sorry ass. Fuckim. Let's you an' me go downtown."

Jose followed, giving that Riker's Island crowd a last look.

27

S even.

    "Stop," he said. "It hurts."

His twitching quake was the ride and she had never squeezed so hard. His back arched with stretch his mouth gurgled the ultimate sweet the ultimate nothings

exploding

    "Stop." Slow empty hollow. Croak.

    "Honey. It feels so good." (her voice like clouds)

Another spasm. A man who would give it all to her. Was moving all by itself inside her, was trembling tickling dancing climbing. Quaked stroked like fingers, and then a rhythm the dying pulse that pushed into her with its last

    (she could swallow him)

the buck of him gave her warm chills

                        it was too good too good too hard to stop but he got quiet like a cave. She put her fingers over his nose. To check for air. And air there was still.

    "Come on," she whispered. "Can't you see it's starting to feel good?"

the burst of his spasm

    What are you doing to me? (through his gasp)

made her laugh tender, stroking his hair, sweet baby. His eyes so glassy spaced and vacant.

    "They call it death by misadventure," she said.

28

They went shopping. They had quite a bit of that Angel grant left, even though Dinky blew quite a bit on the party. They bought CDs. They bought vinyl. They bought books on Tupac and a new one on Biggie. They rode the Staten Island Ferry three times back and forth. They took the train all the way to Coney Island and hung around on the empty boardwalk until the sun went down. Not a lot of words. A little bit of joint, a couple of beers. They could be wordless and close like any Gemini twins. No discussions no issues. They just hung together and that was that.

The party took shape even without them. Brats from school were already hanging out all over Evander. There was buzz and hop, the throb of heavy bass all up and down the block. The pizza place three blocks away could hardly keep up with the demand, as more and more kids from Luis Muñoz Marín appeared. Some of them had the comic book with them. They kept slapping Jose on the back as if he had done them a favor. Jose had nothing to say about the comic book. He tried to laugh, mostly, but Lucy was on him. Not seeing her again really pained him. He was still carrying around that tag.

Sticki & Slick came early and did a sound check. The Chaos Brothers brought their own lights and gizmos, to add to the effect of ghetto blast jamdown. The people at Macondo were very nice, very open. The fact that so many kids in jungle gear were popping up did not scare them. Manuel, the owner, was a short, bearded guy with a pockmarked face. He was really liking the young girls. "It's good to see some life here again," he said, and he stood by while Dinky exercised that DJ equipment.

It was always a trip to work with new equipment. Dinky had to accustom himself, learn the rhythm to every machine, every knob and turntable. The dual CD player was also rad, but Dinky wanted to really hands-on that vinyl for some scratch and scroll, and Manuel had to work hard to find a working cable for that other turntable. It wasn't yet time for the party to start but the crowd was demanding music. He pulsed them wack, he drove them all spasm, but as light turned dusk, kids really started to stream in. Dinky didn't know why or from where but there they were, even some brats he knew from the streets. There was Samson and Jetty and that nutty kid they called Spix. Someone must've got on a cellular because there was Smokey and Trapps and more old faces that stopped by for a hug, a fist handshake and kind wishes. NO POSSE, the flyer said, but there were kids from TTG there and they saw Samson's boys already in the house, playing like they were security.

"Just get along," Dinky said over the mike. "You can kill each other later."

Barbara and Dezzie appeared, Barbara in a blue shimmery

dress so feminine that Jose felt an immediate sense of loss. Dezzie looked sparkly too, and where did she get spandex pants? Barbara was ecstatic about the effect of the new *BUDDHA BOOK* on the masses, and even talked about the effects she was planning to pull off with the next issue, but Jose didn't really hear any of it. He shushed her with a kiss, and she was content to shut the fuck up and cling.

Dinky started with slow jams, moving into a throbby heavy-bass place. Who expected techno? Trip-hop was also his game, but when he cranked the nasty street sounds it always hopped the house. Posse boys from Samson's crew and other nearby worker-bees dove all over that fresh high school pussy that was dressed all nines like that. (When a Puerto Rican woman dresses *machua,* there is no prouder moment than to behold from front from back for every Puerto Rican boy—proof of God and the fitting together of parts.)

Buggy trooped in, followed by more old faces that came as if to pay their last respects. Smokey and Trapps, Junior Smalls and that kid they called The Creeper. There was David with his ferret squirmy all over him, backslapping handclasping Dinky like he had done them all proud someplace. And then Tico came out of the crowd and gave Dinky that tight, little kid hug again.

"You a real manna quality," he said, and Dinky gave him that iron cross pendant he picked up on St. Marks. This teeny gift watered Tico's eyes up fierce. Tico sure was getting mushy in his old age.

Barbara in her dress was an everywhere flash, and Dezzie was attracting posse boys. It was just that there was something up with her. She kept giving Jose and Barbara strange looks and seemed like she wasn't digging their singular coupleness. The nicest moment was when Tico ended up in her lap. (They talked a long time. Dezzie used to watch a lot of Nickelodeon.) Barbara and Jose found hideaways and little cubbies. Right behind Dinky on his DJ station they scrunched together like they were running from an air raid. How much bigger her eyes looked when she wasn't wearing glasses. How much more sparkle in her magic eye.

"Is there any way I can talk you out of goin'na the cops?"

The question made Jose almost pull away from her. She clung.

"No, no, forget it. I was just asking. It's just why, why you gotta do that? Even if people read the comic, you think they gonna know you did that? How come you—"

"Stop," Jose said.

And they both stopped talking, noticing Dezzie's hard stare from across the pulsating dance floor.

"Kiss me," Barbara said.

The mad flash like cop car lights. The stink of beer and buddha and cigarettes. Samson brought ten more pizza pies. Like strong buddha hit, one moment Jose was laughing the next he was crying, his face all wet and flowing and Barbara holding him. And somebody said he had too much to drink and somebody else said, don'chu know? He killed that girl, they found her in a lot or some shit, and Jose went into a corner and threw up all that pizza.

And then it got late, real late. The high school kiddies started dropping like flies. Some left, some crashed, some rolled into a ball and would not move. Who was it passed out the Ecstasy? Posse boys will not leave until pushed, but Dinky knew how to deal with that. One minute it was Jay-Z and the next it was Nirvana come crashing in like the ATF squad was doing a bust. Walls of guitars smashing in loud screech and that dead blond kid with the tired voice growling

love you so much it makes me sick
yaah yaah yaah

and the Puerto Rican kids are all like, what the fuck do we do with *this?*

That cleared the dance floor pretty quick, choked the exits. By the time Mazzy Star was fading into you, the place was mellow private low-lit with only a few stragglers too tired to move. Jose, Dinky, and Barbara were drinking the last of that beer snuggled deep in the half dark. All of a sudden Dezzie comes over and pulls Barbara away. Jose and Dinky watch them under the soft swirly lights, Dezzie gesturing furious, her high-heel foot stomping. Barbara began to cry. Dinky looked at Jose like he already knew what was coming.

Dezzie headed for the exit without even a glance back. Barbara stood there on the dance floor for a moment, alone in her dress. She slowly came over to Jose, her wet eyes as sparkly as sequins. She couldn't look at him too long. Her eyes hopped all around him. She suddenly hugged him. Then she backed off.

"I can't," she said.

"But you came all this way," Jose said.

"I can't."

Dinky was shaking his head. He came right up to her.

"I can't," she said, looking at him helpless. "I'm sorry."

Dinky and Jose didn't say anything. They watched her go. Dezzie waited at the door.

"So what," Dinky said. "Three's a crowd."

"Yeah," Jose said, wiping his face. "Who needs that shit."

And then they saw her, standing by the door. She was wearing a gray trenchcoat that covered her down to her white high heels. As she came closer, they could see she had on those white fishnets. Occurred to them at the same time, she was dressed like a flasher or a hooker that, once she spots a possible john, flicks open that coat for a peek at the garter-belted merchandise.

"I guess I'm too late," Anita said. "For the party, anyway."

They sat on the couch together, watching Manuel and his staff do some cleanup. Anita pulled a small box out of her shoulder bag and presented it to Jose.

"What is it?" he asked, opening it slow.

"Proof," she said.

Inside, credit cards, wallets, IDs, photos. The names the pictures the bits and pieces of her seven kills.

"I can't keep waiting for them to find me." She lit a cigarette like she was disgusted. "I'll get old."

The thunder boomed.

When they walked out onto the street, there was only a hint of light. The clouds rolled thick purple and the rain poured down over them. It made Anita's hair all squiggly. Dinky collected rain in this porkpie hat he had been wearing, and dropped it down her back, making her screech and punch like a teenager. They walked that quiet stretch of 138th Street, chain link fences all raindrop-jeweled. Past Third Avenue, the 41st Precinct stationhouse loomed. Those round globes that said POLICE. Soft glowing like twin moons on either side of the steps.

There was no arguing, no last-minute anything. No sense of stopping or pulling back.

Anita put out her hand. They joined hands one to the other to the other. They walked in step like soldiers, only they weren't. They were young, crazy driven by what was, what is, the South Bronx. The place where young kids faded into brick like old TAGs under whitewashed walls.

There were no words, and there was no need to look back. There was only the three of them. This time, walking right into it.

I have a present: it is the present.

—Jawbreaker, *Save Your Generation*

He has two antagonists: the first pushes him from behind, from his birth. The second blocks the road in front of him. He struggles with both.

—Frank Kafka, *The Great Wall of China*

There's never been a successful escape from Stalag 13.

—Colonel Klink, *Hogan's Heroes*

TO THE FIFTEEN